The Guns of Mars
by
Martin T. Ingham

www.martinus.us

Cover art by Philip R. Rogers
Cover design by Alva J. Roberts

Edited by Jessy Marie Roberts

Second Edition, Released: May 2015

To My Father,
A True American Patriot

Preface

Lorna Forsyth
Grade 8
Tuesday, January 15, 2307
Book Report: "The Life of Morgan Asher," by H.L.
Wallace.

Morgan Asher was born on September 21, 2186, the son of John and Helen Asher. He grew up in and around Seattle, and spent summers in the country. His upbringing was heavily influenced by his mother's uncle, Robert Kragg, who was the CEO of Simworld, the first and largest virtual reality corporation. Upon graduating from business college in 2207, Morgan was given a position as a junior executive at the famous company. He stayed at Simworld until 2213, when a tragic accident claimed the life of his father. Morgan blamed virtual reality for his father's death, as the man responsible for the death was a victim of virtual psychosis, and also Robert Kragg's son.

Morgan bought a bankrupt ranch in western Montana and became a rancher. He remained there until 2216, when he was called back to Simworld by his great-uncle Robert. His cousin, Persephony Kragg, had gone missing in a virtual simulation. Morgan made the fateful decision to enter the program called Fantasan. While there, he learned of the computer virus responsible for the mental condition known as virtual psychosis, and also found a means of erasing it by shutting down the system from within.

When Morgan awoke from suspended animation, it was 2220, and the world was a different place. Simworld and its competitors were losing billions of dollars to purge their systems of the virus he'd uncovered, and many people believed the virtual reality companies had purposely implanted the virus, to make their programs addictive. Morgan subscribed to this theory. He petitioned Congress to cut federal subsidies to Virtual Reality and impose harsh regulations on them. His pleas fell on deaf ears, but his many letters and essays would, in later decades, lead to a new renaissance in many scientific and exploratory fields, and were largely used to justify the re-launch of the American Space Program in 2245.

Finished with political debates, Morgan returned to his ranch for over a year. In the spring of 2222, he returned to the Fantasan simulation, possibly under the false impression that an old friend might need his help. This conjecture remains unsubstantiated, and no one knows what really happened to Morgan after April 29, 2222. Simworld claims they have no record of him ever booting-in during that time, despite sworn testimony from several of the workers on Morgan's ranch saying he did just that.

Many modern historians disregard the claim that Morgan returned to Fantasan, and suspect his disappearance may have been staged to hide him from public view, or to cover up his murder by political and corporate foes. One thing is certain: Morgan Asher has not been heard from in eighty-five years, and it is doubtful we will ever know the truth.

Lorna Forsyth Diary
Wednesday, May 30, 2323

Okay, so it's only been ten years since my last entry, not twelve like I said it would be. I decided to boot out of the Fantasan simulation a little early, and it may sound impulsive and immature, but I met a guy.

You'll never guess who it is. Morgan Asher. *The* Morgan Asher from the history books! It turns out he's been trapped in the simulation all this time, under the affect of a virtual spell. He didn't even realize over a hundred years had passed when my team of adventurers revived him.

At first, I didn't recognize him, since I hadn't seen a photo since twelfth grade American History. After spending a few hours with him, I realized I had never really known him at all.

His handful of letters and the tons of biographies written about him never did him justice.

I don't know what it is about him, but I can't get him out of my mind. I'm thirty years old (even though this body of mine has been on ice for the last decade). I can't believe this is just some schoolgirl crush, but it feels like one—so overwhelming and exciting. It's like one of those storybook romances, where you just *know* he's the one. Oh, now I'm blushing, can you believe it?

Honestly, I don't know how he feels about me, but we've only known each other for a couple of days. I must assume he feels something special, since he asked me to boot-out to the real world with him. I know he's feeling alone right now, and might just want whatever company he can find, but I hope there's something more than that. If not, I might just have to make it something more.

So, yeah, I skipped out on two extra years in a simulated fantasy so I can try to make a fantasy or two come true in the real world. Am I really this impulsive? I hope not. They're not liable to let a lot of unpredictable girls into the space program. I still want to go out there someday, you know, see the real stars and have an adventure in outer space. I've done fantasy, now how about some science fiction!

Anyway, I'm waiting for Morgan to awaken. The Cryopractors just thawed him out, and once he recovers from the process we'll see where he wants to go. I wonder what he'll find out here, a hundred years later. I was only under for ten years and things are looking a little strange even to me.

Well, I'd better go. The nurse just said he's awake and ready to be discharged. He's no doubt itching to get going. I know I am. We're about to see the future.

Chapter One
September 20, 2327

The frigid wind rattled the flimsy material of the pressure tent as Morgan Asher prepared for another evening among the rocks and dust of the lifeless wilderness. His eyes ached and he felt ready to pass out. He wondered if he would ever wake up again. Death was a definite possibility this night, and there were still a few things he needed to say before he succumbed to the eternal rest.

Retrieving a laptop from his duffel bag, he prepared to recount the events leading to his current predicament. His throat was too raw, his breath too shallow to verbally relate his testimony, so he let his fingers do the talking.

"Personal Log, Morgan Asher, Tuesday, September 20, 2327.

"It's been a week since I had to run for my life, out here, into the wasteland of Mars. My food ran out today and my recycled water's starting to taste like urine. The carbon filters for my tent and suit are getting hard to purge and the oxygen doesn't smell right. Or maybe that's just me. I haven't had a bath lately and smell like a sewer.

"I don't know how much longer I'm going to last out here, so I thought I'd better complete my account of recent events. I want to leave a true journal of what went on here, in case those dishonorable Scifes get away with their coup. I want to set the record straight and help defeat their revisionist history."

He paused a moment, trying to think of where to go from there. He'd already jotted down much of the tale during the past week. The guilty parties had been named, his own involvement explained, and now he was stuck with the daunting task of making sense of it all. He still had questions of his own, ones he never expected to have answered in the limited time he had left.

The carbon dioxide levels in his tent were rising and he found it hard to focus. His thoughts drifted momentarily as he resumed his writing.

"My beloved Lorna, if by some miracle you have managed to survive, and someday have the fortune to read this, please know that my only regret is that I'll never see you again, and we'll never have those children you were looking forward to; well, unless Saturday night made the difference, in which case, I hope the kid gets on alright without me. Don't let those dirty Scifes turn it into a little zombie, okay? And I hope the kid has your hair. God, I love that red," he began to ramble.

A few sentences of gibberish later, he cleared his thoughts and continued.

"Everything I have uncovered regarding the traitors and their puppet masters, I have related in this journal. It has a decent buffer, and it doesn't seem to mind the vacuum or the subzero temperatures, so I expect it will survive. I only hope the right people find this someday."

Morgan's vision began to blur, his fingers numb from the cold. He'd written as much as he could. Shutting the laptop, he returned it to the bag and prepared for bed. He lay down on the lumpy ground, only a thin layer of plastic separating him from the dead soil of the Martian plain. He finished removing the last pieces of his spacesuit and used a hunk of chest plate as a pillow, the hard, rubbery material providing little comfort for his head. Flicking the switch on his LED torch left him in the dim glow of the miniature space heater staving off the lethal cold of Martian nights.

As sleep overtook him, both from fatigue and asphyxiation, his thoughts drifted back to where it all began. That fateful first day of Spatial Orientation 101...

Chapter Two
October 26, 2326

New Mexico was never a place Morgan had considered living because the arid climate didn't appeal to him. But he had lived there, for the last two years of his life, in an adobe box on the outskirts of Los Alamos with his wife, the lovely Lorna. They were only a few miles away from the newly established Aries University, where potential Martian colonists trained.

The facility was massive, built atop the rubble of the old government labs which had fallen into disrepair after the chaos of the Last Great War. For over two hundred years, this region of the country had remained quiet and sparsely populated. NASA's new propulsion lab and primary launch center sat several hundred miles to the southeast, in Mescalero Valley, attracting jobs and personnel to the southern part of the state. But space colonization had need of new training facilities, and rather than build in an already crowded region, they moved next door, so to speak. The initial facilities had been built for lunar colonists decades ago, but the new, ambitious plans for Mars required upgrades and expansions, all of which were now complete and in operation.

Lorna had already spent eighteen months in classes, completing degrees in both structural engineering and metallurgy. With these specialties in her portfolio, her chances of landing a ticket to Mars were high. She had dreamt of being a Martian colonist all her life, and it appeared her life's ambition was nearing fulfillment.

Morgan was her husband, and while he wasn't required to have a PhD or any special job skills, he still needed to undergo the spatial orientation course to acclimate himself to a potential life on Mars. It had never been his intention to travel off-world, mostly because in his own time, such a trip had been pure fantasy. The America he'd known a hundred years ago hadn't had a space program in ages, and hadn't been eager to expend funds on researching the possibility. A lot had changed during the last century, and Morgan had slept through it all.

Morgan had mixed emotions about becoming a colonist, and he felt very out of place walking the halls of Aries University. He meandered along, on his way to his introductory class, while thousands of other students rushed around, eager and nervous. After passing a procession of people in spacesuits, he found the right door and entered.

The classroom was large and filled with hundreds of chairs, most of which were already filled with a diverse cross-section of society, people from all walks of life and every ethnicity. These were the spouses of the primary applicants, the proud, the few, who were willing to subject themselves to the harshness of another world, all in the name of love and devotion.

Morgan found a seat in the back row and kept his eyes forward, paying little attention to the strangers around him. It was like being back in high school.

A few minutes passed and a few more students filed in and filled the remaining seats, and then came the instructor, a thin man with egg-shaped glasses and a stained tweed coat. He made his way over to the hardwood desk at the front of the room and picked up a folder, which he surreptitiously tucked under his arm.

"Greetings class," the man droned on in a bland monotone voice. "Welcome to Spatial Orientation 101. I'm Professor Milton Pearson, and I'll be your instructor."

The professor explained the upcoming curriculum. First and foremost, they would undergo a rigorous series of mental exercises and tests. Then there were physical examinations involving machines Morgan had never heard of, followed by extended use of simulators to test their resistance to G-forces. Toward the end of the course, they would all be taken aboard the Tigris Space Station, where they would spend five days in space, during which they would experience simulated gravity approximate to Martian normal, roughly 39% of Earth's standard pull. All of this would determine who had the right stuff for colonization, and which of the many valuable jobs they'd be assigned.

Professor Pearson was an academic with a degree in psychology; a suitable instructor and evaluator for the mental aspects of space colonization, but by no means was he suited to rating the physical requirements.

As if on cue, their "gym teacher" entered the room and made her way to the head of the class. She was a small brunette girl who didn't look much beyond puberty, wearing a sky-blue Air Force uniform and a sparkling smile. She stopped beside Pearson in front of the desk and spun around on her heels in a swift motion. Her eyes surveyed the room, studying all the new faces she was going to instruct.

"I am Colonel Melinda Faris of the United States Space Force. I'll be aiding Professor Pearson in scoring your aptitude tests and serve as your primary guide during the physical aspects of your training. I'll give you a taste of what life in space, and on Mars, will be like. Let's start off with a few questions. Anyone?"

A hundred hands shot up. The Professor decided to yield the floor to the colonel, and sat down behind his desk to flip through his folder.

"Are you the same *Captain* Faris of the first Mars expedition?" a chipper young blonde asked.

"I think that would be obvious, if you'd read your introductory material," Melinda replied coldly. "This isn't going to be an easy course. If you want to make the cut, you're going to have to come to class prepared from now on. But, to answer your question, just so we're all clear, I was the first woman to ever step foot on the Red Planet in June of 2314, and that makes me uniquely skilled to grade your performance."

It had been almost twelve years since the first Mars landing, and Morgan thought it doubtful this child could have been one of those famed astronauts. How could she have been the first woman on Mars unless she'd gone as a toddler? Nobody said anything, but it was no doubt on everyone's mind.

"Colonel, why do we need to take this orientation course?" a young man asked. "I mean, my wife's the geologist. I'm just a meat packer from Cleveland. What's the point in me playing Neil Armstrong when I'll just be a homemaker?"

Colonel Faris answered. "Well, first off, you'll hardly be stuck at home, assuming you qualify for colonization. If you graduate, you'll be assigned one of any number of valuable tasks. Mars needs more than just scientists and specialists—we need quite a few laborers and heavy lifters, people to do the honest work of building and expanding the colony. You might think the work is all done by machines, but even machines need people to run and service them."

On the heels of her answer came a question from a young gentleman in a suit, his New England accent blatantly obvious. "Concerning the civilian labor force you are assembling. Why should we be conscripted into service when there is an overcrowding problem in many of the nation's prisons? Wouldn't it be fitting for them to repay this world for their crimes by helping to build the next?"

"I'll field this one," Professor Pearson said, standing. Turning to the questioner, he asked, "What is your profession?"

"Prosecuting attorney, Harvard, class of '23."

"Really?" Pearson asked with a detectable sneer. "Then you've spent a great deal of time around petty criminals and violent offenders?"

"Yes," the lawyer answered, and before he could continue, Pearson cut him off.

"Then are you insane?"

"Excuse me?" the lawyer asked.

"You must be mad to even consider sending reprobates into space," Pearson said sternly. "NASA is not building a penal colony. There are literally millions of Americans who would do almost anything to be colonists, and you would steal their seats on the next ship in exchange for inmates? No. Space is reserved for the best of humanity. It is no place for those who have not earned it and do not deserve it."

"It was a valid question," the lawyer defended. "Colonial empires have long been built by the dregs of society. I was only curious to know why NASA hadn't considered utilizing such a labor force."

"You have your answer," Melinda said. "Criminal labor is not wanted or needed, since there are more than enough honest citizens eager to go who aren't in prison, yourself included."

The lawyer sat down and shut up, allowing Melinda to continue her introduction.

"Most of you are in this class because your spouses are highly qualified specialists in one field or another. They've already gone through the training and been assigned a tentative seat on the next colony ship, which will leave orbit in roughly two months time.

"You may not be the architects, the geologists, the botanists, or have any specialization useful to colonization, but your contribution to this program will be no less important. You are the new colonists. You will bring human life and culture to a barren world, and within you lies the true foundation of Martian civilization.

"Over the next six weeks, you will learn what it will take to survive on Mars, and be given a taste of what the rest of your life will entail should you choose to go there. Now, I must warn you, not everyone is cut out to be a colonist. Some of you may not be able to handle it, and that is the primary purpose for the orientation course: to weed out the unfit. It is very important you learn your limits now, so we may succeed in establishing a strong and stable colony.

"If, for whatever reason, you are incapable of being a fully functioning colonist, it is important to discover that beforehand, for your own safety and the well-being of your fellow colonists. Your spouses are counting on you, so try your very best, but do not feel ashamed if your best isn't good enough. Out of the first batch of colonists, nearly half of the spouses were deemed unsuitable or opted out on their own. That's why we have nearly double the applicants we need this time around, because living on a lifeless rock in outer space is not something everyone is cut out for.

"Now, who else has a question?" she asked in conclusion.

Several dozen hands shot up again, and Melinda started in front and worked her way back through the room, addressing whatever questions came her way. Most were harmless queries which amounted to hero-worship. Everyone wanted to know more about the famed Colonel Faris, and what it felt like to walk on Mars for the first time. A few wanted to know more about the preexisting living conditions on Mars, and one bold lady expressed her concerns about the damage humanity was planning for the natural Martian environment. Morgan expected she'd be washed out of the program in short order, even if she was a Senator's daughter.

A few students asked substantive questions regarding the upcoming curriculum, which gave Professor Pearson the opportunity to put the class to sleep with technical jargon while Melinda paced around behind him.

Filtering through it all, Morgan got a basic understanding of the class. It was a pass/fail grading system, designed to reveal the useful applicants and discard the rest. At the end of the course, everyone qualified would be offered a job with a paltry salary and free room and board. NASA was preparing a very controlled society from the beginning.

Morgan wasn't terribly impressed or interested in the classroom, and the idea of spending the rest of his life in the heavily restrictive Martian surroundings ate at him. He liked his freedom and had always been wealthy enough to do most anything he desired on Earth—but on Mars, he would be delegated to some menial task, trapped within the confines of a tiny set of pressurized caverns and domes, tethered forever to the dictates of a government agency.

Above and beyond his own desires, this opportunity was

what Lorna wanted, and he loved her enough to give up the world for her. So, here he was, doing just that.

Finally, after the last questions were answered, Morgan put up his hand with the most pressing thought on his mind. He spoke without standing, and with a youthful impertinence unbefitting a grown man. "Colonel, you say you landed on Mars twelve years ago, but I swear you're not much over fifteen. How old are you, really?"

Melinda Faris giggled impishly at the query. "It's no big secret. I'm sixty. Why?"

"Lady, I don't care how much healthcare's advanced, there is no way in hell you're sixty years old with a body like that."

Melinda's smile vanished and her eyes narrowed at his insolent tone. "Stand up," she ordered.

Morgan complied, and everybody in the class turned and glanced at him. His face was one they'd all seen on the news before, the historical figure from a century ago who'd advocated for the technological advancement of man.

Morgan wasn't what you'd call a contemporary citizen. His body had been frozen in suspended animation for over a hundred years, his mind trapped inside a virtual computer program. Had he actually experienced all the years in-between, he'd now be a hundred and forty two, but in reality, he'd lived through less than forty of that.

In his own time, Morgan had been ridiculed and ignored by a world not yet ready to wake up from their addiction to computerized entertainment. Yet, in all the years he had slept, others had heeded his advice, turned away from trivial daydreams, and taken the first steps toward colonizing space.

None of the students seemed particularly interested in him, but Melinda's expression lightened significantly as she locked eyes on him. "Morgan Asher. Of course," she said gently. As she said it, the clock struck eleven, and the class recessed for lunch. The room emptied fast, as everyone was eager to fill their stomachs with the other twenty thousand students, all of whom had spouses eager to get to Mars.

Melinda asked Morgan to stay as the rest of the class left,

and he felt appreciative to have a moment alone with this curious colonel in a child's body.

The petite colonel sauntered down the aisle to Morgan's back seat and stopped in front of him, studying his face. "The great Morgan Asher," she remarked, beaming with pride. It was a reaction Morgan was familiar with. At first, the response had irked him, but the praise he received from select segments of society was growing on him.

"Disappointed yet?" Morgan asked, locking eyes with the girl.

Melinda dismissed the comment and added, "You know, I had no idea you were in this class. Each of the instructors get students at random, so aren't I lucky?"

"First woman on Mars, eh?" Morgan queried dubiously.

"You don't believe me? The history books are on my side."

"I just can't get over how young you look. Seriously, I've seen sixteen year olds with more wrinkles than you."

"Really, Mr. Asher, even in your day and age, you must have seen old minds in youthful bodies."

"Sure, virtual addicts who'd spent decades under sim. Not military officers who'd spent a lifetime in solid reality, subjecting their bodies to a ton of abuse."

"As far as the world is concerned, this is all just plastic surgery. It's what everyone believes."

"You should know I'm not everyone," Morgan said.

"No, of course not, and that's why I wanted a word with you in private. Has your wife told you anything about the 'added incentives' for the Mars program?"

"Nothing specific," Morgan replied, remembering the many times Lorna had alluded to fringe benefits, but been unwilling to get into details due to some non-disclosure agreement.

"Well, what I'm about to tell you must not leave this room. You're not supposed to even hear about this until you're safely on Mars, but you are a unique individual and I feel you have a right to know beforehand."

Digging into her back pocket, she retrieved her wallet and

pulled out several photos. She handed them, one at a time, to Morgan, talking as she went. "This is my yearbook picture from twelfth grade. Striking similarity." She pointed to the next photo. "Now, this was taken shortly after my thirty-fifth birthday. Note the captain's bars on the collar." The next one was large and she had to unfold it. "This was a shot taken just before the first Mars mission."

Her age was obvious in the photograph, as a woman nearly fifty years old. Her short hair was gray, her wrinkles obvious. She still looked quite fit, but hardly young.

Pulling out a fourth picture, she handed it to Morgan. "Here I am, accepting the Asher Prize for Scientific Achievement, almost nine years ago."

Looking at the new picture, the woman was once again a teenager, scarcely old enough to vote. "What is this nonsense?" Morgan asked, confused.

"This nonsense is the ultimate fringe benefit of Martian colonization, and possibly the best kept secret of the United States government. You're no doubt aware of the genetic research that has been ongoing since the first mapping of the human genome in the late twentieth century. Well, twenty years ago, a couple of lab technicians successfully uncovered a means of deactivating the segments of DNA which regulate aging."

Morgan's jaw dropped. He considered her words and looked at her youthful flesh, forty years younger than her natural age demanded. He wiped a hand over his forehead, feeling beads of sweat forming, and noticed the wrinkles starting to form above his eyebrows. He was pushing forty and the signs of age were beginning to claim his features.

"Now, the serum has been tested extensively on Earth among select groups of volunteers, most of whom work for the government, all of whom have been sworn to secrecy. While it works quite well to arrest the aging process on subjects Earth-side, there is something unique on Mars that also reverses the aging process entirely. I can't be more specific than that, but rest assured, if you qualify for Martian colonization, you will be given the gene therapy and have the added bonus of perpetual youth and peak health.

"Now, how's that for a perk?" Melinda asked enthusiastically.

"It's certainly attractive," he said.

"I thought you'd appreciate it."

Morgan handed the photos back to her and slid out of his seat, feeling the need to stretch his legs.

"You can obviously see why this must remain a secret."

"Population control," Morgan muttered, feeling a bit dazed.

"Yes. The world is getting to be over-populated again, even with three billion people on ice in virtual simulations. We have over six billion waking minds on this planet, and if the anti-aging therapy came into common use, there'd be no stopping a boom. If people stopped dying and stopped growing infertile at a regular age, you'd see the planet overcrowded in a couple of decades. Right now, we're starting to find a solution to our over-crowding problem via colonization, but that can only curtail growth so much. Maybe in another hundred years we'll be able to ship billions of people off-world and make this therapy available to everyone, but we need more time."

Morgan's head was reeling. He hadn't run into this kind of future shock since waking up nearly four years ago. Even with the modern marvels, he could never have dreamt age itself could be conquered.

Still, some things didn't add up. How could they keep Melinda's transformation top secret? Exactly how had they explained her going to Mars an old lady and coming back a teenager? Obviously, there was more she wasn't telling him.

"Take the rest of the day off," Melinda advised. "Go home, talk with your wife. Let it all sink in. The real orientation starts tomorrow." With a happy nod, she turned and walked out, leaving Morgan with questions he had an uneasy feeling would eventually be answered.

Chapter Three

The scent of sizzling meat filled the small house built of plaster. Morgan was used to cooking for Lorna, as her rigorous studies had been all-consuming for the last year and a half. Besides, he preferred his culinary talents to those of his wife. Her idea of a tasty steak was one burned on the outside and bloody on the inside, while he preferred a more balanced meat. Lorna's domestic skills were lacking, though nobody, especially not Morgan, had the heart to disparage her gourmet touch.

It was a quarter to seven and the sun was already setting. Despite being late October, the temperature still felt warm to Morgan, who'd spent many years wintering in Montana, where the summer nights weren't always this hot.

The familiar thump sounded on the doorstep and the door swung open. Lorna stepped inside, carrying a duffel bag full of books and instruments, looking ready to pass out. She dropped her bag beside the door and found a seat at the small dining table in the room, which served as both kitchen and eatery.

With one strip steak sizzled to perfection, Morgan stabbed it with a fork and chucked it onto a porcelain plate for his exhausted wife, who looked up at him with bloodshot eyes red enough to match the fiery color of her hair.

Glancing down at the steaming meat, Lorna groaned. "I'm too tired to eat."

"You need to keep up your strength," Morgan said, returning to the stove to prepare another steak for himself.

"I just spent six hours in a flight simulator pulling something around ten gees. I still feel like throwing up."

"I thought you graduated already."

"I did, but some flight surgeon didn't like the looks of my last stress test, so the evaluation board wanted a second run through. Vomit aside, I think they're satisfied now."

Morgan let her relax as he cooked his meat to a thorough brown. A dash of salt and pepper seasoned the succulent strip to perfection, and he sat at the table across from his fatigued wife. He started eating without another word.

Eventually, after a long silence, Lorna said, "Oh, how was your first day of orientation?"

"Interesting," Morgan said after swallowing a hunk of beef, "but about your simulator, I don't get it. We're going to be colonists, not fighter pilots. Why are they subjecting you to such strain?"

"There are a lot of reasons. They want the best possible colonists, those who are physically fit as well as mentally superior. I guess the torture is supposed to add character," Lorna explained, her voice slurred.

"Can I get you anything else to eat?" Morgan asked, wondering if a lighter meal might help her nausea.

"No, really, I'm fine. You go ahead," she insisted.

Morgan inhaled his steak with no problem, and then quietly stared at his wife, seeing the frayed strands of hair jutting out every which way. The exhaustion on her face almost made her look her mental age, which was thirty four, but living ten of those years inside a computer program had left her body young and vibrant. Morgan looked at the leathery hide on the back of his hand and thought how strange it contrasted with her smoothly-skinned complexion. It wasn't like anyone stared at them, or there was anything taboo about their physical age difference, but it still bothered Morgan a little to think about it. It made him feel old.

Lorna obviously had enough on her mind and was too tired for a serious conversation, so Morgan refrained from discussing the bombshell Colonel Faris had dropped on him earlier in the day. There would be plenty of time to discuss the perks of the space program in the weeks ahead.

"Is there anything I can do to make you feel better?" Morgan asked.

"Carry me to bed?"

She may have meant it as a joke, but Morgan took her at

her word, ever in the mood to please. Lifting her from her seat, he walked her a dozen paces over to the bedroom door, and tucked her in to rest.

* * *

There was a cool breeze blowing in the night air, but it didn't bother Morgan as he stood out in the front yard, looking up at the moon. Big surprise, he couldn't sleep, so he had decided to come outside and look at the twilight's splendor as Lorna snored away. A pair of boxer shorts were his only garment, but the neighbors didn't care—not enough to ever stop over and say hello, anyway.

The moon was full and there wasn't a cloud in the sky, allowing Morgan the familiar sight which had only slightly changed from his childhood. Where once it had been a lifeless orb pocked with craters, now in the center of it sat a spattering of structures large enough to see as silvery dots. Those cities were now over thirty years in the making, populated with five million human inhabitants. Three main urban centers were surrounded by two thousand square miles of farmland. It was the prototype on which Mars was being planned, but Mars would take a lot more time and effort to establish such a prosperous, self-sustaining environment.

The initial building materials for Luna's industrial base had been shipped from Earth, an easy feat with modern jetships ferrying people and supplies to the moon on a regular basis, but Mars was still over a month away when it was closest to Earth, and their individual orbits made it unfeasible to send supply ships more than once per year. It would take much longer to build the infrastructure and manufactories there to make the colony self-sustaining and expansive. How many decades would it take before things were sufficiently advanced to permit wide, open spaces?

Eighteen months ago, he'd been among the fields and forests of Montana, enjoying a life of excess as a man of means with the freedom only the wilderness could bring. How lucky he'd felt riding and hiking through the fields and forests, coming home to Lorna every night, sharing his homestead with a family of ranchers who'd been stewards of his estate for over a century. It was the life he had chosen, compounded with interest.

After eighteen months in this hot, arid climate, playing homemaker for his scholastic wife, he was wondering whether he could really take the change. His future seemed burdensome and joyless. Nothing could be wholly absent of joy with Lorna, but he couldn't stop thinking how great their first two years had been, living free in the country. He also couldn't escape the truth of how strained he felt cooped up in a clay box, waiting to be shipped off to a cramped colony with limited freedom and untold trials.

This was the future Morgan had advocated all those years ago. As he'd seen the world stagnated with billions of souls wasting their lives away on computerized fantasies, he had challenged them to wake up and venture toward a grander purpose again. Yet, when he'd discussed it, there had been no chance of him ever going. It had always been intended for someone else, but now he found himself yoked by his own litany. The irony was not lost on him.

Looking at the curtain of night, his head filled with wild thoughts, Morgan asked, "What am I doing?"

The twinkling stars overhead did not answer, but a more earthly voice did. One deep and rich, full of bass, and bold enough for opera. "You lost?" it asked, snapping Morgan's stare away from the stars.

Turning to his left, he saw a white-shirted figure standing on the curb, his dark skin making his body almost phantasmal in the darkness. His smile was bright enough, and the moon helped accentuate his features as he invited himself into the front yard.

Turning back to the stars, Morgan mentioned, "I'm just wondering how I can stand living up there."

"Mars or the Moon?" the man asked, glancing up at the lunar orb momentarily.

"Mars," Morgan replied, turning his attention back to the

stranger with a sonorous voice.

The man whistled in appreciation. "That's far out. My wife and I are prepping for lunar colonization and *that* seems pretty wild. I can't imagine going to another planet." Sticking out his hand, the man introduced himself. "Jim Nicholas."

Morgan shook the hand and introduced himself, expecting instant recognition, though the man's memory slipped and he was left trying to recall where he'd heard the name before. Morgan found it strangely refreshing to meet somebody who didn't immediately recognize him as an historical figure, but it was short-lived, as Jim recalled old high school lectures.

"Oh, you're *him*," Jim said. "The guy they named the city after," he said, pointing at the moon.

Morgan flinched when he thought of "Asherton," the third of the lunar cities. He was already up there, in a sense, beside "Armstrongville" and "Jefferson."

"A little fed up with the hero worship, eh?" Jim asked, staying upbeat.

"I never sought the limelight," Morgan answered.

"I don't think anyone deserving does."

"Yeah, where did you come from?" Morgan asked, feeling a little put off by the friendly stranger.

"I live across the street. After my first day of orientation, I couldn't sleep, either."

"Having second thoughts?"

"Nah, just nerves," Jim said. "I hope I don't let her down."

"Your wife," Morgan surmised.

"Yeah. She never had any doubts; always knew that's where we're headed. Humanity, I mean."

"And you?"

"Ah, it's a nice dream, but I never thought *I'd* be going."

"Maybe you won't," Morgan added. "Even with lunar colonization, there are rejects."

"Sherry would never forgive me. I've gotta make it. Meaning I should probably get some rest before we hit the books tomorrow."

"Yes, I'll see you around," Morgan said.

With a smile and a wave, Jim headed back across the street, and Morgan went inside. He decided to turn in and try to get some sleep, or toss and turn until dawn, whichever was most convenient.

Chapter Four
December 8, 2326

The first international summit on Martian Colonization was going off without a hitch. Held at the historic Houston Space Center, Mars-Con was a coming-together of the world's greatest thinkers. The purpose of the expo was twofold: NASA wanted to recruit elite specialists from around the globe to help assure the viability of their projects, while the politicians hoped to strengthen the bonds between America and her allies. All the while, the military took the opportunity to spy on everyone, hoping to gather intelligence on any hidden advancements made by competing nations.

Colonel Seth Avery had just spent two hours sitting through a presentation on the "Viability of Genetically Modified Lichens during Stage 2 of the Martian Atmospheric Reclamation Process," and was understandably bored. He wasn't a wild-eyed scientist, and having to babysit these experts was turning out to be a bust. He was ready to find a place to hide when a pair of silver suits accosted him out in the hallway.

"Colonel, how nice it is to be seeing you," the gentleman said with a thick, Middle-Eastern accent.

Avery vaguely recalled the scientist's face, but a name escaped him. He was a geologist from the Persian Republic, and his nametag was conspicuously absent. "I'm sorry, what's your name?"

"I am Mahmoud Zahir. This, my associate, Samul Mossadira. Please, we be having a word?" the man asked.

Avery wasn't sure why a Persian scientist would be bothering him, but he decided to hear the man out, considering his words couldn't be anywhere near as boring as the presentation on lichens.

"Is there private place for us to go?" Mahmoud asked,

glancing around suspiciously.

"This is as private as it gets around here, bub," Avery said flatly. "Speak your piece."

"Please, you do not understand. It is concern we have, regarding Consensorates," he stumbled over the last word a little, but it was understandable.

"Colonel," Samul interrupted, "We...I say...our govern..."

"Please, never mind him. His tongue sticks," Mahmoud said. "He is meaning to say, our government has important knowledge regarding the European Consensorate and Mars."

The Persians had finally piqued Avery's interest. Anything involving the Scientific Fundamentalists of Europe concerned him, as both an officer and a patriot. "You have intelligence you'd rather not send through official channels," Avery surmised.

"Yes, imparting this would be impossible at present. As you know, our new President is, how you say, friendly toward the Consensorate, and wary of the far west, but we know the truth. Consensorate is evil."

"How do you figure that?" Avery asked, trying to assess their motives.

"You know history, Colonel. For over a hundred years, the Consensorate has enslaved its people with the *Dictates of Science,'* laws that control how every person lives, what work they do, even who they are allowed to marry. It is disgusting to think that our own president could be in-league with such godless men."

"It's enough to make you yearn for the days of the Mullahs, ain't it?" Avery cracked.

Both Persians frowned, finding no humor in his joke. Samul mumbled something under his breath, turning his gaze away from the American colonel.

"We would not talk to you if this were not so important to both our peoples," Mahmoud said as his colleague continued to grumble.

"All right. What have you got?" Avery asked, less than eager to hear them out, but feeling he had no alternative.

"The Consensorate is already on Mars," Mahmoud said.

"What, you mean they got spies in the program?   I wouldn't doubt it," Avery said.   "Half of NASA is Scife sympathizers."

"No, Colonel," Samul interjected. "They have program as well."

"You think they're finally going to get serious about space?" Avery asked, failing to see the importance. "Let 'em. If they do bother setting it up, they'll still be decades behind us."

"You do not understand," Mahmoud rebutted. "We do not say they plan to get serious. We say they have all along."

Colonel Avery laughed, finding it hard to believe. "If they do have one, it sure ain't much."

"You are wrong, Colonel," Samul shouted. "I have seen it!"

The smile dropped off Avery's face.

"That is why we come to you," Mahmoud said. "The Consensorate is more advanced, more powerful, than anyone suspects."

"You've got proof?" Avery asked.

"First you must offer us protection," Mahmoud said. "Asylum."

"All right, you've got my attention," Avery said. "You boys come along, and we'll talk."

"In private?" Samul asked.

"Almost," Colonel Avery replied. He turned around and made a quick call on his wrist-phone, then turned back around to the Persian scientists. "If you'll come with me," he instructed, leading them down the hallway. Before long, they were in a small conference room, seemingly alone, but observed through a two-way mirror by various interested parties attached to the United States government.

From the comfort of a padded office chair, Samul tried as best he could to relate his experiences. Mahmoud translated what was said with relative clarity.

"Several months ago, after Persia's new President took office, I and several other noted scientists were assigned to participate in workshops sponsored by the Persian Science Ministry, each structured to screen candidates for possible off-world activity. It was widely assumed to be a tool for the Americans, though I soon learned differently.

"As one of the top-scoring geophysicists, I was invited to meet with a visiting dignitary from the European Consensorate. Such foreign agents are common and quite welcome in Tehran, which boasts itself to be one of the more open and up-to-date cities in Asia. Neither aligned with America or the Consensorate, Persia is always being courted by both sides, and a precarious balance of power exists within the representative government."

"So, what did the Scife want?" Avery asked, using the derogatory slang term for the Scientific Fundamentalists.

"He wanted to recruit me for the Consensorate's space program; specifically, to be a part of their mission on Mars. As you can imagine, I was skeptical about the whole thing, but before I could get over the initial surprise, I blacked out. I later awoke in bed with no idea of how I'd gotten there.

"The next day, I talked to the Ministry of Science regarding my memory lapse, hoping they could shed some light on the matter. They had set up the meeting with the Consensorate dignitary, and should have been monitoring our conversation, but they told me nothing. I was asked to go home and rest, and forget about the whole thing. I did as they requested, but that night things started to come back to me. Strange thoughts haunted my dreams, images and ideas resembling faded memories. I recalled faces and places I'd never seen...or had I?

"None of it made sense at first, but after several sleepless nights I was able to fill in the details and fully reconstruct the half-day I had lost. Let me tell you of my experience..."

* * *

Samul was laughing. Mr. Stamos, the Consensorate dignitary, had just told him a joke, or so he thought. What an offer, the chance of a lifetime! To explore the internal workings of Mars as part of the European research colony,

25

it would have been too good to refuse—assuming the Europeans actually had such a colony. In all reality, they didn't even have a space program, let alone the means to visit another planet. So, Samul laughed.

Stamos did not share the joke, and kept a stoic pose as he continued. "You don't think I'm serious."

Samul took in a few deep breaths, extinguishing his jocular reaction. "Of course you make a joke. It was a good one, I'll give you that. Your government wishes to send me to Mars? That is truly original."

"I admit, it is a generous offer, one you might consider yourself less-than-worthy to receive, but you are young and fully capable of growing into the position. We like to select youthful candidates, for the most part. They are more easily groomed and conditioned for a lifetime of service."

Samul stared at the dignitary and saw the man's face hadn't shifted. He was dead serious, which only served to irritate the young Persian. "What is this nonsense?"

"Come, I will show you," Stamos said, standing up from behind his desk. He marched over to the silver sheet beside the main door. As he came within range of its sensor, the metal panel retracted, revealing a small elevator.

There was no sense turning back, Samul thought. He had to get to the bottom of this. He stepped aboard. The door shut behind him, and the chamber began its descent.

During the ride down, Stamos asked, "Are you familiar with the Dictates of Science?"

"I am vaguely aware of them," Samul admitted, having little interest in Scientific Fundamentalism. He didn't care for their all-controlling philosophy, but accepted that others might want to live that way, as servants to a manmade doctrine. Though, he'd never looked into the European system, or sought to comprehend the broader implications of such a system. Political Science was outside his interests.

"Then you understand our employment structure," Stamos said. "That our people are assigned their professions from birth, based upon genetic prerequisites."

26

"I have heard," Samul confirmed. "Why?"

"I thought you might be curious to know why we've singled you out, above all others from your chosen profession. It is because you are the most suitable candidate in all respects, both educationally and genetically."

Samul shook his head, disregarding the man's thin praise. What did it matter what his genome said? He wasn't a geophysicist because of his cells. This is what he wanted to do, what he'd chosen for himself. Why did this foreign dignitary think otherwise?

"You see, you're already one of us," Stamos said with a nefarious smirk. "You just don't know it yet."

The elevator came to a stop, and the door opened to reveal a circular room lined with computer consoles. There were a few men in lab coats milling about, but they came to attention once they spotted their direct superior.

Stamos waved Samul to walk ahead of him, and as they entered the room he shouted an order to his colleagues. "Send us to the Hub." The men began tapping information into their work stations, hurrying to obey.

Samul moved into the center of the room and stood where Stamos instructed him to stand. Both men waited there, on top of a large metal disk, until the men at the consoles finished their work.

Before Samul could ask for an explanation, everything changed. A blinding flash of light enveloped him, and his entire body went numb for several seconds. When the light faded and his senses returned, everything around him was different. The room was roughly the same size, but the walls were a darker shade of gray, and there were different people at the computer consoles. For a second, he thought he'd lost consciousness and been moved, but something told him otherwise.

"Welcome to the Consensorate's Space Hub," Stamos said, squeezing Samul's shoulder.

"Space?" Samul said, shaking cobwebs out of his brain.

"Yes, we were just teleported several thousand kilometers

into outer space."

"Teleported!" Samul snapped. The sudden revelation pumped a wave of adrenaline through him, as the consequences started to take shape. He wanted to scream, but something in the back of his mind told him to be at ease. The calming influence was overwhelming, almost like a drug.

"Yes, it is a science the Consensorate perfected years ago. It's how we are able to stay one step ahead of the Americans without their knowledge."

"I see," Samul said, stepping forward. His legs almost fell out from under him, as he hadn't noticed the change in gravity. The pull was far less than what he'd always felt on Earth, further proving the claims of this European delegate.

"Come along," Stamos said, walking forward with no trouble at all. He knew what to expect, and had enough practice to instantly adjust to the weak gravity.

Samul stumbled along, getting used to his new environment. A wave of elation flowed over him as he continued across the metal floor, and curious sentiments dominated his consciousness. He knew he should be terrified and appalled by these technological marvels, but a little voice was lurking there, urging him to be happy and accepting of it all.

The metal door looked identical to the one that had hidden the elevator in the Consulate's basement, but when it opened there proved to be no elevator there. Instead, there was a long walkway lined with windows. Each of those windows revealed where they were. Samul stopped and stared out at the many stars, and the shimmering blue and white orb that was Earth.

"Now do you believe we have a space program?" Stamos asked.

"How is this possible?" Samul asked. "How could you build such a facility in secret?"

"It was simple, once we mastered the art of teleportation."

28

"You teleported all of this?"

"A little at a time," Stamos replied. *"The tricky part was constructing the receiving platform. Teleporters have a limited range, unless they work in pairs. To begin with, our space planes served as cargo carriers."*

Modern space planes were no secret. Each industrialized nation utilized them for quick, efficient transport, so that part of the explanation was quite logical. But they couldn't have sent up large loads without being noticed.

Stamos continued his explanation. *"For quite some time, each load of passengers we sent up also brought a small quantity of construction material. After a few months, we had enough to construct a telepad, and that was quickly moved beyond the range of American satellite surveillance. Once it was properly positioned, we were able to teleport all that we required to build this."*

"Impressive," Samul said, turning his eyes away from the window.

"But that is all ancient history. Let us get to the matter at hand," Stamos said, urging Samul forward again. They walked the full length of the corridor, and entered a new room with a large conference table littered with files and computer equipment.

"Here, this is what you wanted to see," Stamos said, handing Samul a data pad from the table.

Samul looked over the information, and was further amazed by what he found. Building schematics, personnel records, daily status reports; a whole host of data revealing the presence of a viable colony on Mars. It could have all been faked, but that little voice kept influencing Samul's thoughts, telling him to believe. After everything he had seen already, it was impossible to discount the very real possibility of such an outpost.

As Samul handed back the data, Stamos asked, *"What do you think? Ready to work with us at Eridania?"*

"Eridania?"

"The short designation for our fine Martian colony. I

trust you are eager to go there, and see it for yourself. Am I right?"

Stamos was more than right, Samul realized, as the voice in his head was screaming for him to comply. That controlling influence kept directing him to accept the man's offer, and become a part of the Consensorate's mission on Mars, but something wasn't right. Samul could see these were not his own thoughts, his own feelings. The Consensorate had done something to make him compliant.

When he realized what was happening, Samul worked up enough strength to take control of himself. It was a great struggle, but after a long silence, he was finally able to say, "No."

Stamos flinched, as if he'd been slapped.

"No, I cannot be a part of your program," Samul said, as if he didn't believe his own words. They were what he intended to say, but every fiber of his being was telling him to do the opposite. He was too conflicted to know which course of action was right, but he knew which one the unnatural voice wanted him to take, which propelled him to resist.

"You're joking," Stamos said, sounding less than amused.

"No!" Samul said, forcing his mouth to do his bidding.

Stamos shook his head and pulled a pistol out from under his jacket. The translucent shell of the condensed energy discharger sparkled in the artificial light of the room. "Oh, well. Maybe next time," he said before pulling the trigger.

A flash of lightning streaked out of the gun and soaked into Samul's chest. Once again, his body went numb, and his world went dark as consciousness faded.

* * *

"...So you see, Colonel, the Consensorate is a far greater threat than you know," Mahmoud concluded.

"Yeah, about that," Avery said, doubting the whole story, "maybe you should explain to me why I should believe any of this."

"I understand your doubts. It was hard for me to believe

when Samul told me these things. But I have known him my whole life. He is like brother to me. He would not lie."

"That still isn't enough," Avery pressed. "Why are you telling me this?"

"Because you must stop them!" Samul shouted. "They are evil. They *killed* me!"

"You look pretty alive to me, pal."

"You do not understand," Mahmoud interrupted. "He is not worried about dying. He has already died."

"Huh?" Avery asked.

"As a soldier, perhaps you do not know the physics behind teleportation, but rest assured, the process kills."

Avery may have been a soldier, but he was also a student of history, so he knew a thing or two about the dead art of molecular teleportation. It was a science discovered long ago, but it wasn't openly used by anyone, for several reasons. The power requirements to perform small leaps were astronomical, preventing its general use on inanimate objects, while ethical issues forestalled further research into transporting living beings.

It wasn't so much "teleportation," as it was "duplication." When an object was teleported, its original atomic structure was utterly destroyed, turned into pure energy. Then, energy on the other end was used to recreate an exact copy of the object, but it was just a copy. The person being teleported was, in effect, destroyed, and a "biodigital clone" was made on the other end. The clone was someone with the same exact biological makeup, the same memories as the original, but they were, in essence, a different person. Many religions considered the process an abomination, and some went so far as to call the clones "soulless," beings without genuine life.

Beyond the moral ramifications, most Americans didn't like the idea of dying and having some clone take their place, so nobody had bothered to solve the power consumption issues. They just considered the science a dead-end, focusing money and manpower on other, more viable, technologies.

Clearly the Consensorate hadn't halted their research.

Having heard enough, Avery called in a couple of MP's and placed the Persians into protective custody.

Following the interview with the Persians, Colonel Avery entered the observation room on the other side of the two-way mirror. He sat down in the corner and asked, "Do you really think they're telling the truth?"

"What do the readings say?" asked the man in a black suit. He was the resident CIA observer.

"Oh, they believe what they're saying. That's for sure," the resident psychologist said, looking at a computer monitor. "All scans read complete honesty."

"That doesn't mean anything," Avery argued. "The Consensorate's renowned for their brainwashing."

"It is true, they do know the brain—and aren't afraid to manipulate it," the psychologist agreed.

"So, where does that leave us?" the CIA man asked.

"It leaves *me* with just another pain in the ass to deal with," Avery said, leaning back in his chair. He let the back of his head tap lightly against the wall as he breathed a sigh of frustration.

Chapter Five
April 17, 2327

It was a solemn dinner.

The tests were over, the evaluations complete. Even though the official results hadn't been announced, it was all but assured that Morgan and Lorna Asher were among those to be selected for Martian colonization. In a day or two, they would receive their marching orders and, by week's end, they would be off, aboard a space freighter, headed for their new home.

Lorna had wanted this her entire life, but now that the time drew near, it was a sobering experience. They weren't likely to ever see Earth again.

Morgan sat quietly, picking at the slimy hunks of stewed beef his in-laws had graciously prepared. This was the third meal he and Lorna had attended at the Forsyth's bungalow in the past week. It was understandable, seeing how this was liable to be the last week they would ever spend together. There would be letters sent, video recordings back and forth, but the odds were highly against them ever talking again in person. By the time things were built up enough to allow casual visitors on Mars, the Forsyths would be too old to make the journey. They were nearing retirement age as it was, and they wouldn't be getting the age-arresting gene therapy their daughter and son-in-law could receive on Mars. They would probably die before commercial trips to Mars were ever established.

Simple pleasantries were exchanged over the meal. Lorna's mother, Gloria, kept reminding everyone of how happy and proud she was of her daughter, as if she had to keep reminding herself of why she shouldn't despise this mission that would take her only child away from Earth forever.

Lorna's father was a different story. Norris Forsyth beamed with pride, for his daughter was doing something he could only dream about. She was going to bring life to another planet; and, if that wasn't enough, she was slated to receive treatment to far outlive anyone on Earth. She was the fulfillment of all his hopes and dreams.

That Lorna was also married to Morgan Asher, an inspirational figure from history, was another source of paternal pride. Early on in their interactions, the Forsyths had learned to tone down any reverence, as Morgan couldn't stand it. He could never get used to the importance everyone put on his being. As far as he was concerned, he was just a man who spoke his mind, and the same words that had made him famous had once condemned him a hundred years in the past.

His advocation for a resurgence of scientific endeavors and condemnation of virtual reality had prompted the powers that be to lure him into a trap, freezing him in time for over a century, which was why Morgan didn't like to be reminded of that past. He had only known frustration, consternation and loneliness. His fame was based on a life he deemed irrelevant, and he never wanted to be anything more than a normal man.

After dinner, Morgan found himself sharing a drink with Norris, a non-alcoholic beverage with a strong pineapple and cherry flavor. The folks at NASA called it a "Martian Mons-Topper," and it was quite popular with the scientific-types who didn't want to risk harming precious brain cells with spirits or ferments.

"So, I hear you've sold your ranch," Norris mentioned between sips of the fruity drink.

"There was no sense keeping it, considering," Morgan answered with a sigh. "The Brawns have been there since before I bought the place, and they ran it faithfully all those years I was missing. It only seemed fair that I deed it back to them."

"Then you gave it away?" Norris asked. Being a frugal accountant, such an act of charity caught him by surprise.

34

"They deserved it. Besides, it's not like I need the money. I did keep a twenty acre plot of land in the hills. It's a special place, and the grandchildren might want to come back someday. You never know," Morgan added, thinking it ironic that he was worth millions, yet his money would be worthless to him on Mars; at least, for the foreseeable future.

"I must say, it's truly impressive what you're willing to do for my daughter, how much you're giving up in order to make her happy. I could never ask any man to love his wife more than you love my daughter. Thank you."

Norris was generally emotionally detached. For him to be so open with anyone was rare, and Morgan fully appreciated how much respect this man had for him.

"There's nothing I wouldn't do for Lorna," Morgan assured him.

The door to the kitchen swung open and Lorna stepped into the living room, dressed in casual attire, carrying a fresh pitcher of Mars Mons-Toppers. She set down the drink on the coffee table and asked, "How are you two getting along?"

"Same as always," her father said. "Morgan was just sucking up to me."

"Dad, please," Lorna chided with a laugh.

"We were just having a heart-to-heart chat," Morgan clarified.

"I'm glad the two of you get along so well," Lorna said, grabbing the pitcher to refill her husband's glass. Her steady hands didn't spill a drop.

"So, what do you expect they'll have you doing on Mars?" Norris asked Morgan.

"I don't know," Morgan replied. "Lorna's the specialist, an architectural engineer with numerous side specialties. I'm just the famous husband who gets to tag along."

"Yes, I suppose you're liable to be one of the fifty percent of the people going who will be sweating for a living—building, excavating, or smelting ore. That is, until society starts to take hold."

"That doesn't bother me," Morgan said with a shrug,

35

looking forward to having a regular job for a change. He didn't see the shame in honest labor.

"That may be, but where do you see yourself in ten or twenty years, after there are more career options available?"

"Don't you know?" Lorna interrupted. "Morgan's going to run the first commercial shooting range on Mars."

Norris cocked his eyes oddly, unsure of what to make of the comment.

"Morgan's bringing his guns along," Lorna said, topping off her father's glass with the red liquid.

"Really? I didn't know they were permitting that," Norris mentioned.

"Do you really think they could say no to my husband?" Lorna asked.

"The decision had nothing to do with me," Morgan said defensively. "I just asked to bring my collection along, and when a few bureaucrats on the Immigration and Colonization Board objected, I politely cited history, explaining in no uncertain terms why Mars cannot be the place to throw away any of our Constitutional Rights."

"It must have been some speech," Norris said, saluting with his glass.

Lorna tried to keep from laughing. "Morgan, you can try to be modest, but Mars might as well be under martial law for the interim. The Constitution has nothing to do with them letting you bring along your toys."

"It's not the same as martial law, and even under that, our rights must still apply. I understand the rules have to be different on Mars for now. The developing nature of the colony requires a special sort of order, but that is no reason to throw out the founding principles of America. The directors had to accept my reasoning."

"That settles it," Norris said. "You're going to be the first Senator from Mars."

Morgan took a drink from his glass, dismissing the idea as a tasteless joke. He'd had enough of politics for one lifetime, and was hoping to avoid bureaucratic entanglements in the future.

One could always hope.

***

Lorna shook her head at her father's declaration of Morgan's political future and took the half-empty pitcher back into the kitchen, where her mother was washing the last plate from dinner. Gloria Forsyth had taken her time, pining over the dishes like she wanted to keep herself busy. Her pain was as plain as day.

"Mom, you're going to scrub the enamel off that plate," Lorna said.

In response, Gloria stopped rinsing the plate and set it in the drain board. She turned around and managed to put on a smile, though it was difficult and the strain was obvious.

"This is really hard for you, isn't it?" Lorna noted, unable to ignore her mother's torment any longer.

"Don't worry yourself with me. I'll be fine," Gloria said, still trying to hide her feelings.

"Enough with the brave face, mom. It's not helping."

"You can't let this trouble you," Gloria said. "After all, this is what your father and I always wanted, always hoped for you. We worked so hard and made more sacrifices than you can imagine to make sure you would be here today, ready to leave on the greatest adventure humanity's ever known. I always knew this day would come. I just never thought it would be so hard to see you go."

Gloria walked over to the center island and leaned her arms on the cutting board. "You spent so many years in that stupid fantasy simulation. We haven't had nearly as much time together as we should have. Now we'll never have the time. I won't see my grandchildren playing in the back yard, or be able to hug them when they fall down. You're going to be so far away, and I'll never see you again."

Gloria had to stop talking as the tears began to choke her. She fought to hold them back, and soon recomposed herself. "Oh, but please, don't stay because of me. Mars is your dream—and your father's, too. It's your life."

37

"You know, mom, if things progress on Mars the way they did on the moon, we could have visitors in ten years."

"No, that's not likely at all," Gloria said with certainty. "The colonial plan for Mars is much more controlled and long-term, and the moon is right next door by comparison, just a few hours by plane. Mars is still a month away, at best, and I don't think your father and I are up to that kind of trip."

"Then what am I supposed to do?" Lorna asked.

Drying her tears, Gloria said, "You go. Have the life your father and I helped you attain, and don't you ever regret it."

Lorna gave her mother a tight hug, which helped both their moods. There was something of a finality to it, the last embrace of a parent and child, and they both accepted they had different paths to tread.

Pulling away from the hug, Gloria said, "Come on, dear, let's see how our husbands are doing."

Chapter Six
April 28, 2327

A few days blew by and colonial assignments were handed out. Twenty thousand lucky applicants were chosen, and after a lengthy flight would join the fledgling Martian colony. The settlement had been up and running for two years already, and those first colonists had paved the way for this second wave of immigrants.

Morgan and Lorna were given A-grade preference and shuttled aboard the *U.S.S. Plymouth* on the first day. There were several hundred people huddled inside the Boeing 947 Strato-Strider, a modern space-plane capable of riding to the moon and back without breaking a sweat. It was equipped with several airlocks that allowed it to dock with the *Plymouth* and offload the passengers directly.

The *Plymouth* was one of a kind, the first modern space freighter powered by the revolutionary Humboldt-Greyson Drive®, generically known as a Quantum Tunnel Drive (QTD). The main drive of the ship generated an unstable micro-wormhole, and when you fed matter into the singularity, it tore apart the atomic bonds, creating a tremendous amount of energy utilized for thrust. The best fuel was hydrogen, but large quantities of such a volatile substance weren't carried aboard the vehicle. In order to fuel the vessel, they used hydrolysis aboard ship to extract what they needed from their water reserves.

Ambitious scientists were working on plans to someday attach a Bussard Collector to the bow of a ship, but such technology was not yet feasible. It would be easy to gather hydrogen while in-flight, but the collector picked up a lot more than that. They needed to develop some form of deflective shielding to block out space debris and everything else a ship *didn't* want to collect. It was still a promising idea, and if it were ever realized, a ship could have a virtually limitless source of fuel.

The QTD was the first practical use of wormhole theory for propulsion, and it made the *Plymouth* the fastest spacecraft currently known to man, with a maximum cruising velocity of 71,000MPH. With the relative positions of Earth and Mars in their individual orbits, it would take a little over five weeks for the ship to cross that vast span.

The *Plymouth* was a giant cylinder, full of small cells which housed the twenty thousand passengers. One couldn't escape the similarities to prison, albeit a very comfortable and expensive one, and at the end of their trip, the real adventure would begin.

It took three full days for all the passengers to be ferried up from Earth, and by then, the crew was more than eager to get underway. As soon as the twenty thousand passengers were properly secured in protective harnesses, the *Plymouth* was launched, slingshotting out of Earth's orbit with all jets blazing. After an hour of restrictive gravitational forces, the vessel attained maximum cruising velocity and the late arrivals got acquainted with their cramped surroundings.

Each couple had roughly twenty feet of living space, and there was only one giant washroom, set up like a honeycomb of stalls. Bathing accommodations for twenty thousand people was a daunting task aboard a cramped space vessel. Each person was assigned one hour every three days for washing. The washroom was situated on the interior of the hull, near the aft quarter, and during specified bathing hours, the cylindrical ship was spun to provide limited gravity, just enough to keep the water flowing down into the reclamation drains.

The colonists had plenty of time to themselves and not terribly much to do with it. There was a large commons area, situated in the center of the ship, where people could associate, play a few games and hang out in zero gravity.

* * *

"It's your move," the diminutive scientist said, adjusting

the glasses that kept trying to float off his nose.

Morgan looked at the pieces on the chess board, their magnetic bases holding them to the metal plate in the weightless environment. Without much thought, he pushed a pawn forward one space, and soon saw it gobbled up by his opponent's knight.

"Check."

Morgan's King moved one step to the right, pinning it behind two pawns, and wedged beside his rook. His opponent slid his queen over and threatened the king at an angle.

"Checkmate, I believe," the scientist replied with satisfaction. "Shall we play again?"

"Chess was never my game," Morgan replied, tipping over his king. The piece fell on its side, then the strength of its magnet flipped it upright again.

"I suppose you're a card shark," the scientist guessed, glancing at a nearby table where a pack of passengers were playing poker.

"I'm not much for trivial games," Morgan corrected. "Whatever people are playing, it seems I'm either too smart or too dumb to enjoy it."

"To each his own," the scientist said, unbuckling himself from the seat. He pushed off from the floor and drifted toward the ceiling, which was actually more floor. The room had a circular contour just like the rest of the ship, was a few hundred yards in circumference, and twice as long.

There was a lot of space in the center of the room, which was commonly used for various activities, Magna-Ball for one. Magna-Ball was something of a cross between baseball, lacrosse, and volleyball. Players threw a magnetized ball around the room, catching it with metal staffs, while using compressed air packs to maneuver and run bases that drifted around the room. Morgan had watched a few games, but never felt the inclination to try it.

Morgan left the chess table and drifted over to the corridor opening that led back to his living quarters. Tapping a button on his wristband, he activated the magnets in his shoes so he could walk to his cabin, rather than drift. Floating around was still a new experience and he didn't much care for it. He was a sure-footed man who preferred to stand upright.

Two hundred and thirty two steps he counted, from the opening of the commons to cabin 02-22-405. He punched his six-digit code into the locking pad beside the door and it opened silently, giving him access to the cramped box he shared with his wife. Half of the living space was filled with their possessions. Being A-grade colonists, they had been permitted twice the standard allowance for personal belongings, though they didn't get much extra floor space.

The featureless metal enclosure had a hammock-like net for a bed that hung on the back wall. There was a small magnetic table with chairs off to one side, and a curtain pinned over one corner hid the toilet facilities.

As Morgan strapped himself into one of the chairs, the suction pump sounded from the bathroom, and Lorna stepped out from behind the curtain, wiping her hands with a chemically-treated cloth.

"I'll never get used to that thing," Morgan mentioned. "Having to pee in a tube is not my idea of comfort."

"You think you have it hard, what about me?" Lorna exclaimed, sliding into the seat across from him. "My tube's a little trickier to use."

"If we can survive a month of this, I dare say Mars will be a pleasure," Morgan added.

Lorna shook her head and let the strands of red hair float wildly. "Come on. Isn't this a little bit exciting?"

"It's different, I'll give it that," Morgan said, "but I'll be glad when I'm back on solid ground, just the same."

"I can't wait," Lorna said, her face bright with enthusiasm. "Junior Supervisory Architect. I still can hardly believe it. Hey, have they amended your assignment yet?"

"No. I've been slated as an administrative assistant, whatever that means."

"I bet Melinda Faris knows," Lorna mentioned. "She is the

newly appointed administrator for the settlement."

"Too bad she's not seeing anybody," Morgan said. "She's assigned to crew quarters, where we peons aren't allowed to tread."

"You'll get your chance. In the meantime, I managed to get a pair of magnetic belts today and I'm just dying to try them out. Care to take a load off?" Lorna asked in a seductive tone.

Morgan wasn't entirely sure how the belts would work, but he was certain it would be fun to learn.

* * *

Meals were unremarkable aboard ship. Most couples ate in their quarters, nibbling on dried space-food and sipping bags of water. The stuff hadn't changed much since the early days of space exploration, and no doubt the astronauts of the old republic would have recognized the nutrient-rich flavors.

There were always a few couples eating in the common area, though, and as the days went by, more and more people felt the need to get out and socialize.

It wasn't uncommon to see a number of the crew fraternizing with the colonists, playing magna-ball, or throwing down for a few hands of five card stud. It was unusual to see senior officers, though, as they generally kept to their duty assignments and had a private lounge. Yet, on the eighth day of the trip, the captain and three of his lieutenants graced the commons with their presence, so they could have a meeting with Morgan Asher and examine a few of his fascinating artifacts.

Stepping up to the captain's table, Morgan extended his hand. "Captain Percival Waltham," he acknowledged.

"Morgan Asher," the gray-bearded captain greeted, shaking Asher's hand. "That's a pretty large bag you have there."

"It's what you asked to see," Morgan replied, setting the bag down on the table. The metal objects inside held the sack securely against the magnetic table. Unzipping the bag revealed a number of firearms within.

The captain had learned of the existence of Morgan's guns from his armory officer, who had stored several cases of hunting ammunition in a secure locker, a very unusual event. Of course, the idea of antique firearms aboard ship piqued the captain's interest, and once everyone was settled in, he had ordered an audience with Morgan Asher, or as the senior officers were apt to call him, "the gun-toting colonist."

"So, these are the guns of Mars," Captain Waltham queried, glancing at the weapons.

"A few of them. I have several dozen more, as many as I was allotted by the immigration board."

"Sweet," the youngest lieutenant said. "Is that a P-38?"

Morgan reached in the bag and retrieved the antique weapon. "It's an original, manufactured in 1943. Note the German proof marks on the slide." He handed it to the eager lieutenant who seemed reluctant to hold it, for fear of leaving fingerprints. It was, after all, almost four hundred years old.

"And what is that monstrosity?" Captain Waltham asked, pointing to a bulky semi-auto rifle.

"That is a Remington Model 82, made in 2206, commemorating three hundred years of the Browning Autoloading Rifle. It's the special 'Prestige Grade.' Note the checkered stock, fancy scrollwork, and spider web pattern on the receiver."

The captain took hold of the rifle and turned it around in his hands, then proceeded to point it toward a bare patch of wall to get a feel for the sights. "Where'd you pick this beauty up?"

"My father bought it for my twenty-first birthday."

Morgan brought out two more rifles and handed them to the waiting lieutenants. They were old Winchester lever-actions, nothing terribly fancy, though certainly antique.

"Do any of these still shoot?" one of the lieutenants asked.

"They're all functional. Mind you, they've had a few replacement parts installed over the years."

The lieutenant holding the P-38 handed it back to Morgan. "You're gonna change the face of Mars with these. Before you know it, it'll be just like wild Wyoming down there."

"I hope so," Morgan replied, setting the pistol back in his bag.

The captain shook his head in appreciation and handed the rifle back. "Projectile guns have never been popular in space, for obvious reasons. I have an AK-47 hanging on the wall of my quarters, but of course it's just an ornament. I don't have any rounds to feed it."

"You don't have other guns aboard?" Morgan asked.

The captain snorted indignantly. "I wish. This is a military vessel, but the Brass doesn't think there's any reason to be armed out here. No legitimate threat, they say." He pulled a small plastic rod from his belt. "We wear taser sticks on duty, but I doubt they'd do much more than tickle a man. If I had my way, the armory would be packed with new condensed energy pistols, just in case we run into anything unfriendly."

"Yeah, in case little green men decide to board us," one of the lieutenants quipped.

The captain gave him a grim stare and the officer stopped laughing and grew stoic.

"Of course, the ship is rigged with a number of internal security measures, just in case anyone gets unruly," Captain Waltham added. "In a crunch, we can electrify the deck plates or vent the atmosphere from specific sections, among other things."

"That's comforting," Morgan said cynically, a bit unnerved by the idea of being electrocuted during somebody else's riot.

"Don't worry, we've never had to do anything that drastic, and it requires my personal activation code to trigger a lockdown beforehand. You don't have to fear any of my fine officers flipping the wrong switches."

Returning the last of the rifles to the bag, Morgan asked, "Is there any chance I could see Melinda Faris before we get to Mars?"

"The little lady doesn't want any visitors right now," Captain Waltham answered. "If she ever decides to come out,

I'll let you know."

One of the lieutenants added, "I can't believe they're replacing General Stavanger with her."

"They want to get her off-Earth, that's why," the captain said. "The colonel's an embarrassment to the uniform, with all that cosmetic surgery. Looks like a flaming child!"

"I see," Morgan said, assuming the captain wasn't aware of the "perks" of colonization. "You know, I'm a little confused by the Space Force rankings. You're obviously using old Navy ranks aboard the *Plymouth*, but Melinda Faris is a colonel."

"That's because she's actually in the Air Force," Captain Waltham corrected. "Before the separate Space Force branch was established, space flight fell under the jurisdiction of the Air Force, which is why we still have some hold-over officers. We'll weed 'em out eventually."

Morgan zipped up his bag and pulled it free of the magnetic table top. "Well, it was a pleasure meeting you, Captain. I trust we'll see each other again before this voyage is over."

"Same time tomorrow," Captain Waltham commanded. "Bring out some more of your collection."

"All right," Morgan agreed.

* * *

Lunchtime visits with the captain became commonplace for Morgan, as each day they met in the commons. The captain was generally accompanied by two or three of his officers and they would discuss trivial things, examining the many curios and relics of Morgan's collection. It took a week before they ran out of new guns to see, after which pleasant conversation sufficed.

At no time during the voyage was Morgan or any civilian permitted access to the crew quarters or any vital areas of the ship. The Space Force guarded their secrets and Captain Waltham made no exceptions to the regulations, not even for Morgan. Therefore, they always met in the commons.

Melinda Faris did not leave crew quarters for the duration

46

of the journey. She kept out of sight and out of reach of the civilian colonists she would soon govern, and whatever preoccupied her time was her own business.

At the end of the trip, Morgan realized he was going to miss the old captain, though the reality of getting back on solid ground made him eager to catch the earliest available flight down to Mars. Being A-Grade, he and Lorna received tickets for the third trip.

When it was time to board the flight, Morgan and Lorna grabbed a handful of personal belongings, whatever would fit in their small carry-on bags, and headed down to the *Plymouth's* cargo hold, where the Strato-Strider was being loaded with provisions and passengers. A dozen crewmen were busy hauling crates into the plane's hold; mostly personal belongings this trip, as the A-Graders had sizeable cargo allotments, which explained Morgan's sizeable collection.

A short line was forming on the left side of the cargo hold and it didn't take long for Morgan and Lorna to present their boarding passes and move into the plane for the trip down. Once they were strapped in, they waited patiently for twenty minutes, while the rest of the people made their way aboard.

The lighting dimmed slightly, as the Strato-Strider hummed under its own power and prepared to separate from the large spaceship. Following the pilot's announcement, a noticeable thump sounded, and the plane began moving toward the planet below.

Chapter Seven
June 7, 2327

The afternoon sky was bright and gray, and there were no clouds in sight. Morgan had been expecting it to be reddish or pink, considering it was the "Red Planet," but the orbital appearance of Mars was actually created by the dirt on the ground and not from any atmospheric coloration. In summer months, dust storms made the sky brownish red and could block visibility for weeks at a time, but in the spring months, the sky was generally clear.

The ground outside the hangar bay was covered with reddish sand and dust for miles, as far as the naked eye could see. This once-cratered section of Terra Cimmeria had undergone extensive landscaping over the last few years, as construction of the first Martian colony was in full swing. The terrain had been heavily blasted and leveled, and was now a relatively flat plain, prime for expansion.

The settlement was dubbed Villas Colony, so named after the Ma'adim Villas gorge, a 700km-long sapping channel that could be seen on the western horizon from just outside the hangar bay. The small dome of the colony sat atop a much smaller canyon that provided ample subterranean living space.

This was the sight Morgan and Lorna looked upon, as they finally had a chance to study their surroundings. Their flight had landed several hours earlier, but it was taking some time to get through customs. They stood around a while, huddled together with several hundred other colonists, waiting to be officially scanned and sworn in by the colonial registrar. After staring out at the alien world for ages, they were finally called away from the window to be scanned in and pushed along.

Following their official entry, they were directed to their

quarters by an off-duty miner. The large man stank of sweat and didn't say two words as they made their way through the corridors of the residential district. They stopped in front of a metal door resembling those aboard the *Plymouth*. Entering the domicile, they found it to be a small alcove with a bed, rudimentary kitchen, a television viewscreen, and a computer work station. Another boring metal box.

Next, the miner walked them down the hall to the communal bathroom. They would have to share it with a hundred other couples, but it was much more private than the shower aboard ship. There were half a dozen toilet stalls set up, and several large shower bays so encapsulated they looked like airlocks. Water seemed plentiful enough, but it took a lot of energy to manufacture it. They hadn't found much in the way of natural water on Mars, so they had to create it by extracting oxygen from carbon dioxide and blending it with hydrogen. It was a costly task, and they tried to conserve as much as possible, so the shower water was trapped within the enclosed compartment. It was recycled through complex filtration methods, which preserved it greatly. Even so, each colonist was limited in the frequency and duration of their cleansing periods.

To finish his duty, the miner showed them to the recreation center for their block, a circular room that resembled a mall cafe. With a nod and a grunt, the miner left them to get better acquainted with their surroundings.

Staring around the cramped room and its dozen happy occupants, Morgan yearned for wide open spaces, and wondered what it would take to get him on a surveying team of some kind. He'd been so cooped up for the last thirty six days, he was eager to stretch his legs. Turning to what looked like a large window recessed into one wall, he stared out at the vast expanse of nothing. It was a digital, real-time display of the planet's surface, which gave the illusion of space in this cramped place. The viewscreen in his quarters, albeit much smaller, displayed the same illusion when not otherwise in use.

Their living block was several floors below ground, as was most of the colony. The surface temperature dropped drastically at night, and even with the colony's geothermal heating system, the upper levels grew uncomfortably cold at night.

Morgan wondered how many years he would spend trapped inside this pressurized prison, pushing papers for a living.

Lorna had the interesting job and was eager to do something of value. Working on the great dome project was appealing and Morgan felt it prestigious; such a massive feat of engineering that would take a decade to complete. The ambitious expansion of the cramped colony would enclose a hundred square miles. Most of the materials were being manufactured on Mars, and most people had a hands-on job doing something physical—but not Morgan. He was going to be stuck behind a desk.

Now that they were on Mars, arranging an audience with the new governor wasn't a problem for Morgan, as he was assigned to her directly, and he felt if anyone could fix his situation, it would be her.

Entering the office, Morgan found Melinda Faris settling in, her desk piled high with personnel folders and status reports from the numerous manufactories now operating on Mars. She stopped whatever she'd been doing the second he came in.

"Ah, Morgan, so nice to see you at last," she said. "I trust you'll be ready for work tomorrow."

"Yes, about that," Morgan replied.

"Oh?" Melinda asked.

"I want to change my job assignment," he said.

"I see," Melinda said. "You understand, I'm not in charge of the career assignments. That's the Immigration and Colonization Board's decision for the foreseeable future."

"Some board on Earth that has never stepped foot off world decides who does what out here," Morgan grumbled.

"Not quite," she answered with a patient smile "A good

many of them are former astronauts, and the others have worked tirelessly on establishing this colony. It is their brainchild, their grand symphony. We must respect their wishes, for the moment."

"Could I ask you a blunt question?"

"Fire away," Melinda offered.

"What's the point of being governor if you can't govern?"

Melinda laughed her little girl laugh, evidently finding the comment amusing.

"Seriously," Morgan continued as her chuckles subsided. "You can't be so restricted that you can't reassign personnel here or there. Even if you're not responsible for the initial assignments, you must have some executive privileges."

"We both just got here. Why don't we get set up before planning the revolution, okay?" Melinda replied. "Oh, I'm sure I could swap you around without much trouble. I'd have to fill out some annoying forms and upset a few of my friends on the ICB, but I don't understand why you'd want that. You have been handed a very prestigious assignment."

"An idle job pushing papers is not my idea of prestigious," Morgan complained.

"Look, somebody did you a favor, making sure you weren't handed a strenuous or dangerous job. A lot of people, especially those involved in the space program, regard you as a national treasure. They'd never assign you a menial task, one they deemed to be beneath your dignity."

The concept was understandable, but Morgan couldn't help but find it ridiculous. To think any job on Mars was beneath a person's dignity was absurd.

"This is a fledgling colony, where everyone must work to assure its survival," Morgan mentioned. "Every soul added here means more food, water, oxygen, and energy must be used to keep everyone alive."

"Your point?" Melinda asked.

"How can Mars afford to support a top-heavy bureaucratic class?"

"It can't, obviously," Melinda answered. "That's why the

ICB does most of the paperwork, but even *they* can't do everything remotely. There must be a handful of administrators here in Villas to keep things running smoothly. As it stands, there are a dozen people to handle all administrative duties on Mars."

"Only twelve?" Morgan asked.

"Yes, including you. We are the 'paper pushers,' as you so eloquently put it. I wouldn't call twelve people out of thirty thousand to be an overbearing bureaucratic class, would you?"

"No," Morgan admitted.

Melinda began digging through the stack of thick folders on her desk until she found one marked "Personnel, Aa-Bo." Flipping through the sheets, she found Morgan's page and glanced at it.

"Look right here," she instructed, holding the folder out for Morgan to see. He glanced where she was pointing. "This rates you as a 'Phase-C' applicant."

"What is a Phase-C applicant?" Morgan asked, his curiosity dueling with his frustration.

"According to your profile, it means you have experience with farming, essential skills that will place you with our agricultural program when we get it off the ground in another fifteen or twenty years."

"You mean I'll be a rancher again?"

"Someday. But you must understand that we have a *long* way to go before we can start grazing cattle. You'll likely start out growing vegetables—beans, wheat, corn, other staples that won't gobble up resources. Still, that's over a decade away. In the meantime, it is advantageous that you exercise your other talents. You have a degree in Business Administration, and that makes you a prime candidate for clerical work."

"My degree is a hundred years out of date, and it dealt primarily with corporate finance."

"Even so, it's good enough for government work," she said, closing the folder and returning it to the stack. The papers seemed out of place among the digital technology of Mars, but the government still liked to keep hard copies of personnel records for some reason.

Melinda continued. "Now, I'm going to assign you the position of colonial quartermaster. How's that for a hands-on assignment?"

Morgan knew she was trying to help, so he breathed a sigh of disappointment at being offered one of the best jobs in Villas Colony and said, "I guess I'll just have to put up with it."

Melinda started to laugh again."You certainly are a rare breed of man."

"I can't stand the thought of sitting around all day, doing nothing, feeding off the colony like a parasite."

"Trust me, the quartermaster's job will keep you busy enough," Melinda said.

"It would seem I have no alternative," Morgan said.

"Then it's settled," Melinda exclaimed, sticking out her hand for him to shake. "Come by tomorrow morning. I'll have your duty roster set."

Morgan shook her hand, feeling like he'd just been drafted. "Just out of curiosity, who was the previous quartermaster for the colony?"

"The last governor. He liked to be in charge of everything, which might explain why he had a stroke. Personally, I'd like to sleep more than three hours a night, and survive this assignment."

"What about the age-reversing serum? Didn't it aid his health?" Morgan asked.

"General Stavanger was an odd bird. He never opted for the gene therapy," Melinda said. "Regardless, even a fit, young body can only take so much abuse. Now, if you'll excuse me, I still have a lot of unpacking to do."

With a slight nod, Morgan left her office and spent an hour wandering around the residential corridors, looking for his "suite." The bland hallways all looked the same and he hadn't grown accustomed to the numbering system, which was laid out in a zigzag pattern on each floor. The walk didn't tire him terribly, as his muscles were not overly burdened by the Martian gravity, though the month spent in freefall during the flight from Earth had diminished his stamina, despite the hour-a-day mandatory workouts he'd performed aboard ship.

He finally found the right door and entered the cramped quarters. They weren't much bigger than those aboard the *Plymouth*, though they actually had a kitchen and a real mattress. Stepping into the living/dining/bedroom, Morgan found his wife sipping a bowl of soup. She stopped briefly and waited for her husband to take his seat across from her at the small table.

"How did it go?" she asked.

Morgan glanced down and saw the bowl of lukewarm chicken soup set out for him. His stomach was still getting used to gravity again, and he wasn't very hungry. "I'm the new quartermaster," he mentioned.

"Wow. That's big," Lorna said, followed by a smile.

"Yes, I guess it is," Morgan replied, tapping a spoon against the table.

Little else was said over the meal and they enjoyed a quiet evening together, the first of many they would share on the Red Planet.

Chapter Eight
June 8, 2327

It was cold in the early morning hours, though the temperature was rising fast. It was already sixty below zero, and would be well above freezing by noon.

There was a slight wind, but a heated spacesuit blocked any wind chill factor, and the thin atmosphere dulled the air's howl to a faint whisper.

Colonel Avery hadn't intended to ever visit Mars. The hostile rock over fifty million miles from home, at present orbit, was best left to the pioneering spirits of colonial recruits, brave men and women carefully screened and selected by the brilliant minds of the NASA hierarchy. It wasn't the place for an officer and a gentleman.

There were some dirty little details, however, that only an officer could handle—and Avery wasn't much of a gentleman.

The Persians had handed him more than he'd counted on. He figured their outlandish tale would turn out to be nothing, just more Scife propaganda, or some sort of Islamic plot to subvert the west. Nobody in their right mind would have taken their tale at face value. Still, the top brass decided to see if there was any corroborating evidence. In the process, they uncovered something very peculiar in the center of Lake Eridania, the dusty basin that had once been a lake on prehistoric Mars. Somehow, the contour of the land had changed ever so slightly in one small region. It was nothing anybody would ordinarily notice, and it could have simply been a glitch in the imaging processors of a cartography satellite, but the chance the blemish was signs of human activity warranted further investigation.

So, here was Avery, in charge of a special ops team, marching across the lifeless Martian desert, swerving around boulders and skipping over the reddish sand covering the ground to the horizon and beyond, expecting to uncover a phantom Scife installation threatening to undermine all American extra-stellar colonization. This mission was, of course, off the books. Nobody at NASA knew they were here, and none of the government bureaucrats would admit to authorizing the deployment of troops. Black ops had always gone this way, only this was the first time they'd ever been sent to another planet.

They'd traveled aboard the *Plymouth*, hidden safely away inside crew quarters for over a month. They hadn't fraternized much with the colonists, but when they'd wanted to get out and mingle, they'd done it dressed as non-commissioned crewmen and nobody had known their true identities outside of Melinda Faris and the ship's senior staff.

Colonel Avery and his new space marines kept from going stir-crazy through intense training. From the rigors of the centrifugal exercise room, to the combat and flight simulator, each man kept his wits about him and managed to make it to Mars with enough stamina to handle the forthcoming trek across the surface. They were glad to finally hit the ground running, even if they were stuck in spacesuits.

They'd been deployed in the middle of the Martian night, over thirty miles from the suspected Scife installation. The distance was necessary for the covert operation.

The marines marched across the frozen wasteland for hours, making good time with little strain, thanks to the lighter pull of Martian gravity. By sunrise, they were less than a mile away from their objective. A rocky hillside stood before them, showing no obvious signs of life or that man's hand had ever touched this section of the planet.

"This is it, men," Avery shouted. His voice carried through a closed circuit communications network built into their suits, permitting them to speak to one another and block external eavesdropping.

"I don't see it," Lieutenant Barton said, his deep voice turned into a growl by the communication system.

Colonel Avery tapped a few buttons on his sleeve,

activating a complex sensor array inside his helmet. The readings superimposed themselves on his visor, and enhanced pictures of the landscape ahead revealed several anomalous energy signatures along the ridgeline. "It's there," he told the others. "Keep your eyes sharp for..."

Before Avery could finish, Barton's head exploded. A bullet had zipped through the air and blasted a hole through his helmet. The shot killed the lieutenant instantly, but the sudden decompression increased the gore tenfold.

The dozen men hit the ground, seeking whatever cover they could locate. There were several boulders nearby, which protected them from the sniper in the hills.

"We've been made!" Captain Biggs shouted.

"Not necessarily," Avery said, scanning the hillside with his sensors. "I'm not detecting anything living up there. It could be automated defenses. Fan out and converge below that ridge."

The marines did as they were ordered with expert precision. They moved swiftly and silently, and nobody else took a bullet. Before long, they found themselves at the base of the curious hillside, only to discover it wasn't a hillside at all. Although the outer appearance was rock and dirt, the surface was several inches beneath that image.

Setting his hand against the rock, Avery saw his fingers disappear under the illusion and touch a smooth surface. He ran his fingers up and down and side to side, feeling the contour of the structure. It was fairly flat, sloped at a sixty degree angle, and matched the illusionary hill in front of him.

As the reality of the situation was revealed, the strike team found themselves surrounded. Out of nowhere, a dozen space-suited figures appeared, armed with sleek rifles. The figures corralled the Americans against the dome and directed them to drop their weapons. Seeing no alternative, they complied, and were then marched alongside the hill. A few hundred yards later, they were directed to walk into what appeared to be a solid patch of dirt, yet as they passed through the illusion, they found themselves inside a spacious airlock.

Their captors followed them in and shut the airlock door. Tapping a few buttons on a control panel, the leader of the pack pressurized the airlock and ordered the marines to remove their helmets. A few of the men complied instantly, but several resisted until guns were once again leveled at them.

Colonel Avery was the last man to remove his helmet, and as he did, his nose detected a strange odor. The sweet smell wasn't unpleasant, though before he knew what hit him, he was on the floor, a dark curtain covering his eyes.

* * *

Avery awoke to a light tapping sensation on his cheek. He rocked his neck back and forth and found he was sitting upright in a recliner. His delirium subsided quickly and, as his vision cleared, found himself in an office suite, staring at a blond-haired man in a white suit. "Felling better?" the man asked with a slurred French accent.

Avery didn't reply. As he tried to stand, he found his arms and legs unresponsive. He couldn't feel anything below his neck, giving him a sinking feeling in his gut.

"Ah, you won't be getting up for a while," the Frenchman said. "We took the liberty of injecting a numbing agent into your spine. It will wear off, eventually."

"You dirty Scife. What the hell are you doing here?" Avery cursed.

"Manners, my deal Colonel," he chided. "Is that any way to speak to your gracious host? You are, after all, a guest here."

"Guest, my ass!"

"Of course, how silly of me. Please, allow me to introduce myself. I am Jean Proudhon Budreau, Senior Administrator of Facilite de Mars, the Consensorate's first Martian outpost at Eridania." He spoke gently, as if trying to elicit friendship.

"Whatever you want, forget it," Avery said boldly, his eyes glaring with hatred. "I don't know anything and I'm good for nothing."

"Do not demean yourself," Budreau replied, sounding irritated by the colonel's hostility. "You and your men will serve a grand purpose; grander than any you could have ever hoped to realize as petty functionaries of an Irrationalist State."

Mr. Budreau snapped his fingers and an orderly stepped out of the room. A few moments later, the orderly returned with Captain Biggs in tow, the young marine still in his spacesuit, minus the helmet. The men stood in front of the desk, facing Avery.

"Captain Biggs, express to your colonel where your loyalties lie," Budreau commanded gently.

"My loyalty is to the body of man, first and foremost," Biggs replied.

"Like hell it is," Avery objected. "Your loyalty is to the flag of the United States, soldier!"

"No, sir. All nationality is secondary, sir!" Biggs shouted, standing upright at attention.

Stepping up beside Biggs, Budreau said, "Now, Captain, tell us, what is the first purpose of man?"

"To facilitate the technological and biological advancement of the species," Biggs replied.

"How?" Budreau asked.

"Through the laws of science, dictated by the scientific consensus of the majority."

"Enough!" Avery shouted.

"Quite," Budreau said. "You may leave us, Captain."

Biggs nodded and headed for the door. Before leaving, he turned to the colonel and said, "I'm sorry, sir, but it's just the truth. I hope you'll understand."

Once Biggs was out of earshot, Avery cursed, "You Scife bastards have always been good at brainwashing."

"*Au contraire, mon* Colonel, it is far more than brainwashing. It is an augmentation of the mind and body through digital conversion."

"Digital conversion?" His mind quickly recalled what the Persian geophysicist had told him, regarding the compulsion he'd felt to obey the Scifes. "That has something to do with teleportation technology," he said, hoping to spur some answers.

"Yes, it's a most efficient form of travel, don't you agree? A single unit can instantaneously transport objects anywhere within a thousand kilometer range, for only a few kilowatts per metric ton, and that range can be greatly extended when multiple pads are utilized. But it has a far more useful application in your case, for a simple adjustment of the conversion matrix allows us to adjust the mind, perfect mental pathways to allow rationality and understanding. Thanks to the encephalographic scans we took during your reactions to Captain Biggs, we can now perform a precise reconfiguration."

Colonel Avery's eyes grew wide with hatred and terror. He struggled to move his appendages, but found them useless.

Tapping a button on his desk, Budreau summoned a fresh pair of guards who lifted Avery by the shoulders. "It is time you joined us, Colonel."

Avery remained silent as they carried him out.

***

With his prisoner gone, Jean Budreau sat down at his desk and sighed. Talking to the chaotic American was a trial, though it was his specialty—diplomacy. He'd spent a lifetime dealing with foreigners, serving to the best of his ability. As a reward, his government had stolen the one thing he loved the most.

Picking up a picture on his desk, he looked at the raven-haired beauty within the frame and recalled the joy they had shared for a limited time, the few years they had been permitted matrimony, the passion they had experienced. Yet, it had all ended so abruptly, as the Consensorate Reproduction Board had deemed them an "inferior match." In the blink of an eye, they had taken her away from him, shipped her halfway across the continent to copulate with some Bulgarian neurosurgeon.

Budreau had tried to see her, but it was forbidden. The

Consensorate despised emotional entanglements and felt it counter-productive and dangerous to allow him to see the love of his life. He wasn't supposed to feel anything for her; be glad he was getting a substitute, genetically-compatible spouse instead.

He'd known three other wives since his first marriage, but never had he loved any of them as he had his dear Janet. She was the perfect mate that haunted him to this day, and her memory drove him to his current course of action.

"They have stolen you from me forever," he whispered to the picture as he gently stroked the glass, "but things shall be different here on Mars. You will see. They will never deny love again!"

* * *

There was nothing Colonel Avery could do as the guards dragged him out of the room and down a long, metal corridor toward the molecular teleportation laboratory. He watched helplessly as they entered a bright chamber, octagonal in design. There were computer stations set up all along the walls, and in the center of the room sat a large metal disk that took up approximately a third of the floor space. It was in the center of that disc the guards dropped their human cargo.

As he lay on the ground, Avery began to feel his extremities again. Life was coming back to his limbs. Would he have time to attempt an escape? No, there was nowhere to run, but there *was* a way out. Tucked in his belt, a hidden compartment held a cyanide capsule which would assure his captors would never convert him and his secrets would remain safe.

Feeling was returning to his fingers and he managed to wiggle them a little as the minutes ticked on. Nothing seemed to be happening. The laboratory was vacant, save for himself and the two guards who watched him intently from a distance. He didn't know what was holding things up, but he was increasingly grateful, as his hand began picking at his belt flap, searching for his final option.

Before his fingers could find the secret pouch, several

scientists entered the room and took their stations, each yammering on about trivial concerns, shooting the breeze as they went about their business. They flipped switches and vocalized readings from their consoles, preparing to convert Colonel Avery's body into energy, and then reconstruct it; adjusting his thoughts and memories to suit their whims.

Avery didn't understand the finer elements of the science, but he knew the end result. The man he was, the half-paralyzed Marine Corps officer, would be dead, and a new person, a digital copy, would be born to replace him. He could not imagine a more horrendous fate.

"Salvation," Avery thought, as his fingers located the secret pocket under his belt buckle. A few taps and tugs with his forefinger nudged open the shutter on that tiny compartment, yet it was empty. The precious poison capsule was gone, presumably stolen by his captors for this very reason, to cheat him of his noble sacrifice.

"I'll see all of you in Hell," Avery growled as his last hopes vanished and he consigned himself to the reality of the moment.

With the final preparations set, the scientists activated the molecular accelerator that would pull his subatomic bonds apart.

It was the strangest sensation Avery had ever felt, as the device ripped his molecules asunder, converting his flesh into particles of energy. It didn't hurt terribly much, though he couldn't help but scream as his face melted away and his final thoughts faded with his disintegrating brain. It only lasted a second, but it seemed to drag on into eternity.

Colonel Seth Avery died. As the final atoms of his body were converted into energy, the person that had lived was no more, and many theologians would argue that at this point, his soul was released to whatever afterlife awaited it.

For the flesh, however, it wasn't the end. The impressive basis of the teleporter, the key that made molecular teleportation possible, was the trinary computer core, a massive data storage system similar to those used in virtual reality systems. Before the innovation of the trinary core, there had been no way to keep precise track of all 10^{28} atoms in a person's body and reassemble them into a perfect copy on cue.

The energy of Avery's being was momentarily stored inside the giant metal disc, which served as a massive storage battery; a few seconds later, the process was reversed. The molecular accelerator, with instructions from the trinary core, reconstituted the particles of energy into solid matter and restored them to their original pattern, the only difference being a handful of neurological "enhancements."

When the process was complete, a solid body lay atop the teleport disc. The new clone blinked his eyes and took his first view of the world. The silver-gray of the metal disc beneath him was all he saw and his body was still mostly paralyzed. Yet, everything seemed so fresh and amazing, as he was experiencing things for the first time. It was like being a newborn for a moment. The newness of life was exhilarating.

Although he had only lived for a few seconds, the giant infant knew who and what he was. He was Colonel Seth Avery of the United States Marine Corps.

New thoughts raced through Colonel Avery's mind. Ideas that an hour ago would have seemed alien, or evil, now ruled him. He didn't know they were unnatural, or anything to abhor. As far as he knew, he had always thought this way, believed in the dictates of Scientific Fundamentalism, and put the advancement of humanity above all else. It felt wrong to believe anything else.

He didn't understand why he had fought against his cordial hosts previously, as they walked him to a comfortable set of guest quarters. The guards now joked with him about their latest romantic conquests, and the devious, appealing nature of the opposite gender. He was among friends and colleagues, people closer to him than any he'd known before.

The room wasn't much, but it had soft furniture that comforted his newly revived limbs. He took off his boots and rubbed his bare feet against the soft carpet on the floor, and relaxed in a padded rocker until the arrival of a most unexpected visitor.

"Enjoying yourself, Seth?" the woman's voice asked.

Avery opened his eyes and turned toward the door. There stood Melinda Faris, the last person he thought to see here and now. Her familiar face caused him to harken back to the month aboard the *Plymouth*, during which he had spent many hours in candid talks with this officer of equal rank from the Air Force.

Words escaped Avery, as Melinda walked in and took the chair directly across from him.

Curling her legs up into the seat of the chair, Melinda said, "You're looking well. How have they been treating you?"

Avery still couldn't speak. The thoughts in his head seemed to be freezing his larynx, as two separate sets of thoughts and emotions battled for supremacy. He couldn't think clearly and grabbed at his head in frustration.

"I know. It can be difficult for the first few hours. Take a minute," Melinda said gently. "Try to focus on one thing."

Duty. That was the first thing Colonel Avery's mind latched onto, and it immediately centered on the image of an American flag.

In the blink of an eye, his thoughts shifted back many years to his youth, as he stared at the stars and stripes of the United States, and he recalled his father, "The General," reciting the Pledge of Allegiance with a group of Senators. It was just a stray memory fragment, one of a million floating around in Avery's head, yet for some reason, it was the one thing that brought clarity back to him.

"There," Melinda said with a smile as Avery's expression of agony changed to revelation. "Better?"

"I think so," Avery said, clear-headed, but still a bit confused.

"Tell me, what was your one thing?" Melinda asked.

"Huh?" Avery asked.

"For me, it was apple pie. My grandma used to make the

64

best pie out of apples from the neighbor's farm. I remember sneaking in and stealing a slice fresh out of the oven, burning the skin off the roof of my mouth in the process. I was six."

"What does it mean?" Avery asked, feeling a storm of confusion still echoing at the back of his mind.

"It's just a comforting thought, to help the healing process along. Teleportation is rough the first time around. The mind has to adjust to the new experience."

"It was incredible. Horrible, but incredible."

"I know," Melinda said.

The ugly truth hit him, a revelation that would have ordinarily caused instant revulsion and hatred, though his emotions were oddly tempered by whatever the teleporter had done to him.

"How long have you been working for the Consensorate?"

"I don't work for the Consensorate," Melinda said, remaining calm and pleasant.

"But this place...these people are working for the Consensorate."

"Not exactly," Melinda said. "Yes, this base may have been constructed by the Consensorate, and these people may be Consensorate citizens, for the moment, but their loyalty does not lie with that fascist coalition of European Nation States."

"What are you saying? They're defectors?"

"No, Seth, they are like us—true followers of Scientific Fundamentalism."

Avery's head began to ache as he tried to wrap his thoughts around her claims. As he listened to her voice, the suggestions planted in his mind helped him understand it all.

"How long have you been working with them?" he asked.

"Since my first Mars landing."

"All that time?"

"They were here when we touched down, had been for years. They waited for us to do our initial scouting, then snagged us with the teleporter one by one. They snatched me right out of my spacesuit. You can't imagine how utterly naked I felt when I materialized on that disk in my birthday suit."

"They can teleport you, just like that, from a distance?" Avery asked, wondering why they hadn't done that to him. Why drag him into the lab if they could do it remotely?

"Of course, it wasn't that easy," Melinda explained. "They had to tag me with an RFID chip and acquire a good sight picture, all without being detected. They managed it, somehow. But enough about me. How is your conversion going?"

"My conversion?"

"Where does your loyalty lie?"

Immediately, without thought, Avery blurted out, "To the human race, as a whole." As soon as the words left his lips, he wondered why he had said it.

"And what is your duty, as a member of the human race?"

"To aid the technological and biological advancement of our people however possible."

"And you see no contradiction between that and your being a United States Marine?"

"None," Avery replied hastily, though something deep inside told him there *was* a contradiction. He knew the Scifes had done something to him, but felt it best to play along for the moment and let the "programming" speak, rather than receive further brainwashing treatments.

"Good," Melinda said, believing Avery's mental reconfiguration had been successful. "Now we can work together, for the betterment of our people."

"What do you have in mind?" Avery asked.

"We're going to work with these people, the Eridanian colonists, to forge a new world, true to the dictates of science. We are going to throw out the failed policies of the Consensorate, which stripped away individuality as a means of quality control. Human beings are not just biological machines to be programmed and ordered about, but that's not to say we should live as animals, drifting aimlessly through life, with no desire to enhance the world around us. It is a precarious balance that must be established, and here we shall do just that."

"What's the plan?" Avery asked.

"When the time is right, the Martian colonies are going to declare their independence from their Earth governments. Those of us on Villas Colony, and our counterparts here at Eridania, shall forge the basis of a new united utopia," she said with rapture.

"How will you get our people on board? Teleport all thirty thousand colonists?"

"Hardly," Melinda answered, curbing her enthusiasm. "Most of them are already with us. The ICB is populated with our fellow Scifes, and their orientation screenings made sure the colonists would be understanding. Just a few rotten apples linger about, certain specialists we couldn't do without, and a number of spouses who are borderline. Over time, we'll make them understand, one way or another."

"How do I fit into the plan?" Avery asked.

There was a dramatic pause, after which Melinda answered. "We need you to go back and tell your superiors that this doesn't exist, that you found nothing out of the ordinary at Eridania. We can't have the United States government poking around, getting in the way. If they learn of our plans too soon, we will be undone. Keep them in the dark and quell their suspicions."

"What about the Consensorate? How can we be sure they won't spoil your plans?"

"*Our* plans, Seth," Melinda said. "Don't worry about the Consensorate. We must trust our European allies here to deal with their superiors, just as they count on us to deal with ours."

Standing, Melinda excused herself and wished Avery good luck, leaving the marine to process the new data in private.

Hitting the hallway, Melinda marched directly to the teleport lab, where several scientists were reviewing sensor data regarding Colonel Avery's current state of mind. Jean Budreau was also in the room and shot the lady a smile as she came in.

"How is he doing?" Melinda asked, leaning over a scientist's shoulder.

"It's inconclusive," said the scientist with a Slavic accent. "It is obvious that at least some of the mental reconfiguration has taken hold, but it is still too early to determine if he is with us."

"What do you think, my dear," Budreau asked Melinda.

"We can trust him," Melinda replied.

"You're certain?"

"We're cut from the same cloth. Believe me when I say he's on our side."

Budreau had learned to trust her judgment long ago and accepted her statement as gospel. Everything was falling into place. Their dream would soon begin.

Chapter Nine
July 7, 2327

Three days after their deployment, Colonel Seth Avery and eleven of his men returned to the *Plymouth*, reporting nothing out of the ordinary on Mars. "Those dirty Persians were jerking our chains," Avery told Captain Waltham, and then explained the unfortunate demise of Lieutenant Barton, who had "fallen down a crevasse."

With all crew and passengers aboard for the return trip, the *Plymouth* plotted a return trajectory to Earth. Their next visit to the Red Planet wouldn't be for another two years, when they would bring a wealth of supplies to sustain the fledgling colony.

Life on Mars continued, and the new settlers fell into their roles without too much turmoil. There was just enough space for everyone, but a priority was set on the construction of additional living space. The mining operations provided plenty of open channels in which to build and there were still plenty of natural gorges.

Additionally, room was being planned for a new daycare and school facility, as the first batch of colonists were starting to have children. Breeding had been discouraged for the first two years, but now that life was safely established, procreation was inevitable and desired. The lighter weight of Mars was considered a blessing for pregnant mothers in the third trimester, their added weight nowhere near what they would normally weigh on earth.

After a week on Mars, Lorna decided she wanted to experience the joys of motherhood. Her job wasn't strenuous, her responsibilities limited as a construction foreman. Having children was something she felt ready to tackle, and Morgan was more than willing to accommodate her. They had been engaged in the act regularly for the last two years, yet no children had arrived, which made them wonder. Rather than wait another two years, they scheduled an appointment with a fertility doctor.

The medical offices were thirty levels underground, set at the center of the colony. Here, Morgan met with CPA Will Paulson, an aide to Doctor Grossman of the newly established Martian Reproductive Agency. Paulson was a lanky lad without much muscle tone and a beard stubble that might have been the best he could grow. He was a newbie, having been among the latest batch of colonists from the *Plymouth*.

"All right, give me the bad news," Morgan said as Paulson studied the test results.

"Well, your sperm count's not what I'd call irregular, but it is on the low side of normal. Your wife checked out fine. I'd suggest you just keep trying," Paulson replied.

"But we've been trying on and off for two years already."

"That's nothing to be concerned about. It doesn't always stick, even on Earth, and there are so many new factors to sexual reproduction here on Mars. Any number of things might contribute to reduced pregnancy. The lighter gravity, the recycled atmosphere, unforeseen radiation spikes."

"There's nothing physically wrong with me?"

"No. As I said, keep trying, though I could prescribe something to help nature take its course," Paulson suggested.

"I'm pretty sure Lorna has her heart set on natural conception," Morgan replied.

"Well, it may take a month or three, but you'll get there, I'm sure."

Morgan accepted the answer. He was ready to leave when a question came to mind. "Would taking the anti-aging therapy help?"

"I don't see how," Paulson replied.

"But, in getting younger, wouldn't that increase my virility?"

"Get younger?" Paulson said with an odd twitch. "I may just be a Physician's Assistant, but even I know there's no

70

way to get younger."

Morgan rubbed his neck, feeling someone was playing a joke on him. "Melinda Faris told me her physical age was reversed by the anti-aging therapy; that unique factors here on Mars allowed her body to be rejuvenated."

Paulson shook his head slowly, dismissing the absurd notion. "Look, this anti-aging stuff is still new to me, and it's not my department, but I can tell you it does nothing to reverse your age. Oh, it pretty much arrests it, like stopping a clock, but you can't turn the hands back. You might feel a little younger, since your body won't be degrading further with time, but there's nothing I know of that can reverse your current age."

"Then how do you explain Melinda's teenage appearance?"

"Don't you keep up with the news? Melinda Faris had half her skin burned off in a freak accident during the Aries-2 mission. She needed reconstructive surgery when she got back to Earth, and for some reason, opted for that teen look. It's some extremely impressive work, I'll grant you that, but I can't believe it's more than skin deep."

"Everybody says it's plastic surgery," Morgan added, "but I swear it's more."

Leaving Paulson to his work, Morgan headed back to his place of employment, a stylish corner office in the administrative complex. The office was one of a dozen decorated boxes, roughly the size of a standard set of living quarters, though the metal walls were disguised with wood-textured wallpaper and plastic moldings, giving a more cozy feel. Only the best for the bureaucrats.

There was a short stack of electronic pads on the metal desk and Morgan examined their files briefly before signing them. Standard requisition requests from various departments, seeking permission to tap the stockpiles of resources available. He was growing increasingly bored with the quartermaster's job, as the computer records and warehouse workers conducted all of the hands-on work. He was just a signature.

Around noon, Melinda invited Morgan to lunch, as she commonly did a few times each week, and he joined her in the Governor's Lounge. The Lounge was more of a library than anything else, with books covering three walls from floor to ceiling. There was even a vid-screen in the ceiling, which projected the illusion of a skylight. Morgan considered it the nicest room on Mars.

Finding his regular seat at the oval table in the center of the room, Morgan acknowledged those already seated. Melinda was comfortably nestled in the governor's leather chair, one of the only luxurious pieces of furniture on the entire planet. To her right was Petra Euchland, the colony's chief financial expert; to her left was Timothy Keene, Chief of Police.

"Hi, Morgan. How did things go at the clinic?" Melinda asked.

"Everything's fine," Morgan said, feeling a little self-conscious. He didn't care to discuss his private, marital matters with others, though the governor seemed to take an overly healthy interest in his affairs.

"I'm glad it worked out," Melinda replied as her personal chef approached the table, pushing a tray with a large metal kettle on top. He set it beside the governor and handed out bowls and utensils before leaving.

Melinda enjoyed serving herself, so she grabbed the ladle and filled her metal bowl with the liquid in the pot. The vegetable stew reeked of artificially-infused vitamins, but she favored it and her guests tolerated it. It was comparable to all the current food offerings in Villas Colony, and it would stay this way until the domes were complete and major farming took hold.

"It is times like these I've a hankering for a bowl of lobster stew," Timothy said, smelling the pungent aroma of the food.

"What on Earth is that?" Petra asked, pouring a ladle of the stew into her bowl.

"It is what it is," Timothy said, poking at the stew with his spoon. "There's this little restaurant on the mid-coast of

72

Maine that makes it just right. Any of you ever been to Maine?"

None of the others had been, so Timothy let it pass, sipping the food in front of him, dreaming of something different.

"It must have been three years ago, the last time I was home, just on the outskirts of Ellsworth," Timothy mentioned between sips. "It was right before I shipped out."

"You've been here since the founding of the colony," Melinda replied. "After two years on Mars, do you have any regrets?"

Tim shook his head in the negative.

"I take it you're adapting to the recent changes, then?" Melinda mentioned.

"I'm getting there," Tim said. "Our population just tripled, so a few people are bumping elbows. But I will say this—it's a lot easier keeping order here than on Earth. I spent a decade with the Hancock County Sheriff's Department, one of the lowest crime areas in the nation, but it's got nothing on Villas. Except for a few domestic disputes, I haven't had anything whatsoever to deal with here during the last two years. I was almost hoping the new arrivals would be a little more feisty, so I'd have something to do."

"We're all too busy trying to survive to make trouble," Morgan mentioned, disinterested with his food.

"And don't forget the screenings," Petra added. "Those with overly-violent criminal tendencies don't get selected to immigrate. That quells trouble before it starts."

"If only we screened our political leaders so well," Melinda said, sounding gloomy. "I just received the latest from Earth. Congress has decided to freeze our budget."

"*What*?" Petra shouted, slamming her fists on the table. "How could they do this? What are they thinking? Without full funding, we're liable to die out here!"

"The new Congress decided it was more important to waste our funding on their own pet projects. I have a copy of the appropriations bill President Steyn just signed, if you're

73

interested."

"Reading the bill won't change anything, will it?"

"Why is this such a problem?" Morgan asked, confused.

Petra answered after quelling her emotions. "In the next few years, Villas Colony is going to need progressively more funding. As our construction projects advance, more materials are needed."

"I thought we were making what we needed here, for the most part," Morgan said.

"At the moment, we are. We can manufacture the steel and glass we need, but we don't have the industrial capacity to build the more complex components—not without more industrial machinery. It's just not possible for us to build heaters, air condensers, new spacesuits, or any other of a million little things necessary to complete the dome project with what we currently have. NASA had a progressive funding plan, to allow us to receive materials as needed, but now we'll be lucky to get enough food, let alone building supplies."

"They have cut us off at the knees," Melinda said calmly. "We must find a way to build a set of crutches. The ICB wants our input, so what are our options, Petra?"

"Cut, cut, cut," Petra mumbled. "Well, I can say payroll has gotten out of hand since the newbies arrived. I don't know how we'll stay under budget when we have to pay everyone to live here."

"The ICB already thought of that, and I imagine you'll come to the same conclusion," Melinda said, "but by all means, share your thoughts with us."

Petra turned her head toward Morgan and Tim, her fingers moving nervously as she talked. "Right now, each and every colonist is allotted a financial sum that is deposited in a bank account back on Earth to be used by family members, or left to accrue interest for the future. The amount paid may seem paltry to each individual, but put all thirty thousand of us together and you're looking at some serious coin.

"I'd have to run the figures, but I dare say if we suspend salaries for the time being, we could probably afford the materials we need to complete most of our construction. We might be able to bring our industrial capacity to self-sufficiency."

"And how long would this suspension last?" Melinda asked, as if she already knew the answer.

"At least until the dome is completed, maybe longer," Petra replied. "I mean, it's a fine line, even then, but it's not like we'd really be sacrificing everything. This way, each colonist will have a monetary stake in the project. The people will, in effect, own the industry and the land we vitalize."

"Will we, really?" Morgan asked. "I mean, it's still all federal dollars."

"Yes, but we all signed a contract with the federal government when we became colonists," Petra reminded him. "Each contract specified a set rate salary for every colonist, based on their classification and specialty. Barring a state of emergency, those contracts cannot be renegotiated or rescinded, meaning we are guaranteed to be paid those funds. We can do with them as we please."

"I believe NASA may have had this very contingency in mind when they implemented the colonial salary program," Melinda said. "This isn't the first time Congress has tried to pull the rug out from under the space program. When we were establishing the first lunar colony, a new bunch of lawmakers came in and slashed funding, leaving the project to blow in the wind. If it hadn't been for an influx of money from commercial interests, it would have been the death of Luna, then and there."

"You're saying NASA set up our salaries to pad the project?" Morgan asked

"It's what I would have done," Melinda concluded.

"That's damned underhanded," Tim said. "Some of us wouldn't be here if it hadn't been for the added incentive of a steady paycheck."

"True, but sacrifices must be made," Melinda said. "We

75

are presiding over the next phase in human evolution, after all. We all need to chip in, if we want to have a future."

"A lot of us aren't going to take a cut in pay lightly," Tim added. "We may not have anything to buy now, but come retirement age, this planet will be hopping. A nest egg would come in handy."

"What do you plan to buy?" Petra asked, amused by Tim's defiance. "We'll always have everything we need and simple luxuries. In fact, if we put our salaries toward the needs of the colony, and the next Congress decides to restore our budget, we'll have a healthy surplus to provide all kinds of extras."

"Hey, now you're just talking crazy," Tim countered. "Putting our salaries toward necessities is one thing, but if we get our funding back, I expect my salary reinstated—along with all my back pay! You're not confiscating my wealth to buy luxuries for everybody else. I earn that money. I decide how it's spent."

"Wouldn't you rather everyone in the community benefit by pooling resources, rather than you alone wasting it frivolously?"

"Who says I want to be a part of this 'community' forever? What if, in another fifty years, I get tired of that little gray box I'm living in and want to buy myself a hunk of land and go prospecting? There's a future in micro-dome housing, and plenty of Martian real-estate to purchase."

Petra laughed rudely. "You've been reading too many fantasy novels, Tim. Real-estate on Mars? Really? This isn't the wild west. You can't go out and stake a claim. Private property is never going to be an option in this kind of environment."

"That'll change someday!" Timothy shouted.

"We aren't going to turn this colony into a farce like the lunar settlements. We all know what commercialization has done there, turned it into a corporate sweatshop, where everything is owned by greedy profiteers. We can't allow that kind of ownership here."

"No. Instead, you want to set up a government sweatshop."

Before the fight could escalate, Melinda slammed down her fist. "Stop it! Listen, both of you. The final decision rests with me, as I hold distribution rights to all monies allotted for Mars, including the salaries. I will adopt whatever policies I deem necessary for the well-being of this colony. Is that understood?"

Petra smiled. "Perfectly."

Tim grunted and turned his attention to his soup.

Morgan had never known things to get so heated at the lunch table, and he wasn't certain what to say. Deep down, he wanted to give Tim some backup, but it was clear Melinda was on Petra's side, and he didn't think it prudent to offend the governor. He would remain an observer, and keep his opinions to himself.

The rest of the meal was quickly eaten in silence. With their bowls empty, the Chief of Police and the Senior Accountant excused themselves, leaving Morgan alone with Melinda at the table.

Morgan was about to follow them when Melinda asked him to remain. "You were awfully quiet," she mentioned.

"I didn't feel like picking sides in a petty argument," he replied.

"I think Petra would have appreciated a little moral support."

Morgan was caught off-guard by the comment and couldn't hide his surprise.

"You mean you didn't support her assertions?" Melinda asked, wide-eyed.

"Not entirely. Petra took it way too far, with all that 'good of the majority' and communal wealth talk. I agree, we can't allow a few individual companies to come in and buy the whole planet, but that is no reason to abolish the capitalist system," Morgan replied.

"I'm not saying we should abolish it, but I'm trying to look toward the future, for what's best for humanity as a whole.

We are at a turning point, writing a new chapter in history. If we wish to be successful, to assure mankind reaches the stars, we must start by revising such basic flaws in our economic system.

"Now, I'm no economist, but it is clear to me that the age-old system of profit and loss is a threat to future progress. Our current financial crisis is a prime example of how personal greed can threaten us all. A handful of politicians would rather spend money on freeway off-ramps and corporate kickbacks than provide the essentials for our survival."

"But we've been using a free market system for centuries, and that, more than anything, has brought us to where we are today," Morgan said.

"I think there must be a better way," Melinda replied, turning her attention away from Morgan and onto a nearby bookshelf. She picked through an upper row of the heavy paper tomes and retrieved one slim volume protected by a golden dust jacket. "Here," she said, handing it to Morgan. "I think you'll like this."

Morgan looked at the cover, a flashy prismatic foil jacket that was difficult to read. "*The Black Sheep*, by Neils L. Vanderbilt."

"He was a novelist, specializing in political thrillers and speculative fiction. I think you'll recognize the hero of this book. He's patterned after you, actually."

"Really?" Morgan asked suspiciously.

"Yeah, give it a try. Trust me, you'll love it."

"No promises," Morgan said, feeling less than agreeable.

Melinda smiled and excused herself, leaving Morgan alone in the library, his head full of new questions and a pretty book he dared not judge by its cover.

Chapter Ten

Morgan spent the afternoon reading the words of Neils Vanderbilt, seeing the instant similarities between the protagonist, Albert Archer, and himself. He thought it was strangely plagiaristic of his life, yet wholly inaccurate at the same time.

Lorna arrived home at a quarter to six, as she did most every evening, and made a bee-line for the bed. Morgan lay on top of the bedding, fully clothed, reading the last pages of Vanderbilt's manifesto.

"How was your day?" Lorna asked, peeking at the book in his hands.

"Interesting," he replied, closing the book a few paragraphs short of completion.

"How did things go at the doctor's office?"

"Fine," Morgan said. "They say I'm fine. We just have to keep trying."

"No argument here," Lorna said, leaning against him. "What are you reading?"

"Something Melinda gave me. It's a thinly veiled biography of yours truly, only skewed to suit the writer's false impressions of me, or perhaps to parallel his own ideals."

"How so?"

"For instance, here's the start of chapter two. *'I couldn't stand it, my family feeding off the ignorant masses like a butcher with a head of cattle, marching them into the slaughterhouse. All in the name of Capitalism. I knew I had to get out of the business. I couldn't be an accessory to this legalized crime against humanity. It was my duty to put an end to profit for the sake of profit, and I wasn't going to do it sitting on the board of a virtual reality company, invested in destroying lives.'*"

"A little long-winded, but isn't that essentially why you left Simworld?" Lorna asked.

He flipped ahead a bit. "Somewhat, but the author takes it wholly out of context, making me look like some kind of economic crusader. Like this, from chapter four: *'At last, I understood the measure of a man. As I worked the hard fields with my own hands, raised the crops to feed myself and a thousand others, producing something good for the world, at last I understood. Even though my own pay was little more than what I needed for survival, this was right. It was just and fair, and it gave my life purpose, beyond primitive monetary gain. I knew what it was to live, and I knew from then on what I needed to bring to America; a social conscience to work for the good of all mankind, beyond personal gain.'* Work for mankind without personal gain? Social conscience? This man didn't have a clue who I was. It's like he took the facts of my life and rewrote them to suit his own fantasies."

"Well, like I said after I first met you, the reality's a lot better than the fantasy," Lorna said, picking the book out of Morgan's hands. She examined the cover and added, "No wonder. It's a Scife book." She tossed it halfway across the room and it skipped over the small dining table and eventually hit the door before settling on the floor.

Morgan would ordinarily protest against such mistreatment of a book, but he felt no affinity for the particular text. He only hoped it wasn't damaged, lest he incur the wrath of the lender.

"A what book?" Morgan asked, leaving the tome on the floor.

"Scientific Fundamentalists. You know, like the people who have been running most of Europe for the last hundred and fifty years. Vanderbilt was the head of their American chapter for decades. They've never been too popular in the States, but they have a few million followers, even today."

Morgan took her word for it, embarrassed by his ignorance. After a hundred years on ice, a lot had passed him by, and there were still large gaps in his knowledge.

"Don't be surprised if you run into quite a few of them

around here," Lorna added. "Scientific advancement is their God, and this structured society is right up their alley."

"I'll keep that in mind," Morgan said.

* * *

Lorna was starting to get the hang of her job. Each morning, she was assigned a section of dome to supervise for the day. With her assignment in hand, she was driven out to her section aboard one of the large rovers, along with a few hundred construction workers. She would walk around all day, watching the dome go up, piece by piece, keeping notes on the construction process, busting anyone trying to cut corners. She had fancy gadgets to gauge the tensile strength of the steel, inspect welds, and calculate the angular position of the girders being laid.

Lorna arrived at the foreman's office to get her assignment and received a few peculiar laughs from her fellow engineers. She quickly learned why they were chuckling.

"Good news, Asher," the Chief Foreman said. "Today you get to start supervising the crew building over the sewage spread."

"What?" Lorna asked, unable to appreciate the joke.

"Aw, don't take it personal, or anything," the gruff foreman said. "Everybody takes their turn down there. It's not so bad, really. You'll see."

The sewage spread was a flat section of ground relatively close to the current settlement where the refuse was dumped to fertilize the soil that would someday be a grassy plain for grazing cattle. The sewage was heavily processed and all the water was extracted from the waste prior to being spread. The half-composted black dust covered the ground for a quarter of a mile. Even so, it was nobody's first choice to build in such close proximity to crap, which is why the supervisors rotated the responsibility on a regular basis.

Arriving at the building area officially labeled Section 3, Lorna was thrilled by the site's progress. The metal girders of the dome's framework were largely in place, the long chutes curving upwards almost a quarter of a mile into the air, and the same progress could be seen for a mile in either direction. The thick latticework of metal was bolted down to the heavy concrete foundation, and numerous, temporary support struts in the field assured that the upper weight of the construction would not counter-lever it. When the frame was complete, it was designed to hold itself upright, without any interior bracing.

Built into the concrete foundation, at hundred yard intervals, were silvery metal boxes with long, round shafts sticking into the air. These modern cranes did most of the heavy lifting for the project, and could be extended to a height of almost two miles. The shafts were flexible but strong, giving them the ability to set heavy hunks of steel and glass with precision.

Glass was to be laid over the metal framework, sealing out the native atmosphere, and the first layers had already been set at Section 3. Even as the more distant sections were still working on the lower girders, here they had sufficient progress to lay the first plates. That was the order of business for the day.

Lorna felt it would be a nice change of pace to lay glass, different from the monotony of laying steel.

As her crew prepared to start work for the day, Lorna activated the magnifiers built into her helmet to examine the entirety of the dome construction, and to spy on the other work crews. The closer teams were only a few hundred yards away, while the outermost sites were ten miles distant. They were preparing to lay glass on a few of the nearby sections, but most crews were still working on the framework. Shifting her glance over to her former worksite several miles away, she saw a work crew unloading girders. They'd be picking up where she had left off yesterday, while she tackled this new challenge.

A chirping sounded in Lorna's helmet, and she opened the communication circuit. "See anything you like?" a nasally voice queried.

Lorna searched around until she saw the owner of the

voice staring back from her old worksite. "Hey, Gregg. Just doing a little sightseeing while the crew gets unloaded."

"Yeah, same here," Gregg replied. "This is one pathetic mess you've handed me over here. You barely got the girders up thirty feet."

"It was bare slab three days ago," Lorna defended.

"Don't feel bad, not everybody can handle a crew of torch monkeys like me," Gregg said, trying to sound competitive.

"That's why they've got you, I guess," Lorna said, mildly annoyed by her colleague. "Welding is fun, but it looks like I'll be handling the hard stuff from now on."

"Yeah, real hard directing a bunch of glue jockeys to lay glass." Gregg laughed at his own joke. "Don't sweat too hard, okay?"

"I'll try," Lorna said, signing off.

By the time Lorna was done chatting, her crew was sweating in their suits, off-loading several hundred sheets of glass. The panes were twenty feet square and three inches thick, taking a dozen men to heft one—even on Mars—and they didn't carry them very far. Each plate was picked off the pile and set down on a flat section of ground near the dome foundation, where a crane could grab it and lift it into position on top of the framework. Each sheet was ever so slightly curved, though the gradual grade of the dome made it hard to detect with the naked eye.

After all of the sheets were set on the ground, the builders went to work. The handful of crane operators took their stations and waited while the other laborers climbed up the interior framework. Each man's suit doubled as a climbing harness, and the metal girders had strapping and eye holds that allowed them to scurry to the top of the currently-laid glass panels, approximately forty feet up in the air.

When everyone was at their work stations, things went along without a hitch. The men on the girders began painting the outer sections of the framework with a poly-resin, and once they had their area coated, a crane would lower a sheet of glass onto them and they'd set it into place.

The sheets had lapping edges that allowed them to lock into place, and after a number were set, a glass soldering unit went around and glued them together, superheating the overlapping edges until it was essentially one piece.

Work continued without a break until lunchtime. By then, a new shipment of glass had arrived. The five hundred workers took their meal break inside a large, pressurized mess tent before unloading the second truck, while Lorna and a few underling engineers examined the morning's work for flaws. It was a boring task, looking at glass, though it was necessary to prevent future catastrophe.

The afternoon progressed similarly to the morning, until a windstorm picked up two hours before sunset. Out of the southwest, as usual, the gusts pushed up the black sewage dust.

"Damn it, what is this crap?" one of the crewmen asked.

"Crap, that's what," someone answered.

"It's getting into the glue," one of the dangling workers said as she painted a metal upright with the clear resin.

The black particles were everywhere, billowing around the construction site. It was a local phenomenon, as none of the other work crews seemed to mind the wind. The breeze was insufficient to move the heavy Martian sand, and only this location sat in the path of the desiccated affluent.

"What do you want us to do?" one of the men asked.

"Cap the glue before any more gets contaminated," Lorna ordered. "We'll just have to call it a day."

"We've already got a few hundred feet spread on the frame."

"Leave it," Lorna said. "It's no good with all that crap coating it. We'll clean it up in the morning."

"The chief's not gonna like that," a crane operator mentioned.

"To Hell with the chief," Lorna said, having no affinity for the arrogant engineer. "If he doesn't like it, he can come out of his office and chisel the crap off, himself." She knew this was a nasty setback, but it was temporary. With any luck, she'd get the glass plates high enough tomorrow to avoid future dust storms.

It took another hour for the workers to stow their equipment and supplies. By then, it was nearing sunset. Lorna put in the call, and the rover arrived to pick up the work crew. A short drive brought them back to one of the massive service airlocks. Once everyone was inside, the airlock closed and a light cyclone action helped pull the dust off their spacesuits as the room pressurized. Lorna waited for everyone else to get out before removing her sweaty suit and packing it securely into her personal storage locker along the back wall.

Walking to her quarters, Lorna checked the time at a computer interface. It was a quarter past six. She was late for dinner, but far too filthy to skip her shower, so a quick detour was made to the communal wash room.

She missed the rain. The soft patter of precipitation upon the metal roof of Morgan's home back in Montana she had heard so many blissful nights in the early days of their romance. Rain had always had a soothing effect on her, though she had never realized it until she started her new life here, in a place where there was none. Now the only drops she heard were in the shower room she visited far too infrequently.

Getting out of the shower was always uncomfortable. The communal washing area meant there was always somebody else lurking around to see you get out of the booth, and Lorna wasn't a nudist. She was far too self-conscious and didn't like the idea of strangers looking at her bare flesh.

The towel rack was on the opposite side of the room and she had to cross thirty feet of bare floor to reach it. She was glad to see nobody about, and dried off quickly before anyone else exited their shower booths. She was gone before the voyeurs could catch sight of her pale skin.

Lorna's nose cringed as she walked the hallway from the bathing room to her quarters. The whole of Mars stank with the scent of humanity. It couldn't be helped. All the people in the same cramped space, with limited supplies of recycled air for ventilation, left an odor. It wasn't noticeable all the time, but after the nostrils were cleaned out from shower steam, the smells were unmistakable.

Lorna opened the door and found Morgan picking through a wooden crate that contained several of his guns. He shut the lid as his wife walked over.

"Don't stop on my account," Lorna said as Morgan stood up to give her a hug. Her damp hair left a few drops on her husband's shirt.

"I'm just checking on things. Nothing's rusted, yet. I cooked some spaghetti and it should still be warm."

"Thanks," Lorna said, walking over to the kitchen and filling a plate with pasta strands drenched in pesto. She wasn't a big fan of pesto, but she was famished enough to brave the stuff. "I am absolutely exhausted," she said as she carried the bowl over to the small eating table.

"At least it's Thursday. You have Saturday off, right?"

"So long as we don't get another bad dust storm," she mentioned, and then explained the problem as she ate.

"At least you had some excitement," Morgan said.

"Speaking of excitement, did you talk to Melinda about that book of hers?"

"No, and I'm in no hurry," Morgan replied, wondering how the governor would take his ill feelings toward her favored literature.

Chapter Eleven
July 9, 2327

Friday came and Morgan continued to avoid Melinda, and she seemed to also be avoiding him. She may have wanted to give him space, as he reviewed and considered Vanderbilt's writing. Either way, she did not call on him, and he was grateful to avoid an uncomfortable conversation.

That afternoon, Morgan took a break from the rigors of signing electronic forms, and decided to test out his firearms on the Martian landscape. He considered it a scientific experiment and amused himself with the idea of penning an article for a sportsman's magazine back home.

He stopped by Tim Keene's office and found the Chief of Police to be equally bored and eager to take part in the test, though he had his doubts about the whole thing.

There were several indisputable truths regarding Mars. There was virtually no oxygen, the thin atmosphere being primarily carbon dioxide, and the gravity was less than half Earth normal. Nobody had ever attempted to fire a gun on Mars before, and it was uncertain what would happen in the attempt.

There was a guard on duty at Southwest Airlock #5 when Morgan and Tim arrived. The Chief was immediately recognized by the subordinate, who waved him through. Once in the airlock, he and Morgan donned pressure suits and proceeded out onto the lifeless, rocky terrain.

It was the first time Morgan had had the chance to walk on the face of the planet and he took a few minutes to take in the scene. This side of the colony was still mostly natural, with craters and rocky hills all around. The smooth plain and the lower girders of the dome construction could be seen far to their left.

The glowing sun hung in the western sky, but they still had

at least two hours of good light before it faded to black.

They made sure they were a safe distance away from the complex before unzipping the duffel bag carrying six pieces from Morgan's collection.

"Do you really think this is going to work?" Tim asked dubiously as Morgan removed his 82 Remington from the bag.

"We'll see," Morgan replied, testing his grip. His suit had thin, almost skin-tight, gloves. They had been designed for mechanics and engineers who needed to perform delicate work under airless conditions. They didn't affect one's ability to hold or operate a rifle, either, so they would be useful for space combat, if ever it became necessary.

Returning to the bag, Morgan removed a box of .35 Remington cartridges for his rifle. He took four rounds and placed three of them in the rifle's magazine before examining the fourth. He had spent the morning sealing the cartridges for use in the Martian atmosphere. A small bead of sealer was visible where the bullet was crimped into the case, and a similar bead appeared around the primer in the center of the cartridge base. With these precautions, he was certain the shells would fire, the necessary oxygen sealed tightly in each case with the powder.

"Well, here goes something," Morgan said, after setting the fourth cartridge in the magazine and snapping the bolt shut.

Placing the rifle on his shoulder, he realized how cumbersome his helmet was. It prevented him from getting a good sight picture, as he couldn't place his cheek on the stock. There was no way for him to use the iron sights on the top of the rifle. He wasn't about to let that stop his experiment, however, and after estimating an aim, he gently squeezed the trigger.

The lighter gravity of Mars reduced Morgan's weight by three fifths, but it did nothing to change the explosive recoil of the high-powered hunting rifle, so the blow caused him to stumble backwards and fall over. The padded suit protected him from any harm, and a helping hand from Tim got him back on his feet.

Once he was upright, he examined the rifle to find it hadn't functioned properly. The action hadn't cycled, leaving the empty case in the chamber. Morgan yanked back on the bolt handle, and the case ejected. Releasing the bolt, another round chambered, and he handed the rifle to Tim for a test fire.

After witnessing Morgan's reactions, Tim knew to brace himself against the coming recoil. He leaned forward, as if he were ready to be tackled by a linebacker, and jerked the trigger. He succeeded in absorbing the recoil without losing his balance.

"What were you aiming at?" Morgan asked, unable to see where the bullet had landed.

"Aim? How was I supposed to aim it wearing this suit?"

"You must have had a general idea."

"I was too busy perfecting a good stance," Tim admitted. "Really, though, if we're going to use these things, we've got to figure out a better system of sights."

"What do you have in mind?"

"Well, maybe we could rig one of those new digital scopes to transmit a sight picture into an eyepiece. You know, the kind of setup the army uses for controlling unmanned assault vehicles, only shorter range."

"If you know anybody with the expertise to design it, I'll pay for it," Morgan mentioned, taking the rifle and examining it. Once again, it had failed to cycle. The "autoloading" feature wasn't working.

"You don't think the gravity's making it jam?" Tim asked, as Morgan cycled the bolt manually.

"No, I don't think so. It might be the atmosphere," he surmised. "You know, smokeless powders are designed to burn all the way down the bore of the gun. They supply force all the way through the barrel. Out here, where there's no oxygen, the explosive reaction may be snuffed out as soon as the bullet leaves the cartridge case, reducing velocity and chamber pressure.

"These Remington Autoloaders are recoil operated. You need all the power of the cartridge to cycle the action. See, the entire barrel recoils in this sleeve, and the bolt snaps open when the barrel falls forward. If there isn't sufficient recoil, the barrel won't push back far enough and the bolt won't feed."

"I suppose a faster burning powder might help," Tim suggested. "Most of the velocity would be provided in the initial detonation."

"I suppose I could put in a requisition order for some components. I am the quartermaster, after all. God knows who I'll need to sign off on the importation of hazardous materials."

"If you need, I could put in the order," Tim said. "I am the Chief of Police, and it's sensible that I might need it for security purposes, training and whatever else. Still, it'll be a two-year wait between shipments."

Morgan extracted the last two rounds from the Remington and returned them to his bag, after which he removed a different weapon to test fire. It was an 1886 Winchester, one of his favorite antiques, chambered in .45-70 Government. The bulky thing had a twenty six inch octagonal barrel and weighed almost ten pounds on Earth. Here, it weighted a little less than a short carbine.

He shoved six cartridges into the tubular magazine and placed the rifle to his shoulder. He aimed as best he could and fired, bracing himself to stay on his feet, feeling a stabbing pain in his shoulder from the absorbed recoil. A large cloud of white smoke hung in the air following the shot.

"That sounded louder than the others," Tim noted.

The rapport of gunfire was nowhere near as loud as on Earth. In the thin atmosphere of Mars, it sounded more like a hiss than a boom, but some hisses were sharper than others.

"It felt a lot more powerful," Morgan replied. "These are black powder rounds. Black powder works differently than smokeless."

"It all burns in the initial detonation," Tim said, knowing

the fundamentals.

"I guess cowboy guns are going to be popular on Mars," Morgan remarked.

There were two pistols in the bag and they tested each in turn, though they both used smokeless powder cartridges. The P-38 functioned adequately, because of fast-burning pistol powder, though the hefty Smith and Wesson .44 Magnum didn't live up to its name.

Pistols were easy enough to aim when wearing the spacesuits, so the men were able to learn where their bullets were going. The guns shot high, and they were able to hit targets far in excess of what was standard for Earth. Morgan was most impressed with his final shot, smacking a boulder nearly a mile away.

It was after dark as they made their way back to the colony, but they didn't have trouble finding the airlock, thanks to the handy GPS network in orbit. After removing the suits and donning their regular attire, they went directly to Morgan's quarters to clean and store the guns.

Morgan boiled a kettle of water and was in the middle of pouring it down the barrel of the Winchester when Lorna returned from work.

"What are you doing?" she asked lightly, amused by Morgan's current stance. He was standing on a chair, holding the rifle's muzzle in the sink, pouring water down the bore with a makeshift funnel. The Chief of Police was standing next to him, watching the care Morgan took with each weapon.

"Cleaning," Morgan replied as the last of the water ran out the muzzle. "I need to wash the black powder residue out of this barrel before it starts to corrode."

"You mean you actually shot those things? Where?"

"A mile outside airlock five," Tim chimed in.

"So, this would be the inaugural meeting of the Martian Rod and Gun Club?"

"It's almost like being back in Montana. All we need are some Martian Elk," Morgan replied, removing the gun from the sink. He walked over to the small table and prepared a chemical patch to run down the bore.

"I'm glad you boys had fun," Lorna said, moving into the kitchen alcove. "Morgan, I don't think I've been properly introduced to your new friend."

"Oh," Morgan said, not having noticed. "This is Timothy Keene, Chief of Police. Tim, this is my wife, Lorna."

"It's a pleasure, madam," Tim said suavely.

"Never call me 'madam,'" Lorna joked, washing her hands in the sink.

"Of course, *Mrs. Asher*," Tim said with a grin, standing up from his seat. "I should be going. My wife's expecting me for dinner, and I try to be on time."

Before Tim made it to the door, Morgan asked him to wait. Reaching down into the duffel bag, he retrieved the magnum revolver and held it out for the chief. "Here, take it as a loaner. No cop should be without a real gun, on any world."

Tim thought a moment before accepting. Taking hold of the weapon, he said, "You're a rich Sunner, you know that?"

"What's a Sunner?" Lorna interjected.

"Just some Maine slang, short for something not so nice." With a courteous nod, Tim went on his way.

Chapter Twelve

The bath water was hot, just shy of scalding. The steamy vapor filled the air of the cramped room, the foggy haze obscuring Melinda's view of the mirror five feet away.

Being governor had its privileges, such as this cast-iron tub. It was the only one on Mars, forged from native ore and enameled with poly resin. Everyone else had to use the communal shower rooms, but not her. The private bathroom was one of the few comforts of Earth she could enjoy. If all went as planned, others would begin to share in the extravagance considered commonplace back home within the next decade.

Melinda let the hot water soak into her muscles, waving a hand across the foamy bubbles floating atop the surface. The simple pleasures in life appealed to her more the older she got. When relaxing in the bath, the complexities of existence seemed to fade, leaving her with nothing more than a feeling of contentment and a clarity of purpose.

It felt like the first bath she'd ever taken, and it quite possibly was, for it was the first bath she'd had since her last teleport from the Consensorate's compound. Strict scientists would consider her a reconstituted clone, many religious leaders would consider her a new being, born at the moment of rematerialization, while radical fundamentalists would consider her a soulless shell, an abomination.

Either way you cut it, she held the memories, feelings, and precise physical attributes of Colonel Melinda Faris. For all intents and purposes, that's who she was. She was never one to buy into the metaphysical aspects of existence. Life and death were relative terms. She remembered being alive before the teleport, and she knew she was alive now, so there was no before or after as far as she was concerned. It was all just a fancy means of travel the Consensorate was sensible enough to utilize, while her own government was ruled by superstitions and fears.

An acrid smell permeated the air, tickling her nostrils, the kind of scent left behind by a bolt of lightning. Melinda knew what the odor meant, and felt momentary resentment over her private bath time being invaded.

"I hope I'm not disturbing you," Mr. Budreau said, standing over her.

Melinda slumped down in the tub, setting her chin at the edge of the water and the foam around her cheeks. She blew a patch of bubbles away from her mouth to speak. "Of course you are."

"It seemed the most opportune time to speak with you, without risk of being discovered," Budreau replied without apology. "There are matters of import we must discuss."

"More important than my bath?" Melinda asked childishly.

Budreau wrinkled his nose in irritation. "You have much to account for, Colonel." He lifted a folder in his right hand. "Perhaps you could explain this."

"Whatever it is, leave it by the sink. I'll look at it when I get out."

"You will look at it *now*," Budreau ordered, slapping the folder against the edge of the tub.

"Is it waterproof?" Melinda asked.

"No. You will have to get out of the water."

"Not with your prying eyes. You get out first."

Budreau scowled, but did as she asked. He set the folder down on the counter by the bathroom sink and said, "I will return in three minutes, whether you are dressed or not. Be prepared." Pressing a button on his collar, he sent a remote command to the teleport pad, which promptly removed his physical body from the room.

Melinda was reluctant to get out of her bath, but knew she had no choice. She dragged herself out of the warm liquid and pulled the plug, sending the precious water back to the filtration plant a half a mile away. She dried her skin with a soft towel and slipped on a purple satin robe before picking up the folder. She didn't look at it immediately, but took it with her into the bedroom, where Budreau materialized shortly thereafter.

"Are you ready to be cooperative?" the Frenchman asked after his body fully solidified.

"I suppose," Melinda replied, sitting on the corner of her bed. She shook her wet hair wildly as Budreau neared her, spreading drops of water on his gray suit.

"You impudent American girl," Budreau cursed. "I should have you conditioned, to remove your impertinence."

"You've never needed to 'condition' me before."

"Yes, unlike those stubborn marines of yours, you understand the need for Scientific Fundamentalism without the aid of mental realignment."

"It's the well-being of mankind that interests me. There's no excuse for the waste that exists in our respective nations today. So many lives are spent on trivial games or material pursuits that produce nothing of value. It's got to stop."

"Speak for yourself. My country is quite the opposite. No one is allowed to enjoy the simplest of pleasures, for fear of inefficiency," Budreau lamented. Changing his tone, he asked, "Have you looked at the folder?"

Taking the time to review the documents in her lap, Melinda lifted the flap on the folder and found a number of photos within. They were hazy, long distance shots taken of Morgan and Tim during their target practice.

"I expect an explanation," Budreau demanded.

"For what?" Melinda asked.

"This militant aggression cannot be tolerated. This is exactly the kind of brash behavior that could ruin all our plans for the future."

Melinda examined the photos closely before replying further. "I hardly see how a little civilian target practice could pose any kind of a threat."

"You assured me this sort of thing would not be happening, that you would keep your citizens under control."

"It's just Morgan Asher. We both know he brought his collection along, and we had to assume he'd eventually try them out."

"It is hard to believe the lauded Morgan Asher could be so violently aggressive," Budreau said, returning to his regular stern expression.

"He is a bit spirited, but I don't see that this was at all violent. He was just having a little harmless fun," Melinda said, shutting the folder and handing it back to Budreau. "Now that we've cleared that up, I'd like to get some sleep."

"Nothing is *cleared up*," Budreau retorted. "This situation is still potentially volatile. If word of this leaked to my government, they could perceive this as a threat. In response, they might send a fresh military contingent of soldiers resistant to our persuasive methods."

"How is one man having a little target practice going to affect anything?" Melinda asked, exhausted and bored.

"As you saw in the pictures, this was not only one man. No doubt, it will soon spread beyond two, and eventually may encompass a sizeable minority of the population, if not overtake the majority. This would be the logical conclusion of my government were they to learn of these actions. They would deem this as an American show of force."

"I'm sure you are fully capable of keeping this incident under wraps," Melinda replied, sliding into bed.

"No doubt I can cover up this one incident, but I cannot guarantee I will be able to do so should such behavior persist. If there is a regular show of American arms, word will get back to my government. This activity must end immediately. Until the time comes, no one must know that there are any guns on Mars, outside those held by my security personnel and the handful in your police armory."

Melinda nestled into her bed, wishing Budreau would leave her alone for the night. She lay silently after he stopped talking, hoped he would just go away. When it became obvious he would not, she said the only thing she knew would satisfy him.

"I'll take care of it, okay? Just leave me alone."

"That is all I needed to hear," Budreau replied, pleased

with himself. He pushed the button on his collar. In a few seconds, his body vanished, leaving Melinda in peace.

With Budreau gone, Melinda got out of bed, feeling less than tired, but glad the annoying man was gone. She couldn't stand him, and far preferred it when she was pulling his strings, rather than the other way around. Their joint plans required give and take, even when they shared the same overall goals.

He's right, though, she thought, her mind drifting back to the photographs and the man in front of the camera. Morgan Asher was turning out to be more unpredictable than anyone had planned. Despite his historical renown and stated rhetoric, his personality seemed resistant to the very order he advocated.

Still, she hoped he could be brought into the fold, made to see the value of her dream, and that his overbearing uniqueness would not be the death of her.

* * *

Monday morning, Morgan answered a polite summons from Melinda. He didn't think anything of it, as he was getting used to discussing any number of matters with her, and her office was a nice change of scenery; its various frills and decorations a far cry from the bland metal maze in which they lived.

Melinda sat at her desk, a blank look on her face. When she spoke, her tone was flat and formal. "I received a few complaints over the weekend regarding your recreational activities on Friday afternoon."

"You mean the target practice? It was a harmless experiment," Morgan scoffed, surprised by the topic. He'd been expecting to discuss Vanderbilt's book.

"You might have discussed it with me before you went and shot up the countryside."

"I didn't realize I needed the governor's permission to exercise my rights as an American citizen," Morgan said, defensive.

"You can't behave so irresponsibly," Melinda lectured.

97

"This is a structured environment, with necessary restrictions on its people. Most of the citizens here aren't used to gunplay—nor should they be, in this day and age."

"I have a right to my guns," Morgan challenged.

"Yes, but you didn't really expect to use them here, did you? Based on citizen concern and my judgment, I am hereby prohibiting the discharge of firearms in and around the settlement for the time being."

"I'll fight you on this," Morgan said through clenched teeth.

"You should be glad I'm not outright confiscating them," she warned, and received a nasty glare from Morgan. "Please, Morgan, let's be reasonable. I'm sure after we construct a proper range, you will be able to continue these experiments of yours. But now is not the appropriate time."

Morgan saw no choice but to accept her decision, at least for the moment. Without another word, he strode toward the door, resentment spiraling through his chest.

***

Morgan's defiance left Melinda feeling sullen. She'd anticipated his reaction, but had hoped he would take it better. His attitude was troublesome. She'd been reading of his exploits since childhood, and long revered him as an independent thinker, but it was becoming clear he wasn't the man depicted in the history books. Like many historical icons, he didn't quite live up to everyone's expectations.

Disappointment weighed upon her, but she still had hope. There had to be a way to persuade him, to bring him over to her side before it was too late. He needed to be prepared for what she was going to do for the sake of mankind.

There was always mental reconfiguration, but she didn't want to resort to such a quick fix with Morgan. That cheat was unbefitting such a great man. No, she wanted to win him over with words, and thus reclaim an iconic figure that had long inspired her.

Morgan had to have an Achilles Heel, and Melinda was determined to find it.

Chapter Thirteen
July 15, 2327

The fields were brown with the stubble from recently cut hay. A cool breeze blew out of the northwest and the air was full of orange and yellow leaves. The cows in a nearby pasture were easily heard as the sun rose toward noontime on the small farm in upstate New York.

A boy of indeterminate age played. He knew where he was, who he was, but for some reason, he couldn't tell what year it was or how long he had been here. His young mind was a blur.

The boy walked along the fields, grabbing wind-blown leaves and picking up the occasional field stone to see how far he could chuck it. He was having a fine time until a dark shadow drifted over him, forcing him to turn and look up at a man who seemed a hundred feet tall. He wore an officer's uniform, and his face looked old and weathered.

"Just who do you think you are?" the military man bellowed.

"I'm Seth Avery," the boy replied.

The giant man grabbed the boy by the shoulders and shook him hard. "Like hell you are. *I'm* Seth Avery!"

The shaking abruptly stopped and the boy found himself sitting in a gloomy, featureless room. He was tied to a chair, an American flag wrapped tightly around his chest, a solitary light bulb directly above his head illuminating the patch of floor around him. He looked down at his hands and saw they were old and weathered. He realized he was no longer a child, but the large, uniformed man.

"It's not treason, you know," the voice of Melinda Faris echoed about the room. A moment later, she stepped out of the shadows, sporting a gray uniform belonging to the troops of a long-dead dictatorship. "We're not betraying our people.

We're saving them from themselves. That is the greatest form of patriotism."

"I don't understand," Seth said, his voice still that of a child.

Leaning over him, Melinda flashed a patronizing smile, the kind an irritated teacher displayed to a young student who couldn't grasp the finer points of a subject. "The right to be wrong is not right at all."

Seth sat there, confused. Before he knew what was happening, the flag pinning his arms to his sides was on fire and the flames were consuming him. He struggled to get free of his bindings, but the material of the flag didn't burn; rather, it emitted the flames that fanned out to engulf his body. As they reached his face, he felt his body dissolve in the heat.

And Colonel Seth Avery awoke.

It was the third nightmare this week, and Avery was getting tired of being tired. Checking his wristwatch, he saw the time was two in the morning. He'd managed four hours of sleep, at least.

Reaching down the side of his hammock, he unclipped the straps that held his body in place during the night. With a slight nudge, he floated out from under the covers.

Whenever he couldn't sleep, Avery found himself headed to the weight room, as there was little else to occupy him on the spaceship. He'd already spent two months on board, with another two ahead of him before he returned to Earth. The long journey back gave him plenty of time to consider his options—and be haunted by recent events.

The gym was a spacious room filled with exercise equipment intended to help the ship's crew stay in shape during long space voyages. There were stepping machines, treadmills, weights, and a myriad of other devices, each of which Colonel Avery used on a daily basis. There was even a centrifuge in the back. Even so, he found his muscles shrinking, and he would need a few weeks of intense work to get back into shape once he returned to Earth. It was an occupational hazard of space travel. No matter how hard you tried, your body couldn't keep muscle tone without the constant pull of gravity.

Avery liked the late-night workouts. It was quiet and he didn't have to wait for someone else to let him use the equipment. He went at his own pace, for as long as he wanted, or until his body gave out.

Two hours he spent in the machines, trying to keep his mind singularly focused. Before it was over, he ended up running five miles on the treadmill with three magnetic jackets on his shoulders. As his legs grew numb, he realized how much he'd overdone it, and was happy to strip out of the magnets and float freely in the middle of the room. He promptly fell asleep and didn't awaken until he heard the commanding voice of Captain Percival Waltham.

"I'm sorry, Skipper," Avery said, shaking the cobwebs from his head. "I was having trouble sleeping, so I gave myself a workout."

"I can see that," the captain said, dabbing beads of cold sweat out of the air with a towel.

Avery glanced at his wrist watch and saw it was 07:00 already, though he hadn't felt more than a moment pass since ending his run.

"I know my ship has been placed at your disposal for the duration of your mission, but I'd appreciate it if you would keep me apprised of your activities. The crew's getting a little restless and I don't need a breakdown in discipline."

Avery had used the gym almost every night for the past month without logging in an official schedule, though this was the first time he'd been caught sleeping. "I'll keep regular hours from now on."

Captain Waltham snorted dubiously. "That's it? You're not going to challenge my authority?"

"Excuse me?" Avery asked, trying to float closer to the captain, but finding it hard, as he was stuck in the middle of the room with nothing to grab.

"All you did during the flight out was remind me that you were really in command, that I was under orders to assist you in whatever way you deemed necessary. You were damned arrogant and I didn't much care for you."

"I never got that impression," Avery replied, reaching the top of a weight machine and pulling himself down to face the captain.

"That's because I don't let my personal feelings get in the way of my duty. I'm an officer, same as you."

"Then why are you telling me this now?"

"Because you've changed, and I don't like that, either," Waltham replied as Avery drifted in front of him. "Since Mars, you've been quiet and agreeable; nothing like the man I spent the first month hating. A man doesn't just change his entire personality overnight."

"You want me to be a bitter pain in the ass again, Skipper?" Avery asked lightly.

"Something happened to you down there, didn't it?"

The smile melted off Avery's face. A little voice in his head screamed in fear, knowing it had been exposed. "That's classified," he snapped, hoping to divert the captain's suspicions.

"It always is," Waltham replied.

Avery saw no sense in sticking around for more of Waltham's interrogation, and pushed himself toward the door.

"Take some free advice, Colonel," Waltham said before he could escape. "Decide whose side you're on before we get back to Earth. It'll make everyone's job a lot easier."

As Avery made his way back to his quarters, he pondered the captain's words and felt a new wave of apprehension.

What did Waltham mean about choosing sides? Did he know about the mission? About the Consensorate? Had one of the others broken their oath, spoken of the events on Mars? If that were the case, Captain Waltham might be of a mind to throw them all out an airlock. His suspicions complicated things.

Avery had already chosen his side, had known what he must do since returning from the Consensorate's compound.

He understood what they were trying to do to him, but it hadn't worked. He was still himself, and those little voices and fake feelings implanted in his head had been quickly put aside. The dominant force of Seth Avery's personality had overpowered their mental conditioning.

Revenge was on his mind, coupled with devotion to duty and loyalty to America. He was not about to let the Scifes get away with their actions, but he couldn't tip his hand too early. There was no telling how many spies they had among the *Plymouth's* crew, or throughout America, so he had to play along until he figured out who he could trust.

Anyone could be a double agent. The power the Scifes had with their teleportation technology was frightening. There was no telling how many powerful officials in the government or military had been compromised. Few people had Avery's "give 'em hell" attitude to help them through the rebirth.

Can I trust Captain Waltham? Avery wondered in the privacy of his cabin. It was a question he had to answer quickly.

Throughout the day, Avery questioned each of his men privately, seeking to find out who among them had spoken of their experiences openly. He grilled them, demanded answers, and eventually he got what he wanted. Two men confessed to having a candid discussion in the public area, within earshot of several enlisted crewmen, though they didn't think anyone had overheard them.

It wasn't solid proof, but Captain Waltham could have learned of their connection with the Scifes through eavesdropping. He could only hope, the only other possibility being that Waltham was in league with the Scifes and was testing Avery's conditioning. If that were the case, coming clean would condemn him. But if Waltham weren't a double agent, he was doubly screwed if he didn't confess.

Avery had to go with his gut. He decided to have a frank talk with Waltham. He brought along a pistol, just in case he was wrong.

The captain's cabin wasn't much different from any other

officer's quarters on board. The cramped quarters had a few extra feet of floor space, a few paintings bolted to the walls, along with a decorative AK-47, but overall it was just another room.

Captain Waltham invited Colonel Avery into his chambers and asked him to take a seat. Avery hooked his legs around the base of the chair sitting by the captain's desk, prepared to give a full confession.

"Before I begin, I'd like to ask you something , man to man," Avery said, letting his hand drape down his side and linger in the vicinity of his pistol.

"I'm listening," Waltham said, his own hands disappearing under his desk.

"Exactly where do your loyalties lie?" Avery asked.

"I was about to ask you the same question," Waltham said, stone-faced.

"Cut the crap. Are you with the Scifes or not?"

Waltham growled and grabbed the gun hanging under his desk. It was his personal sidearm, a stainless steel Liberty Arms 10mm, not one of the weak taser sticks his crew was assigned. He set the compact weapon on his lap and said, "You've got a lot of nerve!"

"You better believe it," Avery growled back. "You just tell me straight out. Who are you working for?"

Waltham raised his pistol and leveled it at Avery's chest. "I am a loyal officer of the United States Space Force. Now give me one good reason why I shouldn't put a hole in your heart, you Scife turncoat!"

Avery had seen his share of combat, but never before had he felt the pangs of fear as he did now. Of course, the enemy was usually aiming at you from farther away. Point blank was something new to him. He tried not to let it show as he answered. "If I were a Scife, I'd have shot you already."

"Not good enough," Waltham said, keeping his aim. "I know damn well what you are. I've had your room bugged for weeks, ever since your men started whispering sweet nothings in the commons. I don't know everything, but I've got a pretty good idea what's going on, and so do the Joint Chiefs."

"You reported back to Earth?" Avery asked, disbelieving.

"You're damn right I did. I expect they'll have your tribunal set up by the time we enter orbit, and you know what they do to traitors."

Avery most certainly did. The punishment was death by hanging, an old military tradition dating back to the founding of the first American Republic.

"You and your men will be confined to quarters until we reach Earth, after which you will be formally charged with treason."

Ignoring the threat of the pistol pointed at him, Avery slammed a fist against the desk. "Listen here, you son of a bitch—*I am not a traitor*. Those Scife bastards tried to screw my mind, but it didn't work. Now I'm gonna get my revenge against those suckers, and no second-rate freighter captain is gonna get in my way!"

Captain Waltham laughed at his arrogant display, leaving Avery grimacing in frustration. "There! That's the Colonel Seth Avery that pissed me off every day for a month," Waltham said as his laughter subsided.

"I'm not a traitor. Believe me," Avery asked, trying to reign in his temper.

"I can't say I'm inclined to, at the moment," Waltham replied, returning the pistol to his lap, "but I am listening. Why don't you start by telling me how you plan to get your 'revenge' against the Scifes."

Avery smiled. "Well, that all depends on you, doesn't it? If you're such a patriot as you claim, how'd you like to help me pull a double cross on the Scifes that tried to turn me?"

Chapter Fourteen
September 11, 2327

About the time the *Plymouth* entered Earth's orbit, Morgan felt a needle stab into the roof of his mouth and the unpleasant burn of Novocaine as it was injected. The dentist was someone nobody wanted to visit, but it was a necessity of life.

There were only four dentists on Mars, but their schedules weren't very hectic. Most of the colonists were young, their teeth well-maintained. It was rare when a dentist had to break out the laser drill and treat a cavity, though that wouldn't be the case forever.

Morgan sat through the procedure, smelling the odd stench of burning molar, then feeling the light tapping as the filling was forced into the void. When it was all over, the dentist gave his patient a quick review of the newly patched tooth. "I used gold. I hope you don't mind. We have a fair quantity from the excavations, and it's not like it will cost you anything extra."

Morgan looked at the image on the video screen, showing a clear picture of his mouth from moments ago. The cavity had been on the interior side of his top-left twelve-year molar, and there was now a small patch of gold along the gum line. "Yeah, how's the new moneyless society working out for you?"

"I suppose it's only logical," the dentist said. "How else is a fledgling colony like ours to survive if we're all out to make a fast buck? It's not like we need money for anything."

"That's what our illustrious governor says," Morgan replied.

"She hasn't steered us wrong yet."

"She's only been in charge for three months."

"Yes, well, if you'd been here for the first two years of the colony, you wouldn't be complaining," the dentist chided. "It was rough setting all this up for you new arrivals, and General Stavanger was a veritable slave-driver compared to Governor Faris."

"I'm sure he was," Morgan replied irritably. "Are we done?"

"You're all set," the dentist said, sounding uneasy. "I'll schedule you for a routine cleaning and check-up for this time next year, if that's all right."

Morgan nodded and left the dentist to his business.

A lot had changed on Mars over the last few months, and things were starting to feel more like a prison. The Immigration and Colonization Board had begun "rubber-stamping" all of Melinda's proposed policies, giving her a free hand to govern her controlled society. She started with the financial problems, following Petra Euchland's advice in reallocating all salaries to industrial acquisitions. Most of the citizens didn't care because they hadn't joined the colonization efforts for the money. They were the scientists and explorers, those who had sought to be bold pioneers. Compensation was a secondary consideration. And as it was currently of no use to them, it was the furthest thing from their minds.

A select segment of society, however, was not so thrilled. The construction workers and the miners, many of whom had come because of their spouses, were largely capitalists. They didn't take kindly to the news that they would now be slaving away for the glory of the State. Many rebelled. Work slow-downs cropped up and an entire excavation crew went on strike.

Melinda could have done horrible things to the malcontents, but she chose to let things work themselves out peacefully. She did not cut anyone's rations, didn't lock anyone up for treason. Instead, she sat back and waited a week, while all who rebelled suddenly came to their senses and fell into line. Just about everyone who took an active part in a work slowdown or strike changed their minds overnight and went back to work, accepting the new financial policies as necessary and fair. It was declared a "victory for common sense," though it was all too convenient to be natural.

Morgan's mind hadn't changed, and he had no intention of letting it be changed. Melinda tolerated his occasional contrary suggestions, but he was smart enough to hold his tongue most of the time.

* * *

Lorna was one of the "content pioneers," for the most part. She didn't always agree with the administration, but understood the importance of their mission and the need for sacrifice. She performed her monotonous job every day with the self-assurance that it was all for the greater good, but often agreed with her angry husband when he expressed his misgivings about their current leadership.

Around the time Morgan was having his tooth drilled, Lorna found herself sitting outside the governor's office, following a most peculiar summons. She had shown up for work an hour earlier, and been redirected here, though she couldn't fathom why.

Lorna had only met Melinda Faris a few times in passing, and most of what she knew of the governor came from Morgan. She welcomed the chance to have a longer conversation with the famous "first woman on Mars."

Eventually, Melinda's youthful head poked out of the office door. "Mrs. Asher, it's nice to see you again. Please, come in and have a seat," she said cordially.

Lorna complied, trying not to show how nervous she was as she crossed the room and sat down in the padded chair in front of the desk.

"I'd like to discuss your crew's progress," Melinda said immediately.

"Is there something wrong?" Lorna asked.

"You are progressing rather slowly, don't you think?"

"We are well within our recommended quotas, and I don't see how we can work any faster without compromising the quality of the work," Lorna said honestly. She was proud of her crew and knew they labored at their full potential every day. She couldn't understand why the governor considered their work unsatisfactory.

"What if I told you that Mangrove's crew is laying five times the number of plates a day as you?"

"That's not possible," Lorna retorted sharply.

"Please, don't be offended," Melinda said sweetly. "It's true, though I must admit Mangrove has a certain technological advantage that you lack."

"I'd like to see this advantage," Lorna said.

"Oh, you will. In fact, I believe a demonstration is in order."

Melinda flipped a switch under her desk, activating a radio transponder in Lorna's chair, sending a signal to her collaborators at Eridania. In response, they locked onto Lorna's position with their teleporter and disintegrated her in a matter of seconds. A few seconds later, she rematerialized in front of the governor's desk, a new person, with a few slight adjustments to her thoughts and memories.

Lorna looked around, bewildered for a few minutes, as she tried to make sense of what had just happened.

"It's molecular teleportation," Melinda explained. "A wonderful new technology, don't you agree?"

Lorna remained speechless as her newly reborn brain considered the possibilities.

"You're wondering, how is this at all possible? Matter transference is still mostly theoretical by American standards. It is fortunate for us that the European Consensorate did not waste a hundred years playing with virtual computer programs, and instead invested serious time and energy into this practical science."

Lorna worked up the courage to speak, her voice quivering from fear and astonishment. "You're saying my body was just broken down into pure energy and then reassembled?" Her eyes widened and her short fingernails dug into the arms of the chair.

"Yes. It may take a little while for you to calm down. I know from personal experience that the first time through is the hardest. You get used to it."

"How can you get used to dying?" Lorna asked, having a fairly good understanding of why American science had shied away from exploring the technology.

"Nonsense," Melinda said, her voice kind. "There is no dying involved, merely a temporary pause. It is no more death than being frozen in suspended animation. When your body is reformed, you wake up, and you're still you."

"Forgive me if I don't particularly appreciate your demonstration," Lorna said, terrified.

"You'll thank me later. Think for a minute about the value of this technology. Consider how much faster your work will go if you don't need massive cranes to slowly set metal beams and sheets of glass. Think of the ease of merely teleporting them into place."

Listening to Melinda's words calmed Lorna's emotions and kicked her analytical skills into gear. "That's why Mangrove's making such progress. But how did you get your hands on this technology?"

"It is a gift."

"From the Consensorate? But why would they help us? They hate Americans."

Melinda waved her hand dismissively. "Their government may dislike us, but the people are a whole other matter. There is a large underground movement who disapprove of the fascist and oppressive nature of the Consensorate. It is these dissidents who are offering us the use of their technology as a gesture of good faith, so we can all live better."

"I don't understand," Lorna said, confused. The mental adjustments performed on her during transport were still trying to take root, but she was prone to skepticism.

"Our friends have offered their assistance in the construction of our great dome as a magnanimous gesture, to help us establish a new society here on Mars. Both sets of colonists are going to unite someday soon. Together, we'll forge a nation based on fairness and logic."

"I see," Lorna said, the mental conditioning integrating into her thoughts. She found herself unable to restrain a smile, overjoyed by the news.

"Now, there is one little problem I need you to address," Melinda said.

"Anything I can do to help," Lorna said, eager to please.

"It's your husband," Melinda said. "As you know, he can be quite stubborn at times. I'd like you to talk to him, make him see reason, if you can. Subtly, of course."

"I think I understand," Lorna replied, her conditioning filling in the details.

"Good, I knew I could count on you," Melinda said, pleased her latest scheme seemed to be working. "Take the rest of the day off. You'll start fresh tomorrow, with the aid of the teleporter. Then you'll really show some progress."

"Thank you," Lorna said, brimming with excitement.

"Oh, and please, don't tell anyone about our friends just yet," Melinda added. "I know it's a big secret, but it's ours to keep. Promise?"

Lorna nodded her head in agreement and went out to enjoy the day. It was uncommon for her to have a weekday off, and the newness of life she felt gave her the urge to see other living things. She headed down to the lowest habitable level, nearly five hundred feet underground, at the bottom of the chasm.

The entire lower level contained the plant nursery, twelve acres of saplings and shrubs in raised planter beds, and grass on the ground in between. A few uneven stone paths led the way through the chamber and a few dozen botanists fiddled about, watering their favored plants and playing with fertilizers. It was calm and quiet, full of natural life; just the scene Lorna sought.

The light overhead seemed more natural here than it did on the surface. The mix of full-spectrum and ultra-violet bulbs gave the feel of a sunny summer day on Earth. The colors were more vibrant and real than the washed out appearance of the Martian day. The air was much fresher, too. It was natural, filtered by the abundance of plants, not recycled by mechanical means. Someday, all Martian air would smell as sweet, just as soon as the main dome was constructed and enough oxygen had been extracted from the atmosphere to fill it.

"Ten years just turned into two," Lorna thought optimistically. Her mind dreamed of the speed at which she could build, with the miracle technology she had just been offered. It would take no time at all to move the girders and glass plates. What other wonders could the teleporter perform? Perhaps they could bond the pieces together, eliminating the need for welding? In theory, almost anything was possible.

Lorna stopped by a small bed of roses and saw a solitary bud on the verge of opening. The plant was nearly two years old, one of the oldest plants around. She leaned over and smelled it. It was the most fragrant thing she'd smelled in her life.

She was riding a natural high and she no longer bothered to consider the cause. The philosophical thoughts about her teleportation had faded, were almost forgotten. She was who she was, and nobody could tell her different. It was just good to be alive, and everything felt so new.

She walked over to the northern wall of the chasm and felt the smooth granite. It was moist to the touch from condensation. The room was humid, in stark contrast to the dry environment everywhere else.

A few hundred feet further down was a solid metal wall. The botanical labs sat on the other side, but they were inaccessible to the general public. Beyond them sat lifeless dirt and rock, and a series of natural caverns that had scarcely been explored. *What natural wonders lay hidden down there*, Lorna wondered.

Several botanists greeted Lorna as she neared them on her walk. They exchanged pleasantries, and she was invited to enjoy the scenery as long as she didn't touch anything. They were accustomed to the occasional visitor, though a few guests had the strange idea to pick a flower or pull up a sprig of grass for their quarters. Such behavior was intolerable.

Lorna had no desire to harm anything and continued her jaunt in peace. She passed a long row of saplings, numerous varieties of apple, pear, and plum trees, their little green leaves rich and glossy as only a hothouse plant would shine. These trees were perfect, grown in a controlled environment free of parasites and unpredictable weather. Their fruit would someday rival the best on Earth.

Reading the placards made her mouth water. She hadn't had fresh fruit in months. The small supply brought aboard the *Plymouth* hadn't lasted a week among the settlers, and there wouldn't be more for over a year. In ten years, these saplings could supply the much-desired produce, and a hundred years down the line, their progeny would blanket the countryside.

Lorna smiled as she considered how long she might live. She hadn't received the age-arresting gene therapy yet, but she'd get around to it. She had chosen to have her first child before trying it out, fearing it might somehow interfere with reproduction, despite the doctors' assurances to the contrary.

"Morgan," Lorna whispered. Thinking of him filled her with more joy. She couldn't wait to tell him the great news. He would have his wide, open spaces so much sooner!

Leaving the peaceful greenhouse environment, Lorna headed back up to the administrative complex and found the quartermaster's office. She rang the doorbell and received an automated message from the intercom beside the portal. "The quartermaster is currently out. Would you like to make an appointment for a later date?"

Lorna left the automated message hanging and continued on her way, trying to think where Morgan could be. She checked back at their quarters to find them empty and began asking around. Eventually, she tracked him down at the police barracks.

As was becoming second-nature, Morgan was visiting with Tim Keene, talking about their future prospects on Mars and how they were going to get around Melinda's restrictive mandates. Under a new sedition law, much of what they discussed could be seen as illegal, though the chief wasn't going to arrest himself or his fellow conspirators.

Lorna rushed in, unable to curb her enthusiasm. "Morgan, I've got the greatest news."

"Are you pregnant?" Morgan asked, thinking nothing else could bring her such elation.

"Oh, not yet. This is more important," Lorna replied. "Come on, let's talk in private."

Morgan excused himself from Tim's company and followed Lorna back to their quarters, where she revealed the big secret.

"Two years. That's how soon the dome will be completed with this new technology. Can you believe it? We'll be walking around in open fields before you know it!"

"Slow down," Morgan said, trying to process the new information. "There's viable teleportation technology here on Mars? You've seen it?"

"Seen it? I've been through it. It's the most amazing thing!"

"Through it?"

"Oh, yeah. Melinda thought a firsthand experience would be the best kind of proof."

"Lorna, we have no idea what that thing could do to people. Are you sure you're all right?"

"Of course," she said, beaming.

She didn't seem all right to Morgan, though she could have just been full of adrenaline. There were many strange wonders on this world Morgan would have never believed possible. First, the anti-aging therapy, now this miraculous teleportation device. It was like something out of a daydream, and he half-wondered if someone were playing a trick on him.

Morgan placed his hands over Lorna's on the table. She sat and smiled profusely. "Did Melinda happen to tell you where this teleporter technology came from?"

Lorna paused for a moment. She had never lied to her husband before, not about anything, and she didn't want to start. Melinda had made her promise to conceal the truth, and she felt honor-bound to keep her promise—but this was her husband. She could trust him to keep a secret, she reasoned.

"The Consensorate built it," she replied.

"The European Consensorate?" Morgan asked, disbelieving his ears.

"Yeah, they have a colony on Mars, too." Lorna explained what Melinda had told her about the Scifes, their technology, and the planned unification of the colonies.

Morgan's face slumped as the harsh realization set in. It all made sense—Melinda's restrictive rules, her affinity for Scife literature, and all her rhetoric about the evolution of mankind. Frightening suspicions came to his mind, things he prayed were only products of his over-active imagination.

"Come on," Morgan said, standing up and pulling Lorna with him. "You've got to tell Tim everything you just told me."

"No!" Lorna said, yanking back her hands. "I promised Melinda I wouldn't tell anyone."

"You told me," Morgan replied.

"That's different," Lorna said.

"This is too important to keep to ourselves. We have to get the word out before we're Scife slaves."

"You don't understand at all," Lorna chided. She was ready to cry.

It was enough to freeze Morgan in his tracks. "Lorna, I'm sorry, but we have to do something about this," he said.

"No, we don't," Lorna answered. "We can accept Scientific Fundamentalism and enjoy the better future it brings."

"A better future?" Morgan questioned. "What's gotten into you? Just a few weeks ago, you chucked one of their sacred documents across the room in disgust. Now you're worshipping them?"

"It wasn't like that at all. I don't see what you're worried about," Lorna said. "The Scifes have a lot of good ideas."

"Like governmentally-arranged marriages and forced embryo adoption? Do you want our kids to *not* be our kids genetically, because we might not be eugenically compatible?"

"I never really thought of that," Lorna said, confused. A moment later, her conditioned mind supplied her with clarity again. "No, I can't believe that would happen."

"Stop and think a minute, Lorna. A month ago you couldn't care less about their philosophy, and now you're defending it blindly. What happened?"

"I'm not allowed to change my opinion?"

"Not like this. Not in the blink of an eye."

"You're worried, I know, but don't be. The Scifes aren't our enemies. They're not going to make us slaves. They just want to help us."

"I don't trust them, not after seeing what they've done to Europe, not after spending the last month reading up on their beliefs and behaviors. I don't see how Scientific Fundamentalism can ever be compatible with free will. It is at the very core an all-controlling philosophy."

"I really hope you're wrong," Lorna said, regaining her regular composure. "I'd hate to miss out on what they're offering."

"I think we'd be better off on our own, without their offerings."

"What are you going to do?" Lorna asked.

"I'd better go have a talk with the governor," he answered.

* * *

It was well after sunset before Morgan worked up the courage to see Melinda, the woman he'd almost considered a friend up until a few hours ago. As a member of her administrative staff, he had clearance to call upon her when needed, so the officer guarding the lift to her private quarters let him pass without question. The ride down was brief, opening to a cramped hallway.

He was nervous standing outside her quarters, with no clue what he was going to say to her, or how she would react. Eventually, he rang the chime and waited several minutes for the door to open.

Melinda was dressed in a satin nightgown that glistened in the lamplight. Her hair was tousled and her eyes were puffy, showing she had been sleeping before the door chime summoned her. She didn't seem upset, and when her eyes locked onto Morgan's familiar face, she smiled.

Her feminine beauty could not be denied. For a moment, Morgan caught himself staring, as he rarely did at a woman other than his wife. Yet he had never seen Melinda outside her baggy army fatigues or the conservative pantsuits she preferred as of late.

With a cordial wave and a kind word, Melinda invited Morgan into her domicile, and he entered with mixed emotions. He looked around and was amazed by all the space. The governor's "mansion" was four times the size of standard living quarters. The living/dining room was filled with many pieces of furniture. There was a large wooden desk, almost identical to the one in her office, sitting near the door to her bedroom on the right. To the left, a long counter partitioned the living area from the kitchen, and the floor was wall-to-wall carpet, an ostentatious luxury in Villas Colony.

There was more wood in the governor's quarters than anywhere else on Mars, and the cost to bring it all here must have been astronomical. So much for not having an overly-prosperous ruling class.

"Can I get you a drink?" Melinda asked, walking over to a section of wall between her desk and the kitchen partition. Sticking her fingers into a small notch cut into the wall, she slid down a four foot section of the wood paneling, revealing a liquor cabinet. The contents were varied, the finest selection of alcohol on the entire planet, far superior to the stuff rationed out to the average citizens on an irregular basis.

Morgan shook his head. Melinda took down one brandy glass and poured herself a minuscule sampling. She sipped the drink and shivered happily as it made contact with her tongue. "Oh, that's good. Still, I wouldn't want to drink it every day," she admitted, before downing the rest.

"Melinda, I'm not here for a social call," Morgan said.

"Oh," she replied, putting down her empty glass.

"I want to know what the hell you did to my wife today," he said, sounding more uneasy than angry.

"Oh, that," Melinda said lightly. "I assume she had a talk with you."

"Then it's true? About the teleporter and the Scifes' control of it?" he asked, agitation seeping into his tone.

"She wasn't supposed to tell you *that*," Melinda said, sounding disappointed.

"What are you doing, aligning with those people?"

Melinda lowered her head thoughtfully. "You must think I'm a traitor."

"The thought crossed my mind," Morgan replied.

Melinda stepped forward and placed an arm on Morgan's shoulder. "Believe me, it's nothing of the sort. I love America so much, but I must do what I believe is best for mankind."

"You may believe that, but I don't see it that way."

"That's because you don't have all the facts."

"Then why don't you provide them?" Morgan demanded, shrugging her hand off his shoulder.

Melinda returned to her liquor cabinet and poured herself a fresh snifter of brandy. "I need to know I can trust you," she said, pouring a second glass for her guest.

Morgan accepted the glass but didn't drink. "I could say the same."

"Then it's settled," she said, tapping her glass against his. "What's said here, stays here. Agreed?"

Morgan shook his head in affirmation.

"Do you want to know why I'm really dealing with the Scifes?" She raised her free hand and waved it over her face. "This is why." She paused and took a slurp of her drink, providing a dramatic pause.

"By now, I'm sure you've learned the truth behind the gene

therapy—that while it arrests the aging process, it cannot reverse age. But no cosmetic surgery known to man can be responsible for this body of mine. This rejuvenated look is more than skin deep. I've even lost an inch I put on when I was seventeen."

"Did the Scifes do it to you?" Morgan asked, looking at the drink in his hands. He wondered if the alcohol would soothe his nerves and took a sip, then regretted it.

"In a sense. It was an unintended consequence of our first meeting." She went on to explain her first arrival on Mars, about the Scifes already having a base established, and them using their teleporter technology to abduct her. "I remember opening my eyes that first time afterwards. The sights and sounds...everything was so much sharper and clearer. The scientists said it happened to everyone, but as I spent the afternoon with them, I kept hearing offhand remarks about my age. They made jokes about Americans sending children into space. I thought it was some strange kind of European flattery until I saw my reflection in a darkened monitor. This sixteen year old face stared back at me, and I realized my sensations weren't just euphoria, but truly revitalized.

"Unwittingly, the Scifes had uncovered the single greatest medical breakthrough in history, and it was truly a combination of Scife and American innovation.

"You see, about a year before leaving on the Aries mission, I had accepted the then-experimental gene therapy, to arrest my aging process. It was working just fine and my cells were still adjusting themselves when the Scifes first teleported me. Their teleporter was confused by my cellular flux and reassembled my body as you see it now.

"Of course, I couldn't very well tell the world about my discovery when I got back to Earth. Not only was the genetic therapy a State secret, but our government has something of a non-interaction policy regarding the Consensorate, and it's doubtful I would be standing here today had they learned the truth behind my transformation. I told nobody about the Scifes, nor did any of my fellow astronauts.

"The best American geneticists considered this a fluke, a natural mutation in my genome, and experts have spent over a decade trying to reproduce it. But the answer lies here, on Mars," she concluded, downing the last of her brandy.

"So, you're just working with them to get your hands on their technology?" Morgan asked with suspicion.

"We both need what the other has. They have the teleporter, but we have the gene-therapy—something their scientists haven't been able to invent yet. We have a free society that respects emotion and individuality, but they have structure and discipline we lack. It's only logical we work together for the benefit of all, combine the best of both cultures into one perfect union."

Morgan ruminated on her words and sipped at his drink. It all left a bitter taste in his mouth. She told a good story, but not everything added up.

"I'd buy that, if you weren't so sympathetic to their philosophy," he reasoned, recalling Neils Vanderbilt and the recent economic policies. "How do I know you're not really a Consensorate agent?"

"I don't deny that I happen to share many of their ideals, as they share many of ours. We both have the desire to advance humanity, but not at the expense of our American values. I have things well under control. In a few decades, when we're all perpetually young and spreading across the face of Mars, you'll agree it was the right thing to do."

Morgan handed her the half-full glass. "I have the feeling we're going to get burned over this."

"I know what I'm doing," Melinda assured him. "Trust me, as I'm trusting you, all right?"

He didn't want to trust her. Everything in his gut told him this was wrong, that the Scifes were not to be trusted. But what could he really do about it?

"If there's anything I can do to help assuage your concerns..." she offered, her voice trailing off.

"There is something," Morgan said, recalling the initial reason he came to see her. "I want your word as an Air Force officer that you will not send me through that teleporter device, ever. I don't know what exactly it's done to Lorna, but she isn't quite herself."

"I'm sure it's just post teleport euphoria. She'll be fine in no time."

"Promise me, just the same," Morgan said.

"You have my word, as an officer and an American."

Morgan accepted her oath and agreed to keep what he had learned to himself. He realized her promise wouldn't mean much if she were lying, or if her Scife allies were lying to her.

Morgan was never one to break a promise, but for the first time, he wondered if he could afford to be honorable.

Chapter Fifteen
September 12, 2327

"It's treason!" Morgan told Tim Keene. He'd gotten the chief out of bed in the middle of the night to tell him everything Melinda wanted to keep secret.

"I knew something was up," Tim said, warming his hands on his second cup of coffee. "The writing was all over the walls. Now it makes sense."

"The question is, what are we going to do about it?"

"I don't know if there's anything we *can* do. This conspiracy obviously stretches far beyond our little colony. There are a lot of Scifes at NASA, but I never imagined they could sell us out like this."

"I don't expect that it's official policy," Morgan countered. "A few subversives have sneaked their way into the system, but if we expose their actions here and now, before things go any further, we might stand a chance of undoing the damage and saving ourselves."

"What about the teleporter?" Tim asked. "You say it did something to Lorna's personality, that it's somehow controlling her?"

"Yes. It's just too coincidental that she went all Scife-sympatico on me right after being teleported. And that could explain a lot of things, like how a thousand miners could suddenly go from a total strike to utter contentedness overnight. Melinda's brainwashing people with that thing."

"How are we supposed to stand up to this kind of a threat?"

"I'm still working that out, but we can't just sit here and be taken over by the Scifes," Morgan said defiantly.

"We may not have a choice. The *Plymouth* isn't scheduled to return for another eighteen months. That's a long time to stage a coup, and I don't see that Melinda's the type to just step down. We'd better be prepared for the long haul here."

"You want to sit around and wait for Melinda's Scife buddies to turn you into a zombie?"

"I didn't say that," Tim rebutted. "Do you remember a criminal complaint I sent you last week, regarding the theft of several thousand ration packs from storage?"

"I chalked it up to an accounting error. What of it?"

"Promise you won't report me to myself," Tim said, risking self-incrimination.

"You've been stealing from the colony?" Morgan asked in a harsh whisper.

"Like I said, I knew something was afoot. I needed an escape route, so I've been quietly creating a survival stash over the last few months."

"Do you plan to run off and start your own colony somewhere else?"

"Maybe just take an extended vacation," Tim replied. "I've got enough supplies to keep half a dozen of us alive out there until the *Plymouth* returns. If we go into hiding, bide our time until we can get some help, we might just succeed."

It was a wild idea, one that would test the character of any man attempting it—to brave the open wastes of Mars for such an extended period of time. It had never been attempted before. Sure, teams of researchers went out for months, but they always had a warm bed waiting for them afterwards.

Morgan was willing to entertain the notion, though he hoped for an alternative. "Okay, let's just say we go ahead with this escape plan. We're still going to need to get the word out about Melinda's activities if we want Earth to send help."

"Somehow I doubt your testimony alone would catch their attention. We're going to need solid proof," Tim concluded.

The ever elusive proof. How could they get it and keep their minds intact? Melinda hadn't gotten this far without being cautious, and anyone who had threatened her order thus far had a convenient, abrupt change of heart. Who knew what kind of safeguards she had created to protect herself?

She might have the power to flick a switch and teleport you away.

As he sat there, a plan came to Morgan's mind. It was drastic and risky, but it was the only thing he could think of that had any chance of success. It might prove suicidal, but these were desperate circumstances, and they had to try.

"I think it's about time we brought in the great equalizer," Morgan said.

* * *

Melinda sat at her desk Tuesday morning, anticipating another uneventful day in her administration of Villas Colony. Things were going smoothly, and all signs of dissent had been quashed. She felt safe and secure.

At nine fifteen, a knock sounded at her door. The doorbell didn't chime, and when she asked the caller to enter, nothing happened. She wondered if there might be a malfunction of some sort with the automatic door controls and got up to open it manually. When she did, the color vanished from her face as she found a gun barrel pointed at her.

"Step back," Morgan ordered.

Melinda complied, taking three full steps backwards, keeping her eyes locked on the revolver's barrel.

Morgan remained in the doorway as he spoke. "Before you do anything stupid, like have your Scife buddies teleport me away, you should know I have several associates stationed on the other side of these office walls, each equipped with infrared scopes. If I disappear, they shoot, and you die."

Melinda wiped the fear off her face and folded her arms across her chest. "You're bluffing."

"Want to bet?" Morgan asked, taking one step inside the office and slamming the door behind him.

Melinda knew from his tone of voice that he was serious, and she decided not to call his hand. "What do you think you're doing, Morgan?" she asked, insulted more than anything.

"Over to the desk, now," Morgan demanded, taking another step forward.

Melinda stepped backwards until her legs bumped into the hardwood desk. She slid around behind it and sat in her chair, eager to slip her hands out of sight.

"Keep those hands where I can see them," Morgan shouted.

Melinda complied and set them on a bare patch of desk. "Really, Morgan, is this the way you want to be remembered? As the armed terrorist of Mars?"

Morgan kept his cool. "Open the laptop."

"Why?"

"I need proof," he said, not elaborating on what kind.

Melinda complied, seeing she had no alternative. She opened the laptop and unlocked the hard drive with her password before asking for further instructions.

Morgan dug around in his pocket and removed a cube-shaped object with a square jack sticking out of one side. "Plug this into the back," he said, setting it on the desk.

Melinda did as she was told, and as soon as she had the object in place, was ordered to lean back, away from the keyboard. She put her arms in the air and watched as windows popped up on her computer screen. Her files were being accessed remotely.

It only took a minute for the files to be copied, and as the download ended, Melinda put her wrists together and pointed her open hands at Morgan. "Now that you have what you came for, please let me live," she pleaded, feigning concern.

"I never wanted to hurt you," Morgan said.

His answer put a smile on Melinda's face. As he removed his interface device from her computer, she slid her hand onto a nondescript button on her collar and activated a concealed transmitter. By the time Morgan glanced up, her body was engulfed in a streak of shimmering light as the teleporter pulled her away.

Morgan cursed under his breath and darted for the door. He reached the hallway in seconds, grateful he hadn't found himself nabbed, or worse, surrounded by Consensorate soldiers.

It had all been a big bluff. There were no snipers surrounding Melinda's office, no help for the new outlaw.

He and Tim had spent half the night working out the details of the plan, and so far, it seemed to have worked. The modified uplink had given them access to Melinda's computer, and with any luck, the contents would be dissected in short order and crucial evidence would be uncovered.

The only question was, would they have enough time to flee? They'd been counting on Morgan's ability to hold Melinda at bay for a while, long enough for a computer expert to locate the right data for their vindication. With evidentiary data in hand, they were hoping to use it as leverage for their escape, while an accomplice remained behind to relay the evidence to Earth at a later date.

Arriving at the door to his quarters, Morgan removed the small uplink from his pocket, dropped it on the metal floor, and stomped on it. The bits of plastic and circuits cracked under his heel, assuring that nobody would use the device to trace the hacker on the receiving end.

It was mid-morning and Lorna was safely at work, so Morgan found his quarters vacant. He wanted to take her with him, but her brainwashing posed a grave threat. He didn't know how she would react after learning of his criminal behavior, but he couldn't afford to stick around to find out, no matter how much he wanted to remain. He was trying not to think about her, but there was no getting her out of his head. She deserved better than this; at least a face-to-face farewell, but it was not possible.

Damn Melinda Faris and her Scife conspirators! Morgan thought as he grabbed a bag of personal effects and headed out into the hallway again. There was no time for regrets or second thoughts. Tim would be waiting for him at Airlock #5 with a halftrack rover ready to take them to places unknown. They'd be roughing it like no one else in history, but they'd be free.

As Morgan neared the elevator at the end of the corridor,

he was halted by an authoritative shout. "Freeze, or we fire!"

Morgan's run was over before it had even begun. He raised his hands over his head and turned around to see several of Tim's fellow officers pointing condensed energy weapons at him. The newly developed firearms purportedly caused extensive nerve damage, even on a low setting, so he didn't think of testing their effectiveness. He stood motionless in surrender.

The senior lieutenant kept his pistol pointed at Morgan while his colleagues rushed toward their fugitive. One grabbed Morgan's hands and cuffed him while the other grabbed his bag. The lieutenant read Morgan's Miranda Rights off of a laminated card, stumbling over the words. Never before had they needed to apprehend a dangerous criminal on Mars.

As Morgan was dragged away by two junior police officers, he told the lieutenant, "Thanks for not shooting me."

"Thanks for not resisting," the lieutenant replied. "We all have our jobs to do, like it or not."

Chapter Sixteen

The cell was pretty boring, just another metal box identical to the standard living quarters, minus the furniture. There was a bench to sit on and a small camera wired into the ceiling to keep tabs on the occupant.

This makeshift prison was a recent addition to Villas Colony, for there was never supposed to be a need for one. The idea that any of the carefully screened colonists would warrant imprisonment was beyond the realm of the ICB's imagination.

Until ten hours ago, Melinda Faris wouldn't have thought it possible, either. She'd encountered resistance to her rule, even idle threats, but she could have never envisioned such a violent act occurring—and from Morgan Asher, of all people!

Stepping into the cell, Melinda stopped and stared at Morgan. Only yesterday, he had been a trusted friend and fellow administrator of their fledgling society. Now he was little more than a petty thug, holed up like a rat. Such a fate was unbefitting a man of his stature.

"They warned me about you, you know, but I didn't believe them."

"Who is 'they?'" Morgan asked, defiance lingering in his voice.

"Some good friends who tend to be more pragmatic."

"You mean those lousy Scifes pulling your strings."

Melinda rolled her eyes. "Those 'Lousy Scifes,' as you call them, aren't pulling anyone's strings here. If they were, we wouldn't be having this conversation. They want to condition you with the teleporter."

"And you don't?" Morgan asked dubiously.

Melinda stepped closer, showing no fear, expressing no anger or resentment. "I want to convince you I'm right the old fashioned way, not with some technological shortcut." She paused a moment, trying to find the right words to explain. "I mean, you're one of my heroes."

Morgan groaned. "Oh, here we go again..."

"Yes!" Melinda barked in frustration. "Yes, like it or not, you've been an inspirational figure for three generations of progressive Americans; those of us who've wanted to build a better world, and move our nation forward beyond its addictions to entertainment."

"I was a figurehead and not much else."

"Modesty doesn't suit you. So what if you're a figurehead? It doesn't matter. Not to me, and not to the millions of Americans who grew up believing in your dream of a better tomorrow."

"And now you spit on that better tomorrow," Morgan cursed. "Plot to overturn everything I believe in, everything I've fought for my entire life! The whole purpose of a better tomorrow is for Americans to live free again and not be slaves to their own vices. My dream wasn't Scife fascism. It was the advancement of American liberty."

Melinda spit on the floor, disgusted by his rant. "Liberty be damned! It's a stupid, outdated concept. A million minds with a million different opinions, all with the right to be wrong. Such chaotic thinking leads to nothing but stagnation and cultural death. Look at how it has restricted our growth over the last two centuries. We are a hundred years behind the Europeans in some respects because of our petty bickering and short-sighted liberties."

Melinda closed her eyes and breathed deeply, to settle her nerves. She was rarely flustered, but Morgan's actions had brought out the worst in her. Part of her admired him for that ability; such strength of spirit, though it was very frustrating to be on the opposing end of his arguments. Would he ever see the light? She wanted to at least give him the chance.

***

Morgan had never heard Melinda speak with such passion and conviction. This was her true persona, everything he had surmised from her offhand comments and governing policies.

It assured him he had done the right thing by attempting to expose her treachery. If she went unchallenged, freedom would be an alien concept on Mars.

It was clear Melinda's mind was closed, so Morgan saw no sense in further discussion. He bit his lip and left her speech unanswered.

"You might be interested to know that we've got your coconspirator locked up across the hall," Melinda added, sounding proud of herself.

"Which one?" Morgan asked, trying to sound brave. "I've got an army of followers."

Melinda grinned, fighting to hold back laughter. "Oh, please. You don't have any support, except for Mr. Keene." Morgan's face dropped in an exaggerated expression of dread. "Oh, yes, we have the good chief in custody, caught him red-handed with the copied computer files. Not that you would have found any incriminating evidence in my database, anyway."

"What are you going to do to him?" Morgan asked.

"Oh, we'll see," Melinda said with a sly inflection. "I suppose he'll have to be conditioned, just like any other malcontent. I need my Chief of Police back on the job."

Morgan remained silent, biting back an angry retort. Melinda gave three hard taps on the door which summoned the officers on the other side to unlock it. "Of course, you must understand that after the way you've acted, we'll need to confiscate your guns," she said before leaving the room.

"Will you destroy them?" Morgan asked.

"No, I'm sure the police department can make use of them. Who knows? If you behave yourself, you might get them back someday." With that, she stepped outside.

"Fat chance," Morgan replied after the door slammed shut.

* * *

Tim Keene hadn't been surprised when his men had come to his office holding a warrant for his arrest. He didn't question the document's validity, as he knew what he had done, and arrest was a logical result of his behavior.

He'd been dreading capture all along, ever since agreeing to go along with Morgan's harebrained scheme. He would have rather made a discreet departure from the colony and infiltrated at a later date for the evidence, but Morgan had vetoed his idea, feeling they had to strike immediately to stand any chance of success.

Had it been worth it? Tim wondered. It would have been worse if he had done nothing; sat back and waited as Melinda conspired against her people, betraying them to foreign agents whose true agenda was shrouded in uncertainty and contrary to the values Tim held in his heart.

So far, his former subordinates were treating him well. They made sure to grant his simple requests for food and drink, as well as his desire for an electronic note pad he used to pen a letter to his wife.

His very pregnant wife.

Above all, it was urgent he jot down his thoughts to the woman he loved, giving her more of an explanation. Getting himself locked up for theft and conspiracy to commit murder wasn't the best thing to happen to an expectant father, and he didn't want her to think it was all for nothing.

Dear Deirdre,

You have no doubt learned of my arrest, and heard one or more incomplete stories regarding the circumstances behind it. I can only imagine what you're feeling, and hope your kind understanding has not left you.

I must admit, I am guilty of many things. I did behave rashly and assisted in the execution of a criminal act, even though my station charged me with the responsibility to prevent such an act. But I do not apologize for what I did, as I would not have even considered it, had I not deemed it necessary.

We have all heard the rumors about the Scife influences in our colony. They stopped being mere rumors for me last night. It will not be long before they can no longer hide their presence. It was these subversive elements that spurred the actions that led to my arrest, for I know what these people are and what they have planned.

I could not allow our children to become slaves to the insidious Scife doctrine, and so I did the only thing I could do. I fought back, and I failed, but please do not feel I have failed you. All I have done is for you and our dear unborn Theodore. To sit back and do nothing would have been a betrayal to you both, and I could never have lived with that. I only pray that I live to make it up to you, though I know not where my future lies.

Please pray for my safe return to your arms, that I may be a husband and father, whole in my being, and failing that pray that history shall exonerate me.

May God bless you and protect you.

Your loving husband,

Tim

He read the letter back to himself several times, but didn't change a thing. It was the message he wanted to send. Before going to bed, he summoned one of the officers outside his cell and asked him to deliver the letter. Tim knew the young officer to be a man of honor, and felt assured he would fulfill the request.

Tim balled up his jacket and rested his head upon it, uncomfortable on the thin, bare mattress. Before he could get any rest, the door opened and his eyes locked onto a pair of size six army boots belonging to none other than Melinda Faris.

"Sorry to wake you," Melinda said softly, "but we need to talk."

"What about?" Tim asked, sitting up. "Are you after an apology or something?"

"It would be a start, but I don't expect to get one," Melinda replied, taking a seat on the bench near the bed. "What I really came here looking for is a name."

"A name?" Tim asked innocently.

"Don't play dumb, Timothy. We scanned your computer.

You missed a file in your temporary memory that clearly shows you downloaded a significant portion of my data to another remote system, and whoever received it was skilled enough to mask their address. I want the name of that person."

"There is no name," Tim said without hesitation. "I simply downloaded the files to a secondary computer, in case of this contingency. *I* still have the data Morgan stole from you."

"I don't suppose you're going to tell me where your other computer is."

Tim gave her a nasty stare for an answer.

"Why are you doing this? You, of all people, should be able to appreciate the kind of order I wish to bring here."

"If you have to ask, you'll never understand," Tim replied.

"Oh, I understand, Tim. I admire your idealism, even though I don't share it. I'm not going to press you for any more information tonight. It's such a shame we can't see eye to eye," Melinda said, standing up to leave.

She didn't speak another word as she crossed the room, leaving Tim to his sleep.

As she left, the former Police Chief let his mind drift back to his wife, wondering if she'd truly received his message, and what she would do about it.

* * *

Even with the insulated walls and geothermal heating ducts, the outer sections of the colony were cold at night. It was understandable why most of the personal quarters were located in the center levels of the chasm, away from the harsh exterior that could get close to the freezing point in places.

Useable space was still in short supply, and what few rooms they had vacant for the prison cells were on the upper levels, near the exterior walls. It got nippy after dark, and the frosty air was harsh on the two young officers stationed as guards. By midnight, they found it intolerably cold, and one left his post to hunt down extra coats. They were both under orders to stay put without prior authorization, but neither man wanted to wake up their lieutenant and end up on his crap list.

The one remaining guard shivered at his post, dreaming of the warm clothing and hot cup of coffee his partner would soon bring. The thought of trouble never crossed his mind.

Footsteps sounded from down the hall, drawing the attention of the young officer. A round figure approached, bundled in a heavy coat. As she neared, the young officer recognized her.

"Mrs. Keene," the officer greeted, rubbing his cold hands together.

"Tony, right?" she asked with a friendly grin.

"Yeah, that's me." He blew warm breath onto his frigid fists. "What can I do for ya?"

"You can let me see my husband," she said.

"Well, I'd like to oblige, ma'am, really, but I got orders. Nobody gets in these cells without the say-so of Lieutenant Weitz or the Gov."

Deirdre Keene pulled a revolver out from under her coat, the sturdy .44 Magnum Morgan Asher had given her husband. It made her slender hand look like a child's as she gripped the handle. "Open it. *Now!*" she shouted.

Tony didn't take her seriously and folded his arms across his chest. "Come on," he mocked her, "whatcha gonna do, lady?"

She sunk a bullet into the metal flooring between Tony's feet. He jumped and checked if the ricochet had damaged his privates.

Deirdre's hands trembled as they continued to clutch the gun. She looked scared and sounded desperate. "Please, don't make me do that again."

"Jeez, you'll wake the dead with that thing," Tony said as he opened the door to Tim's cell.

Deirdre motioned for Tony to enter the cell ahead of her, but before he had the chance, Tim stepped out, having been roused by the gunshot.

"Deirdre, what are you doing here?" Tim asked, his face displaying his disbelief.

"I wasn't going to let them melt your brain," Deirdre replied, as if he'd just asked an absurd question.

"I never thought you could be so impetuous," Tim replied, giving his wife a nod of approval.

Deirdre turned her eyes back to Tony. "Get in the cell," she ordered.

"Shouldn't he unlock Morgan's cell first?" Tim suggested, seeing no point in leaving his friend imprisoned. They were in this together, after all.

"Oh, right," Deirdre replied.

Tony didn't need the gun waved in his face as an incentive. He complied with their request, ready to turn the tables with his taser at the ready.

Morgan was already on guard, lurking beside the door, sending a swift elbow into Tony's face the moment he identified him in the gloom. Stunned, Tony relaxed his grip on the taser. Morgan easily took it away, sending the young officer stumbling back out into the hallway, clutching a bloody nose.

With Morgan free, Deirdre ordered Tony into the cell and locked him inside. With the guard locked safely away, the easy part was done. Now the real challenge presented itself— how would she get these men to safety? An upper airlock was only a few hundred feet down the corridor, so it was the logical place to go. Where they went from there was the real question.

When they reached the outer chamber to the airlock, Tim grabbed his wife's hand and pulled her into his embrace. "We've got a stockpile of supplies outside," Tim explained, dropping a kiss on her nose. "Food, water, oxygen, tools— enough to keep us going for months if need be."

Deirdre shook her head. "I'm staying."

"But they'll kill you after this," Tim argued.

"I'll be okay," Deirdre said, staring lovingly at her husband. "As it is, I don't think there's a suit that would fit me," she added, tapping her bulbous belly.

Tim stared back at her, nodding his understanding.

Deirdre knew it had to be eating him up inside, just as it was paining her. Their hearts ached to be together, but this was how it had to be. It was the only sensible course of action. There was no way she could leave with them, not in her present condition. If she hadn't been about ready to give birth, things might have been different, but as they were...

"Come on!" Morgan said, pulling on his helmet.

There was little time to waste. Tim pulled Dierdre close and embraced her one last time, letting his fingertips graze over her extended abdomen, before rushing over to the rack of spacesuits to find one his size. She watched as he pulled the loose-fitting suit over his clothes, and even from the distance, she could smell the sweat from the last wearer.

Before fitting the helmet, Tim found the small patch of cloth that held the suit's transponder and yanked it free. Its removal would help prevent remote tracking.

Deirdre attached fresh oxygen tanks to each man's suit and slapped the revolver into Tim's hand before leaving the room. Closing the door, she didn't look back, but kept on walking, ignoring the tears streaming down her cheeks.

* * *

"I really hope we don't have to shoot anyone," Tim told Morgan as the room depressurized.

Morgan nodded. "Me too."

As the last of the air was sucked out of the chamber, one entire wall retracted, exposing the pure twilight of the Martian night. Both men ventured out into the darkness outside the airlock. Hundreds of overlapping footprints and tire tracks covered the ground, and high overhead sat the partially-built dome, its girders and panels scarcely visible in the night.

They walked for half a mile before finding the edge of the dome, and followed along the glass wall until they found an opening leading to the undeveloped expanse.

The sky was so clear on Mars; its thin atmosphere did little to obstruct the view of the stars. It was almost as good as being in outer space for viewing the naked light of distant suns. The pretty sight gave momentary respite for the fleeing fugitives.

"How much farther?" Morgan shouted, his voice barely perceptible to Tim's ears. They didn't want to use their suit radios, for fear of eavesdropping, so they had to touch helmets and yell to communicate.

Tim checked the display panel on his left arm, and then set his helmet against Morgan's. "Quite far, I'm afraid. We're on the opposite side of the compound. We'll have to circle around to get to our supply stash."

"How far?" Morgan asked.

"In a direct line, only about three miles, but we should give the colony a wide berth. Ten miles would be on the safe side."

"Lucky I only weigh about eighty pounds," Morgan quipped.

They marched through the night, swinging around Villas Colony in a half circle, heading toward the secret supplies Tim had smuggled out over the last few months. It had been fairly easy to amass such a depot. Tim had made it a habit to take walks in his spare time, and always brought a large pack along that he filled with rocks, after stashing the goods he carried. Deirdre was a geologist, so he had used the excuse that he was collecting samples for her. It was the perfect cover.

It was almost dawn before they neared the supplies, and the sky was turning pale gray on the horizon. Behind them, the hills in the distance seemed to glow as the light of the sun began trickling over them. With the light came added sight. In the distance, they saw the stack of stones covering the crevasse storing the pilfered supplies. Only there was a large object sitting upon the cratered plain now, one that spelled doom for the rebel fugitives.

Tim tapped a few buttons on his arm panel and a new display appeared on the interior of his helmet. He magnified the image and examined what lay ahead. He cursed when he spotted half a dozen men armed with modern rifles, standing around a small halftrack rover.

"I thought nobody knew about this place," Morgan said.

"Nobody did, not even Deirdre," Tim replied, gritting his teeth. It was a nasty complication, one he hadn't been expecting.

They had to get to the supplies. They wouldn't last a day without them. The only other option was surrender, and they were in too deep for that.

The riflemen hadn't seen them yet, or at least it didn't appear so. The six figures milled about, as if they'd been stationed there a while and had grown bored. As inattentive as they were, it gave Morgan and Tim a chance to get close before they were spotted. They weren't a hundred feet away when one of the guards finally caught sight of them. A muffled warning siren blared to catch their attention.

They looked over at the group of men, and saw that one of them was standing out in front of the vehicle with both hands in the air. After he knew he had their attention, the man tapped at the control panel on his sleeve, seeking to communicate.

"This is one hell of a jam you've gotten yourself into, Chief," Lieutenant Weitz said.

Tim turned on his suit's radio and responded. "Yeah, Armin, it is at that. What are we going to do about it?"

"I'm under order of the governor to bring you in alive," the lieutenant said. "I don't suppose you're going to come quietly."

"Are you gonna shoot me down if I don't?" Tim asked.

"Stand by," Weitz said, changing his radio's frequency. He talked privately with two of his fellow officers. Moments later, they raised their rifles and fired. The short, blockish devices were modern Condensed Energy Dischargers.

Morgan remained hidden behind a crater's edge, but Tim stood up and walked out in the open, allowing the officers a clear shot. He didn't raise his pistol or make any aggressive move as the men pulled their triggers.

There was one technical glitch about CED weapons. They

needed a relatively thick atmosphere to allow the energy bolt to remain charged. In the thin air of Mars, the modern weapons were absolutely useless.

Switching his frequency, Weitz said, "Aw, geez, Tim, looks like we can't arrest you after all." The five officers around him looked at each other with clever smirks, clearly in on the joke.

Tim smiled. Lieutenant Weitz had known full well the CED weapons wouldn't function in the open. He had served as Tim's second in command for the last two years, and was one of his most loyal friends.

Playing into the orchestrated display, Tim raised the revolver and said, "Stick 'em up."

"We surrender," Armin said, throwing aside his rifle. Seeing no alternative, his men followed suit.

With the officers at his mercy, Tim ordered his former subordinates to load the half-track rover with the supplies he had stored in the crevasse. The handful of loyal men were perfectly willing to pitch in, and they worked hastily until the back of the vehicle was fully packed with the goods.

"You may need this," Armin said, handing Tim a small device that resembled a radio. "It'll scramble the airwaves for a few miles. It's not much, but it should keep them from tracking you initially."

After accepting the gift, Tim opened the driver's side door of the rover and ducked under the dash. He yanked out a small, clear tube and handed it back to Armin. "Here's the transponder, just in case."

"It'll take us a couple of hours to get back to the colony, and with the radios jammed, I should be able to give you that time to gain some distance. Get as far as you can and watch your ass out there. When the time's right, I'll make sure Melinda's files get into the right hands."

Tim nodded in appreciation as he activated the scrambler. Armin backed off with his men and watched as the fugitives drove off into the rising sun.

Chapter Seventeen
September 13, 2327

Melinda always enjoyed paperwork. Where others scoffed at having to file reports, she cherished that most fundamental aspect of her job. She had something of a journalistic flair and enjoyed relating the facts as she saw them. It provided a sense of power, especially now, where she held a monopoly on what Earth learned regarding life on Mars. If she wrote it, it was so, as far as anyone beyond the immediate events were concerned. Who would contradict her?

Yet, drafting her latest report made her feel dirty. She rewrote it, over and over, wondering what she would say about recent events. She kept going back and forth in her mind, wishing she could erase the betrayal she felt, even as she contemplated how much to divulge. Did the people back home really need to learn that Morgan Asher, an American legend, had become a petty outlaw? Without divulging her own questionable dealings on Mars, it was impossible to do anything but paint him as a lunatic. That wasn't anything she was prepared to do. She deleted her drafts and put down a short message noting nothing of interest was happening at the moment.

She did not fear any critical oversight. She was beyond the reach of outside scrutiny. The ICB had her back, and half its members were her former Aries-2 astronauts who knew how vital her leadership was to the fledgling colony, and how vital the Consensorate's technology was to America's future.

What she said was taken at face value, plain and simple.

Once the report was complete, she forwarded the file to the communications room, where her trusted staff would send it off to Earth with the next communications stream.

A flash of light caught her eye, alerting her to the arrival of an expected guest. She folded her laptop and leaned back in her chair as Mr. Budreau marched in from her bedroom.

"*Bonjour. Je vous souhaite le,*" he said cordially.

"You sound awfully happy this morning," Melinda remarked, trying to sound as pleasant.

"There is no sense in beginning a bad conversation on a bitter note. I only wish your policemen were more assertive in their confrontation with the traitors."

"What were you expecting, for my men to fire on them?"

"That is exactly what I expected."

"Well, they tried, but CED weapons don't work in the Martian atmosphere."

"Yes, a fact your new police chief conveniently overlooked."

"Are you suggesting he wanted them to escape?"

"It would appear so, at first glance—unless you wish me to believe he is utterly incompetent."

"It was not on purpose," Melinda assured the Frenchman. Armin Weitz had been conditioned. He couldn't betray her so blatantly.

"If you would only allow us to teleport the fugitives, we would not be needing this conversation. We should simply tag them with an RF chip and be done with it. Then they will be here, under our control."

Melinda shook her head and put up her hands, "I don't want to argue about this again."

She had put her foot down the previous night and stopped the Scifes from capturing Morgan and Tim with the teleporter. It had seemed the easiest and most logical way to retrieve the fugitives, but she didn't feel it was right. Morgan had made her promise to never send him through, and unlike him, she planned to keep her word. He was still that same iconic figure she'd grown up admiring. How could she betray her childhood hero, even if he'd turned out to be less than admirable?

Clearly, Morgan wasn't ready for the life-altering phenomenon of being demolecularized and reassembled, and he would never forgive her for summarily forcing such an

141

experience on him. A mental reconfiguration could make him forgive her, but any fraudulently conditioned version was simply unacceptable.

"Where are they now?" Melinda asked. The American tracking satellites were conveniently out of commission at the moment, leaving her to rely on her Consensorate associates.

"Our satellite shows they are roughly fifty miles east. We do not have much time if we wish to catch them. The dust storm is already pelting our compound, and when it gets worse, and it *will* get worse, our communications will be disrupted—including our satellite imaging. Our telepads will be inoperative within the hour, and teleporting men to apprehend these fugitives is the only way to catch them."

"Then I suggest you send your men immediately. And could you please try to bring Morgan back alive, without the teleporter?"

"If I discovered one of my heroes to be a traitor to our beliefs, I would gladly see them conditioned" Budreau mentioned.

"We Americans don't do things that way. We prefer logic and reason to win over the best and brightest, as much as possible."

"Are you sure you're one of us?" Budreau asked with an uplifted eyebrow.

"No," Melinda said, causing her companion to flinch. "We may share similar beliefs and desires, but we will never be identical in our thinking."

"Oh, of course," Budreau said, not sounding wholly convinced. "Excuse me," he added, stepping into the bedroom momentarily. He answered the vibrating phone in his pocket, keeping his voice low to avoid eavesdropping. After listening for a while, he issued some commands and ended the call, returning to Melinda who fiddled with a paper weight in boredom.

"My team is prepared to apprehend your men," Budreau said. "However, if you do not wish them harmed, and you do not wish them teleported, we will require some form of persuasion. The wives, where are they?"

"One's locked up for instigating the jailbreak. The other is doing her job, constructing the dome."

"Have them brought to me immediately," he commanded, as if he were telling a waiter to bring him a croissant.

"Why?" Melinda asked, suspecting the worst.

"It is quite simple. We will use the women as part of the team. They will be properly conditioned and sent to talk sense into their husbands. If the husbands are so sick as to kill their own wives, I will not feel the least bit of remorse over their deaths. Now, send for them."

"No," Melinda said flatly.

"*What*?" Budreau shouted.

"Mrs. Keene is over eight months pregnant. She's in no condition to be thrown into danger, and I need Lorna's expertise on the dome construction. I'm sorry. You'll just have to think of something else."

"You dictate outrageous terms and then tie my hands to make the task impossible!" He spit out some colorful curses in French and German.

"Don't you have any tranquilizer darts?"

"The only darts we use have radio transponders attached, so we can acquire a teleporter lock."

"You have become dependent on the teleporter. It seems to tie your hands more than anything."

"Yet you begged us to have one of your very own. You have made great use of our technology in the past. I do not understand your reluctance to use it now."

"I have my reasons," Melinda said. "And don't pretend to be so selfless. We agreed to share our technologies equally, and I daresay it's a fair bargain."

"I suppose," Budreau said, sounding less than thrilled.

"I gave you genetic research most people on Earth don't even know about. You should be a little more appreciative. You'll be living a very long time, thanks to me."

"Assuming it is genuine. Our doctors are still not fully convinced of your *fontaine au jeunesse*."

Melinda fought off a laugh and said, "You just hate to admit that Americans came up with it first."

Budreau wrinkled his nose in offense.

Chapter Eighteen

The landscape was so bleak, and it was always that way. It was nothing to write home about, this lifeless rock they'd traveled millions of miles to inhabit. *What a horrible mistake*, Morgan thought. He hadn't wanted to come. He should have tried to talk Lorna out of it. They'd have been safe and comfortable on Earth, free to live out their lives without fear of international conspiracies. But it was her dream to see Mars, and pleasing her had been his only concern. He'd given up an entire world for her, and look at where love had led him—right into the hands of death.

As desperate as his situation seemed, he knew there was still hope. If all went as planned, he'd return someday and free Lorna from Scife bondage. Then, they could have that family they'd been wanting, and forget about all this madness.

But what if things didn't work out?

Now wasn't the time to be having such thoughts, so he swallowed the emotions and focused on the task at hand. He'd have time for doubts and regrets later, assuming he survived.

They'd been riding for almost three hours, moving around rocks and canyons, trying to get as much distance from Villas Colony as possible. They'd managed about fifty miles, according to the odometer. Not nearly enough for comfort.

A few minutes into the trip, Tim had handed the wheel over to Morgan and gotten into the wealth of supplies. He sorted through as much as he could in short order, picking out the absolute necessities, and filling several large packs for them to carry when they had to go on foot.

"You know, we're going to have to ditch this thing pretty soon," Tim said, gesturing to the rover. "Even with the transponder pulled, it's pretty easy to spot. Plus, I wouldn't want to be driving this thing when the dust storm hits. Walking will be hard enough. I'd rather not drive off a cliff."

"We can't carry all the supplies we'll need," Morgan said.

"We'll stash them and come back as needed. I know, it's a big risk, but we have no alternative."

"You said to head east. Any particular reason?" Morgan asked, swerving around rocky obstacles. The digital display helped plot a course, but it wasn't perfect.

"I figured we'd head for Zephyria," Tim replied. "It's a mountain range. It translates to 'land of the west wind.'"

"Why are we going there?"

"Geological scans indicate an extensive network of caverns in and around Zephyria, or so my wife once told me. It seems like a good place to hide. Far enough away for serious breathing room, but close enough to get back when the time comes."

It was getting hard to drive over the terrain. The craters were deep and there were a number of boulders to avoid, as well as a lot of fissures and crags. Hellish was an accurate description.

A bright light twinkled ahead in the distance. At first, Morgan felt it was just the sunlight reflecting against his helmet or the windshield, but after a few minutes of travel, he started to see movement. Before long, he could tell there were people there. He changed course, hoping to get away from them, but soon saw moving objects directly ahead in his new direction. A third course change yielded the same result. They couldn't get away from the enemy.

The rover came to a stop and half a dozen soldiers materialized in front of it. Their suits were indistinguishable from the generic type used by the Americans, though there were subtle differences. Each man held a peculiar-looking plastic rifle, similar to standard issue Consensorate military hardware, but they weren't energy based. They threw lead.

The leader of the group stepped forward and communicated to the fugitives. "Surrender, or you will be fired upon."

"Are those our only options?" Tim asked cynically.

"Surrender, and you will not be harmed. Resist, and you

will die," the voice added. There was a detectable, guttural accent with the words, denoting a German upbringing.

Melinda had sent the Scifes out to do her dirty work.

Morgan glared at the man standing in front of the rover. He couldn't see the face inside the helmet, not with the solar glare, and it provided a ghostly feel to the situation.

"What is your response?" the leader asked impatiently.

Morgan answered by kicking the rover into gear. Slamming his foot down on the accelerator, he pushed the vehicle over the leader of the group and sped toward his comrades. The rover was slow to accelerate, but still faster than the soldiers in close range. The heavy tracks crunched over all five of them before they could raise their weapons to fire.

"Sorry for the bumpy ride," Morgan quipped, adrenaline pulsing through his veins.

The rover headed east again, crossing nearly half a mile before more resistance was encountered. Suddenly, a barrage of bullets pelted against the engine, causing the motor to seize. The rover rolled to a stop near a rocky hillside.

More bullets came at them from out of the south, a few penetrating the door panels. Tim caught a bullet in his right calf and screamed sharply as the projectile ripped his flesh and spacesuit. Air and blood spewed forth from the holes. He pressed against the punctures, trying, in vain, to stop the air loss with his hands.

Another volley of lead left Morgan and Tim scrambling to get out of the rover. They managed to bring along one giant duffel bag packed full of survival gear, but the other goods were still trapped in the back.

The shooting paused momentarily, giving them some breathing room. Morgan reached over the driver's seat and grabbed for the second survival bag Tim had prepared, but before he could get a firm grip on the duffle's handle, a bullet shattered the passenger-side window and whizzed past his head, forcing him away. He abandoned the bag, finding shelter behind the large vehicle.

The soldiers stopped firing and waited for their targets to show themselves.

"I wonder why they aren't throwing grenades at us," Morgan mused. "If they lobbed a single one of those at us, we'd be finished. Either the blast would kill us, or the flying debris would tear up our suits, and the atmosphere would do the job."

"Maybe they're giving us a fighting chance," Tim suggested, digging into a first aid kit. A hunk of sterile wrapping made a tourniquet, and as he yanked it tightly just below his knee, the air stopped gushing from the bullet holes. He felt the excruciating pain of explosive decompression on his lower leg. Sudden exposure to the thin atmosphere proved destructive to his soft tissues.

As Tim screamed in agony, Morgan spotted a most conspicuous object in the survival pack. It was another revolver, and it wasn't one of his. He grabbed it and examined the small thing, a Colt Police Positive .38 Special. There was a box of shells tucked in along with it, so he decided to load the weapon.

"And I thought I had the only real guns in Villas Colony," Morgan muttered, snapping the cylinder shut.

"You're the only one crazy enough to advertise," Tim replied as his leg grew numb.

"Why didn't you tell me?" Morgan asked. Before Tim could answer, a few more bullets pelted the rover. The Scife soldiers were growing impatient. More glass shattered and a few projectiles ricocheted against the rocky landscape.

There was a sizeable boulder nearby and Tim ducked behind it for added protection.

With his friend safe behind the rock, Morgan ventured forward. He rushed to the side of the rover and crawled alongside the engine compartment, trying to keep out of the line of fire. He peered around the front of the rover and caught a glimpse of his opponents. They were crouched behind a wall of tightly packed stones perfectly arranged for their protection. There were six soldiers, resting their rifles atop the rock wall.

Inching back over to Tim, Morgan asked, "How's the leg?"

"It's just a flesh wound. Ordinarily, it would be nothing to worry about, but out here, I'm screwed."

"Hey, don't talk like that," Morgan said, fearing his partner was right. "Once we take care of these goons and pitch a pressure tent, we'll patch you up."

Tim smiled. "I never would have pegged you as an optimist."

"I'm not, but I'll be damned if I'll let these bastards win."

"I appreciate the sentiment, but we both know this is it for me. Look, I've got five shots left in this Magnum of yours. Take the goods and get out of here. I'll try to hold them off long enough for you to sneak away."

"Hey, enough with the good soldier crap. You're not sacrificing yourself. Besides, have you had a look around here? I don't think I'll be doing much sneaking."

Tim reached over and dragged the pack onto his lap. Inside, he found a small block of plastic explosive. It was the stuff the miners used in their excavations, and he'd brought it along with blasting in mind. He stuck a small detonator into the block and handed it over to Morgan. "Well, you're the one who mentioned grenades."

Morgan felt the weight of the explosive in his hand and wondered if he and Tim wouldn't get blown up as well. Still, it seemed the best chance at taking out all their enemies at once.

The Scifes hadn't fired for a while and the silence grated on Morgan's nerves. He moved back over to the front of the rover and had another look at the enemy. Only four of them were visible at the wall. He didn't know where the other two had gone, but hoped they were merely hiding out of sight as he tossed the explosive in a high arc, sending it directly behind the Scifes' defensive construct. Before the payload hit the ground, he was running in the opposite direction.

Tim pressed a button on his sleeve, sending the radio signal to trigger the detonator.

The blast shook the ground, sending a wave of debris flying out in all directions. Morgan was several feet away from the sheltering boulder and was knocked over when the shockwave hit. Scrambling to his knees, he turned and saw the rover rolling side over side toward him, and he barely had time to dive out of the way as the large vehicle thundered by, continuing down the gradual slope of the ground, until it finally ran out of steam and stopped in a crumpled heap.

Standing up, Morgan looked over to where the Scifes had been. He saw a pile of rubble littered with body parts and charred spacesuits. The threat was over. Morgan felt things were looking up until he glanced over at Tim's position, and his joy turned to despair. The boulder behind which Tim had been hiding had been pushed over by the blast, and much of the heavy rock now lay atop the crushed body of the man whose exposed legs twitched slightly, and then stopped moving entirely. It looked as if the rock had killed him quickly, which was a small consolation.

The duffel bag of survival equipment had survived, so Morgan threw it over his shoulder and carried it along as he went to investigate the remains of the rover.

The vehicle was a mess, as was the wealth of equipment stored within. The roof had collapsed down to the bottom of the windows, trapping any useful goods within. Morgan tried vainly to pry open the doors, but nothing budged.

He didn't stick around long.

More soldiers were liable to come along, and he had no intention of going out like his friend. No, the Scifes weren't going to have the satisfaction of claiming him. Live or die, he'd do it on his own, out among the barren wastes.

A stiff wind blew at his back as he headed out, the prevailing edge of a summer dust storm traveling with it. His suit protected him from the harsh spray, and as his vision grew short, he felt hopeful that it would also be enough to mask his trail and prevent his foes from tracking him.

Jogging, he headed east, away from civilization as he knew it, wondering how long his meager supplies would last.

* * *

Morgan walked alone as he crossed the barren hills of Mars, treading ever closer toward the Zephyrian mountain range to the east. There were no distinguishable landmarks, not through all the dust blowing around him. For several days, he walked half-blind, seeing just far enough ahead to avoid stepping into any ravines or smacking into boulders. With a bit of luck and his suit's compass, he managed to stay on an easterly course until the sun finally broke through on the fifth day, after which he relied more on that life-giving orb than technology to guide him.

At night, he rested in a pressurized tent. It would be suicide to walk in the darkness. There were too many things to trip a man, and the terrain had many fissures that could twist an ankle or swallow him whole. The twin moons were small things, and provided insignificant light when they did appear. Both of them together could not provide half the illumination of Luna.

The nights gave Morgan ample time to reflect on recent events, and he found his mind lapsing back over the full scope of his life. He had only a few regrets, and most of them had been beyond his control. He thought of Lorna, wondered what she was doing and what she was thinking. Did she blame him for leaving? Was she struggling to understand? How would she ever know the truth if he didn't see her again? He couldn't stand the thought of her alone with those treacherous Scifes, so he often forced his ruminations onto less volatile concerns.

Morgan had known many people in his life, and so few remained among the living. He thought of the lives he'd seen extinguished; some by his own hand, others by his related actions, or inaction. He thought back and wondered what it all meant.

Morgan considered how cheap life had become since the advent of virtual technology. Before running over those Scife agents with the rover, he hadn't killed anyone—not in real life. He had slain his share of simulated characters and virtual travelers in the past. Such behavior had desensitized him to killing, made it almost trivial. He didn't regret his actions, but he regretted not regretting them. The callousness of it all bothered him.

The days wore on as he moved ever closer to the Zephyrian mountains, for what reason he couldn't fathom anymore. It wasn't like he had enough with him to hide there. He'd be lucky to make it that far before his supplies ran out and left him dead on this dead world. He'd be joining Tim before long, and he accepted his fate.

Of course, he could always turn around, surrender to Melinda's will, and hope her Scife allies didn't kill him out of spite. *Would it be so bad, to give up?* The thought crossed Morgan's mind as he marched on, moving further away from that option. After five days of walking, he approached the great divide where he had to make the final choice.

It was mid-afternoon, and he stared down at the rocky crater. This was as far as he could go and still have the option to turn back. His supplies were diminished, his CO_2 filters were beginning to saturate, but he still had just enough to get back, if he turned around.

But he'd have to do it now.

The thought of a warm bed was comforting, and the thought of seeing Lorna again brought a smile to his face— but then he remembered why he was out here, and those who had driven him to it. He recalled how strange Lorna had been after those monsters sent her through the teleporter, changed her in untold ways. Was there really anything to go back to?

Even if he turned around, it was uncertain if he would make it. He did the math in his head, studied the readings on the arm of his suit, and realized he had to make his decision quickly. Forward or backward, it was as simple as that.

Deciding on a course of action, Morgan took three steps forward, choosing his fate. He had committed himself to death.

Chapter Nineteen
September 21, 2327

It was hard to wake up on the eighth day. Morgan felt numb all over and his eyelids refused to lift. He could sense the faint rays of sunlight refracting through the translucent material of the tent as the tissue covering his eyes glowed red against his pupils, but his body refused to listen as he tried to move.

"Morgan!" a woman's voice shouted. The unexpected sound made the muscles in his neck and shoulders respond. He rose to face the voice, curious to see who was there. Even when his eyes opened, his vision was too blurry to see her features, but there was definitely someone sitting there at his feet.

"You're not going to lie there and die on me, are you?" she asked, her tone sharp and familiar. He was having a hard enough time believing there was someone there at all, let alone recognize the voice. As his eyes cleared, he saw the soft pink of her skin, the shimmering black hair, those penetrating blue eyes, and he could not deny it.

"Rheena?" he asked in disbelief.

"Yeah," she replied, smiling awkwardly, as if embarrassed.

"But you're dead," Morgan said, pulling himself into a sitting position.

"In some ways," she replied, "but you didn't expect me to just pop out of existence altogether, did you?"

"You're saying you're a ghost?" Morgan asked, feeling ready to pass out again.

"If that's how you want to explain me," she answered, looking around the cramped tent.

Morgan remained silent as he put on his spacesuit. The air was still cold and the insulated suit provided greater

153

warmth, so he rushed. He wanted to get moving again, anyway. He didn't know how much time he had left. The CO_2 levels in his air were already up to nineteen thousand parts per million and rising at an alarming rate. Before long, he'd feel more than simply drowsy, never mind that the added exertion would only hasten his demise. He wasn't about to die standing still.

Sealing his suit, he looked at the woman beside him—Rheena Liszt. She'd been dead for over a hundred years, yet there she was, as young and healthy as he remembered her. She looked no older than thirty, but her mind was aged and wise, thanks to virtual technology.

Morgan reached down to the micro-compressor and prepared to suck the air out of the tent. "The oxygen's going. Can you conjure up a spacesuit or something?" he asked Rheena.

"I don't need to breathe anymore," she replied.

"But you're doing it right now," Morgan said, seeing her chest rise gently.

Taking a deep breath and letting it out, she said, "Force of habit. Go ahead, I'll be fine."

Morgan flipped a switch and the compressor hummed and sucked the air out of the tent, placing it all into a small metal cylinder. A minute later, he pulled the lynchpins out of the tent framing and the plastic canvass slouched down over him. He unzipped the end of the tent and went outside with the sum of his belongings, where he finished folding up the material and stashed it on top of his other meager supplies.

"That looks heavy," Rheena mentioned as Morgan hefted the bulky pack onto his shoulders.

"It would probably be a hundred pounds on Earth," he replied, adjusting the straps for comfort. "Here, not so much."

"Wow," Rheena exclaimed, staring at the world around her. She turned in a circle, looking out at the rocky hills and cratered plains, then left her eyes on the sunrise. "This is all so real, isn't it? I know they've had virtual simulations of this stuff for ages, but to actually be here and see it..." Her voice trailed off. She knelt down and brushed her hand against the ground, unable to cause any disturbance on the dusty surface. "I wish I could touch it, feel it!"

The rational centers of Morgan's brain couldn't accept Rheena's presence, even as she stood right in front of him. He found himself looking for some logical explanation for her presence, and the most obvious excuse was oxygen deprivation. He was hallucinating.

Even so, what could he do about it? For whatever reason, his mind had invented the image of Rheena, and she seemed real enough. Maybe he didn't want to die alone, so he'd recreated a long lost friend to share his final hours. His groggy mind kept going over it until Rheena grew tired of standing still and urged him to walk on.

"So, what have you been up to the last hundred or so years?" Rheena asked, joyfully walking along.

"Well, I was asleep for most of it," Morgan said.

"Really, what happened?" Rheena asked.

Morgan stopped walking and faced her. "You already know what happened, since you're just a hallucination of mine."

The happiness drained from Rheena's face. "No, I don't. And no, I'm not," she said, her smile fading.

Morgan started laughing, but fought to restrain himself. "Look at me. I'm arguing with my imagination."

Rheena growled. "If I still had teeth, I'd bite you. Then you'd see how real I am." Her ludicrous statement left them both laughing and eased the tension. After a lengthy chuckle, she added, "No, really, it's me."

Morgan raised his hand and motioned as he spoke. "If you really were Rheena Liszt, you'd figure some way to get me out of this. You'd conjure up a flying dragon, or cast a spell to whisk me back to Earth, or some other damn thing."

"That only worked in Fantasan." She stroked her cheek, looking thoughtful. "But I may be able to help out, just the same. Come on," she said, her happy expression returning.

Morgan followed her, along the side of a hill. After a few minutes, he noticed the sun to his left. They were moving south, though the direction didn't seem to matter. He'd been walking for a week and hadn't found any mountains. The dust storm must have knocked his GPS askew. He could be hundreds of miles off course.

Rheena led for hours. Morgan related his recent experiences as the sun rose to prominence and the hills gave way to cratered plains covered with rocks and dust.

Around midday, Rheena stopped and pointed at the ground. "Dig here," she said.

"Why?" Morgan asked, giddy.

"There's something here, I can feel it."

"Really? What am I going to dig with?"

"You don't have a shovel? Then use your hands."

Morgan looked at his gloved hands. "These things aren't made for excavating. I'm not going to have my suit cut open on a jagged rock, digging at your whim."

"Well, use something, anything," Rheena implored. "If you want to live, you've got to dig."

It was the craziest thing in the world, but what did he have to lose? He removed his pack and picked through his belongings, looking for anything he could use to move dirt. At the bottom of the bag, he found the first aid kid, locked up in an airtight metal box. He released the clamps and dumped the loose contents into his bag, and then used the box to scrape into the sandy soil.

Had he been less delirious, he might have thought twice about listening to his imaginary friend. But as it was, he moved dirt for the better part of an hour, his arms getting heavier and heavier as the CO_2 poisoned him. His chest was pounding and his respiration was rapid, far beyond what was normal for the leisurely digging. His eyes went blurry and he ached, but Rheena egged him on, her words of encouragement giving him the strength to fight through the pain and confusion.

Three feet down, he finally hit something. At first, he

thought it was another stone, but after scraping away a little more dirt, he could see it was smooth and round—a thin rod of metal. He dug at a frantic pace to uncover whatever it was hidden in the dirt. "What is it?" he asked Rheena, his words slurring, as he tried to widen the hole, to expose more of the object.

"I'm not sure," Rheena replied, "but it's big."

Another half an hour of digging revealed the metal bar to be the handle to some sort of hatch. He brushed the dirt aside and stared at the polished silver alloy. It looked as if it had been made yesterday. *Could this be something built by the Consensorate?* Morgan wondered. *Perhaps an entrance to their secret base?*

The mechanism was hard to open, but after Morgan threw all of his weight on the lever, it pulled up. Stepping to the side and gripping the edge of the hatch, he was able to break the seal. A loud gust of air blew out at his feet and he peered inside the hole. A set of metal rungs led down the side of a round tube. Another hatch was visible at the bottom, roughly thirty feet down.

"Go on," Rheena urged. "I'll meet you down there."

Morgan followed her suggestion and put his feet on the first rung. It was rough, the traction allowing his boot to get a good grip. He moved down a few steps and heard Rheena's voice. "Close the top hatch before coming down." He did as she suggested, plunging them both into total darkness, but the rungs were evenly spaced and he had no trouble reaching the bottom.

The second hatch sat in the side of the wall, directly across from the ladder. Morgan's hands searched for the handle and yanked hard after finding it. It took a bit of elbow grease to get the door to budge, and when it did, another a rush of air was forced into the tube, but no light. Whatever lay beyond was shrouded in total darkness.

"Rheena? I can't see," Morgan said, gasping as he stood in front of the opened hatch.

"Neither can I, but there's a floor in here," she said.

She hadn't led him astray yet, so Morgan stepped forward and felt the flat floor under his feet. He stopped, keeping his arm against the opened hatch as he rested a moment. Light appeared from above as he caught his breath. The ceiling panels of the room began to glow, awoken by his presence.

His eyes searched the room. It was a featureless box of metal, with several closed doors leading to other unknown rooms. In front of one of those doors was a mummified corpse dressed in a blue satin robe, clutching a small brown bag.

Morgan glanced away from the dead body and saw Rheena standing beside him. His eyes asked her for direction and she jerked her head, gesturing for him to investigate the corpse. He took one step before collapsing, feeling the life go out of his legs. Carbon dioxide poisoning had removed what little strength he had left.

"Take off your helmet!" Rheena cried, as Morgan flopped on the floor, trying to stand.

What did he have to lose?

Reaching up to his neck, Morgan flipped the clamps and released his helmet, allowing the native atmosphere of the room to flow around him. It was cold and dry, but it was clean. Several deep breaths brought a pounding headache and renewed strength. It took a few minutes for his legs to regain their composure, but when they did, he made his way over to the body across the room.

It looked ancient, and it was hard to tell if it had been a man or a woman. The robe could have been worn by either gender, and the body's height would have been close to six feet. The brown leathery bag was clutched tightly to the chest, as if this person had spent their last breath trying to protect it.

Morgan gently pried the bag from the corpse's clutches, and after some crunching and cracking, the desiccated arms released their hold and he was able to pull the object free. Examining the outer material, it looked like a large purse, made with some synthetic fiber that hadn't deteriorated with the body.

Holding it with both hands, Morgan felt how heavy it was. As he pried it open, he saw why. Inside lay a stack of metal tablets, each glistening yellow in the artificial light. They looked like sheets of gold.

Morgan arranged twelve tablets on the floor. Each was barely a millimeter thick, and they had strange symbols etched into them. Although he couldn't read them, he recognized a few of the letters.

"Are these Greek?" Morgan muttered, running his fingers over the tablets. "I think they are. That's an alpha, right?" he said, pointing to the oddly-shaped A.

"That's an omega," Rheena said, pointing to another plate. "And a beta..." She paused and gave a puzzled look. "My God, Morgan. What have we found here?"

"I don't know, but I could swear I'm still hallucinating."

But it wasn't a hallucination. At least, it didn't seem to be after Morgan had sat there for the better part of an hour, breathing the cool, fresh air. He waited patiently for everything to fade away, for Rheena to disappear, but nothing changed.

Had he gone insane? he wondered. *Had the oxygen deprivation caused substantial brain damage?*

His world was suddenly so fantastic. It was almost as if he were inside a virtual simulation...

Then it hit him. What if none of this was real? What if he'd been duped all along, had never woken up from his last virtual trip? Such a thing had happened to him before, all those years ago, during his first visit to Fantasan. He'd awoken into what seemed to be the real world, only to find he was caught inside a pocket simulation. Only through dumb luck had he discovered the truth and been able to escape.

What was real, then? Had he truly slept for a hundred years? Was this really the future or just some programmer's daydream? Was Lorna actually his wife, or just another computerized character?

It was too much for him to accept, that these last few years were counterfeit memories. It was equally as improbable as

159

this current turn of events with Rheena and the alien tablets. Whatever the truth, he had to accept what he saw as reality, for the time being.

He could sort it out later.

Morgan remembered he had left his pack on the surface, and decided to retrieve it before exploring the strange, alien complex. His spacesuit had a built-in compressor, so he vented the contaminated air he'd been recycling for a week and refilled his tanks with the fresh air of the curious chamber.

He headed up the shaft and pushed open the top hatch. It was hard to open as the dirt had started to cave in around the hole, and the very real risk of imprisonment came to Morgan's mind. If he went back down in there, the hatch might become buried again. How would he ever get out?

He didn't have much choice, he reasoned. He wouldn't live long if he remained on the surface, with no food and recycled water no longer fit to drink. His air scrubbers were fried, leaving him with only a few hours of air if he didn't return to the chamber below. Perhaps he would find some means of survival in the unexplored chambers. At the very least, it would prove a more entertaining end, spending his final hours exploring the mysteries that lay below.

There was no real choice. He had to go back and confront the unknown. It was far preferable to the certain doom that awaited him on the surface.

When he returned to the chamber, Rheena was there waiting for him.

"I wonder how much air is stored down here?" Morgan said aloud, not expecting Rheena to respond. He recalled the huge quantity blown outside when he'd opened the upper hatch. He checked the control panel on his left arm and brought up an atmospheric reading of the chamber. The mix was approximately 29% Oxygen and 70% Nitrogen, with a few trace elements accounting for the rest. The pressure was 75 kilopascals and rising. Whatever the source, the air was replenishing.

160

The air pressure stabilized at 100.9 kPa and Morgan removed his helmet. He shut off his suit's systems, hoping to conserve energy. He didn't know if the artificial light of the chamber could power his systems, and without solar energy to recharge his batteries, they would eventually run out of power. He only had a sixteen hour reserve.

"Are you making any progress with the tablets?" Morgan asked, walking over to Rheena.

"Not much," she replied, "considering I don't know Ancient Greek—assuming that's what this is. Some of the symbols look something like it, but do either of us know enough to tell for certain?"

Morgan was no linguist, so he knew the answers wouldn't be forthcoming right away. In time, they might figure it out, but there'd be plenty of time for that later.

There was exploring to do.

With a gentle nudge from his foot, Morgan slid the mummified remains away from the hatch. He yanked the lever and the portal opened. Beyond lay a long corridor with dozens of doors on either side. The overhead light panels blinked on one by one, revealing the vast length of the complex.

"Amazing," Rheena said in awe.

They started down the corridor, glancing at the hatches as they passed. Each one looked the same, holding no apparent numbers or symbols to differentiate them.

"Rheena, you say you're not a hallucination, but there's something I don't get. Why are you here?"

"I wasn't going to let you die out there," she answered.

"But how did you know I was in trouble? You claim you haven't been watching me and don't know what's going on in my life recently, so how did you know to show up and help me now?"

"Let's just say there *are* people who keep an eye on you. They let me know you needed me."

"What, I've got a guardian angel working for me?"

"Something like that," Rheena said, stopping in front of

one particular hatch. "Try this one."

"Did the power on high tell you to stop here?"

"In a manner of speaking, yes," she replied, a little irritated.

Morgan opened the hatch and stepped inside. The room beyond was certainly different than any he'd already explored. There were large tables set in the center of the room and both side walls were covered with small metal hatches like giant checkerboards. Each hatch had a digital readout in the center, displaying a few of the same symbols they'd seen on the tablets.

"What is this?" Morgan asked.

"I have no idea," Rheena said.

"Didn't your people tell you?"

"*They* don't give me specifics. They just guide me, show me where to go. They wouldn't have led us here if it weren't important."

Morgan examined one of the smaller hatches. The fancy readouts were just labels and had nothing to do with the opening mechanism. A simple tug of the handle did the trick, and as the hatch was pulled open, a drawer slid out, revealing a bin full of some sort of rooted vegetable.

That feeling of unreality struck Morgan as he picked up one of the carrot-like objects. It was cool and firm to the touch. "What do you think?" he asked Rheena.

"Go ahead, it's safe," she replied.

He was starving, so real or not, he decided to give it a try. A crunching bite sent a strange flavor into his mouth. It was sweet and starchy, something of a cross between a carrot and a potato.

"This is incredible," Rheena said after he swallowed a bite. "This must be some sort of stasis unit for preserving food. I wonder, how long has it been here?"

"What powers it?" Morgan added between bites.

After a thorough examination of the "pantry," they identified enough food to sustain Morgan indefinitely. There were entire drawers full of fruit, vegetables, meats, breads, and several other items not readily identifiable. Morgan assumed it was all fit for human consumption, as he had no means to test for poison. At least the potato-carrot hadn't killed him yet.

At the far back of the room, they found a row of metal sinks with golden faucets. Turning on a tap brought a fresh stream of clear water. Morgan cupped his hands and drank a mouthful. There was a slight metallic aftertaste, but it was better than the recycled sewage his suit had stored. He stuck his head under the tap and thoroughly quenched his thirst.

Before moving on, Morgan grabbed a loaf of crusty bread to eat along the way.

Directly across the hall was the dining room, a spacious cafeteria with tables and benches made of the same stainless material as the walls. Set along the wall near the door were a series of electric stoves. The top ranges were easy to operate, utilizing simple dials to regulate the temperature, but the ovens were another matter. They utilized digital readouts to program time and temperature, and one needed to understand the alien symbols to operate them.

Subsequent rooms yielded several bunk areas, military-style accommodations for several hundred people. There was also a large store room of clothing, much of it useable.

They still had much more to see, but Morgan was exhausted. In need of a good night's sleep, they retired to one of the bunk rooms.

"I'm glad you can't smell me," Morgan said as he removed the lower half of his spacesuit. "I hope we find a shower room tomorrow."

Rheena nodded and turned her attention to the metal frame of a bunk, studying the ancient tool marks in the round upright shafts.

"So, what's it like, being dead?" Morgan asked as he removed his socks.

"I can't tell you," Rheena replied.

"You're not allowed, right?"

"No, it's that I literally *can't* tell you. When I'm here, in what is essentially my human state of mind, all the memories and knowledge of the next life are removed from me. It's like waking from a dream too late. I know that I know, but I can't remember *what* I know. Does that make any sense?"

"Your memory is taken from you to make sure you don't reveal anything you're not supposed to," Morgan surmised.

"I guess," Rheena agreed.

"This has been the strangest day of my life," Morgan said, lying down. As he closed his eyes and sleep overtook him, he had the unshakable feeling that it was only going to get stranger.

Chapter Twenty
September 22, 2327

Morgan awoke after a long sleep, feeling stronger and more alert than he had been in days. The lingering effects of CO_2 poisoning were fading fast, and the previous night's bread eased his hunger.

His eyes opened to see the bright ceiling. He didn't know how to turn off the lights, but he had slept all night, regardless. He felt it important to find the off switch, to save energy, just one of many things he sought to learn about this place.

Turning on his side, Morgan saw Rheena sitting on the next bunk over, staring at him. He jumped nervously, having forgotten about her.

"Oh, you're still here," he said, sitting up.

"Good morning to you, too," Rheena replied, bristling.

"Sorry," Morgan apologized. "I just figured you would have spirited off, back to wherever you came from, now that I'm safe and sound."

"I'd like to stick around for a while," Rheena said. "It's been a long time since I died, and I kinda miss the land of the living. It's rare that anyone has an excuse to come back."

"Did you just sit there all night?" Morgan asked, rubbing his eyes.

"Pretty much," Rheena said. "I tried to do some scouting, but everything's pitch black outside of this room, and the lights don't turn on for me."

"What about the rooms we've already visited? Did you examine any of the equipment in there, or study those tablets?"

"The lights turn off automatically after you leave the area. There must be some kind of bio-sensors keyed to the system."

With renewed strength, Morgan scouted around the bunk room. After opening several empty closets, he located the shower room, though it had seen better days. The room had been set up like a honeycomb, much like the showers aboard the *Plymouth*. There were several dozen individual stalls, but the plastic material used for divider panels had broken down over the years. The metal frames were still there, as was all the plumbing made out of gold alloy, but hunks of crumbling plastic cluttered the floor and blocked the drains.

Morgan removed the degraded material with haste, eager to wash off the week's worth of filth from his flesh. After scraping the last translucent hunk from the porous floor of the first stall, he began to disrobe.

"Could you wait outside?" he asked Rheena, hesitating as he pulled off his shirt.

"It's not like I haven't seen you naked before," Rheena replied, unmoving from her perch atop a sink counter.

"Well, I'm married now. So please..." Morgan persisted, waving toward the door.

Rheena huffed and marched to the door. She stood in front of the closed portal and tapped her foot, as if waiting for someone to open it.

"What?" Morgan asked.

"I can't open the door," Rheena said.

"Can't you just pass through it?"

"You could at least give me the illusion that I'm still alive?" she asked, pouting.

"For crying out loud!" Morgan growled. He stomped over and opened the door. As his ghostly friend stepped out he said, "You know, the *real* Rheena never acted so childish."

Rheena grew a wicked smirk on her lips. "You didn't know me when I was eighteen."

"No, I knew you when you were a hundred and eighteen, so why don't you act your age?" he challenged, shutting the door.

Morgan stepped over to the shower stall again and removed his remaining clothes. As he pulled his legs out of his underwear, he spotted Rheena's head sticking through the door, her eyes staring at him. "Do you need a towel?" she asked.

Morgan chucked his pants at the door and her head vanished, leaving him to wash privately.

There were two unmarked valves, and it took Morgan a minute to regulate the water. Once the temperature was to his liking, he stepped under the bulbous shower head and let the water flow over him. It was a most relaxing sensation, feeling the dried sweat dissolve and wash away, though he found himself wishing for a bar of soap. Ten minutes was all he spent on washing, but it did the trick. His nose no longer cringed with each breath, and he was eager to explore further.

As Morgan turned off the shower, he realized Rheena had been right. He needed a towel. His mind wasn't entirely together yet. He couldn't dry himself with his dirty clothes, and he felt reluctant to put them back on, even in the chilly air. He needed to get replacement attire, so he opened the door to the bunk room and found Rheena standing there, her arms folded across her chest.

"Looking for your modesty?" she asked.

Morgan ignored her comment and walked, stark naked, across the cold room, out into the hall, and over to the clothes storage. By the time he got there, his damp body had mostly air-dried, but he was chilled to the bone. He shivered as he picked through the assorted garments, seeking warm attire.

It wasn't an easy task.

Much of the clothing appeared feminine; skirts and blouses in a wide array of fancy colors that didn't tempt him in the least, and they were far too thin to protect him from the nip in the air.

After his search, Morgan found some warm clothes that fit him—a pair of beige pants with extra-long legs he had to cuff and a fancy tank-top that belled out at the waist in an odd fashion. He also found a warm jacket adorned with gold tassels and strange embroidery.

There were some things missing from his wardrobe, in

particular underwear. There were quite a few pairs of boxer-shorts, but the material had deteriorated over the years, and they were like over-bleached rags that disintegrated when they were stretched. The same held true for the socks, leaving his feet bare against the metal floor, sending him on a new hunt for footwear. It took a while, but he finally found several drawers stuffed with boots. He found a set his size, though they were stiff and uncomfortable.

As Morgan paced around with the boots, trying to get accustomed to the rigid plastic, Rheena looked down at the pile of disintegrating underwear he had dumped on the floor. "It makes you wonder why they didn't have stasis bins for these."

Morgan walked over and brushed the underwear aside with his boot. "It's another thing I don't get. Why did they bother with the food bins in the first place? If this is some kind of research outpost, why didn't they just use canned goods, or some simpler form of preservation? Why go through all the trouble of setting up those bins?"

"Maybe they preferred fresh food," Rheena surmised.

"Lucky for me," Morgan said, feeling his stomach begin to grumble. It was about time for breakfast.

Morgan hadn't had a real meal in days, so he decided to put together a hearty breakfast. He dragged out some thin meat strips that resembled bacon, a loaf of white bread, some of the potato-carrots, along with a jar of oil and some salt, and he brought them into the kitchen/cafeteria, where a long line of stoves awaited his testing. He poked around the cabinets near the ranges and found cooking utensils. A good assortment of knives aided his preparation of the food, and a shiny metal skillet was set on one of the ranges. He dripped a few drops of the oil into the pan and spread it with a big, half-moon spatula. The scent drifted up, teasing his nostrils, and he could swear the stuff was olive oil.

When it was all cooked, he had a feast. Freshly sizzled bacon, home-fries and a whole loaf of toast satisfied his hunger. His belly full, he resumed his exploration of the compound.

A few doors down the corridor, he found a spacious room full of antiquities. It was akin to a museum; there were paintings hung on virtually every bare patch of wall, and there were numerous statues and sculptures.

The artwork could have been from any human painter. There were many landscapes drawn, pictures of farms, forests, towns, and several animal portraits that resembled Earth wildlife, with a few exaggerations.

Rheena pointed out a small picture hung in the corner. It depicted a human male wearing clothing not unlike those that Morgan had scavenged, with a golden sash added for decoration. The eyes were sharp blue and followed him around the room, as only a masterful piece of artwork could.

Several other paintings along the walls depicted scenes of people who had roughly the same look as your typical homo-sapiens. There were subtle differences—metallic skin tones, pronounced foreheads, pointed teeth; all minor details that might have been artistic license. They were by no means photographs, and there was no telling how accurate the depictions were. Still, the beings looked more human than not.

Morgan stopped to study a bronze sculpture reminiscent of an ancient astrolabe. The varied rings around the sphere were covered with ornate scrollwork and symbols, all of which was difficult to see on the tarnished metal. The surfaces were almost black from oxidation.

As he stepped back out into the hall, Morgan remarked to Rheena, "This isn't just a research station. It's a time capsule."

Farther down the hallway, the remaining doors were locked. A key would have to be found, or else their contents would forever be a mystery.

A hundred yards from the museum, Morgan found the end of the corridor, and one more unlocked door. It was dark inside and the automatic lighting wasn't working. He left the door open, and tried to see what he could. There were many monitor screens, their darkened surfaces reflecting Morgan's image. There were seats and tables spread out into the darkness.

"The war room," he guessed.

"Or simply a command center," Rheena countered, peering into the darkened areas. "I think this room is important."

Morgan walked over to one of the computer stations closest to the door, and strained his eyes to make out the Greek-like symbols on a shadowed keyboard. "Powering this stuff up might be the easy part. Figuring out what it does will be a whole other matter."

"I'd say we have plenty of time," Rheena said.

"Maybe a lifetime," Morgan agreed.

Chapter Twenty-One
October 2, 2327

Lorna was taking the loss of her husband well, or so she let those around her believe. Inside, she felt torn up and betrayed. Part of her wanted to cry at his absence, another wanted to curse him for his actions. How could he have been so selfish, behaved so irresponsibly? He had betrayed her trust, abandoned her, for reasons she could no longer understand.

She had worked late the day of Morgan's betrayal, coming home almost an hour after dark to find a police officer standing at her door, waiting to explain things personally. Lieutenant Weitz tried to break the news gently, but Lorna's emotions were far too unstable, and she chased him away before he could finish. Lorna had been unsure what to make of the report and waited until the next morning to go see her husband—but by then, it was too late. He'd escaped.

With her husband AWOL, Lorna buried herself in work. The raging dust storm suspended construction of the dome for almost ten days, during which she helped supervise a subterranean crew expanding their living space. She took her frustrations out on her subordinates, demanding perfection and haste beyond the norm. By the time work resumed on the dome, she had calmed down and let her laborers do their jobs in peace, as she moped about the construction site.

Nearly three weeks after Morgan's departure, Lorna found herself invited to Sunday brunch by Melinda Faris. She felt a bit uneasy accepting the invitation, but knew she couldn't very well refuse.

"I am pleased you decided to come," Melinda said as she poured her guest a glass of orange juice. "I wasn't sure how you would feel about me, after everything that has happened."

"I don't blame you for any of it, if that's what you mean," Lorna responded. "Morgan is strong willed."

"Tell me about it," Melinda replied, returning the pitcher to its place-mat. The two women were alone in the governor's library, and it was the first time they had spoken privately since Lorna's initial encounter with the teleporter.

"Is there any word on my husband?" Lorna asked after sampling her drink. It tasted fresh enough, even though it was made from powder.

"Sadly, no. We discovered Mr. Keene's body, as you know, but we've had trouble tracking down Morgan. Dust storms have been the prevailing factor, hiding his tracks, and our satellites haven't had any luck, either."

"Is there any chance he's still alive?"

"I don't know," Melinda said, sounding sad. "Our Eridanian friends are still looking for him, so there's hope."

Lorna nodded and turned her attention to the meal of reconstituted eggs and fruit salad from a can. It was better food than one usually found on Mars.

"I'm glad you don't hold any animosity toward me," Melinda said. "I really am heartbroken over all this."

"I know," Lorna said.

"Morgan was a good man, just misguided and impulsive. I'd hate to sully his name back on Earth with this."

Lorna looked up from her eggs with an inquisitive stare.

"I've decided not to divulge the true nature of this incident to the ICB. Everyone who knows the truth of what happened is on board with this. I hope you will be, as well."

"How are you going to explain it?" Lorna asked with mixed emotions.

"An unfortunate accident. Two men out exploring got lost in the dust storm. That's an understandable excuse for their loss. I'll not let the people back home think ill of either of them."

"Whatever you think is best," Lorna agreed reluctantly. She abhorred what Morgan had done and hated the thought of a cover-up even more, but she didn't want to press the issue.

"I knew I could count on you."

There was a calm in the room as the two ladies finished their meal. It wasn't awkward, even though they hardly knew each other. They had a curious, instant rapport.

"I read the senior foreman's latest report," Melinda mentioned after finishing the last of her fruit. "I see we're making some real progress."

"Yes, the teleporter technology is astounding. I expect we'll be done in less than two years, once our own pad is up and running."

Melinda raised her half-empty glass for a toast. "To the dream," she said.

Lorna raised her glass and then downed the rest of her juice.

"This is nice, don't you think?" Melinda said. "Just the two of us."

"I guess," Lorna said.

"I've never had many friends, and the few I have are back on Earth. The life of an officer can be a lonely one, and as governor, I've found it difficult to know who I can trust. I tend to keep everyone at arm's reach. But I'm hoping things can be different between us. You understand what I'm trying to do here, for our people and all of humanity, and we have both felt the sting of loss and betrayal."

Melinda's long lament left Lorna's mind harping upon a curious vibe. Natural suspicion dominated her thoughts as she pondered the governor's meaning, and several scenarios played out in her head.

Lorna knew Morgan and Melinda had spent much time together over the last few months, but she had no idea how much of that time had been in private. Melinda's current behavior left Lorna with an uncomfortable question. There was no tip-toeing around it, so she just came out and asked, "Melinda, did you have an affair with my husband?"

Melinda was caught off-guard by the question, and the shock on her face helped assure Lorna of the believability of her response. "No, my dear, I would never steal another woman's husband. There's nothing more despicable. Besides, as handsome and intriguing a man as Morgan was, he was never quite my type."

"What exactly *is* your type?" Lorna asked, revising her opinion of Melinda, still feeling awkward.

"I prefer my mates to be a little more submissive, with a bit more kindness and sensitivity. Such traits compliment my overly dominant personality, and I really loathe conflict in a relationship. I get enough of that from my day job."

"I see," Lorna said.

Seeing Lorna's forlorn expression, Melinda added, "I hope you believe me. Your husband was nothing but faithful, as far as I know."

"Yes, I never doubted it," Lorna assured the governor, covering her lingering suspicions.

"I'm glad," Melinda replied gently. "Morgan was a wonderful man, and if you should ever need someone to talk to, I want you to know I'm here for you."

"Thanks," Lorna said, her misgivings fading. She couldn't help but feel inclined to trust this woman, even when her behavior was questionable. After a few moments, she was smiling again.

"Good," Melinda said, standing. "Now that we've gotten that cleared up, why don't we have a little fun?"

"What do you have in mind?" Lorna asked.

"A fresh batch of movies came through with the last data burst from Earth, and there's a new one about Vincent Van Gogh I'm just dying to watch. Care to join me?"

"Sure," Lorna said, unable to resist.

* * *

Three hours into *The Life of Van Gogh*, Melinda was paid a visit by Mr. Budreau. He teleported directly into the center of her living room, blocking her and Lorna's view of the video screen, which sat on the wall opposite the couch.

"Could you move to the right a little?" Melinda asked indignantly.

The Frenchman turned and looked at the screen, continuing to block the view. "An excellent choice of cinema," he remarked as he recognized the film, "even if it was made in America. Most of your films are illogical nonsense with no redeeming value. But this," he said, pointing at the screen, "this is a man who deserves to be known!"

"I would never have imagined you'd be a fan of a decadent artist like Van Gogh."

"He was not simply decadent. He was a man of many passions, far beyond what the Consensorate Hierarchy would ever dream of tolerating. To them, feeling is a crime, and that is why I and my comrades now work with you, to correct that fatal flaw in their logic. Speaking of work, do you know what time it is?"

Melinda looked down at her watch and realized how long she had been viewing the film. "Damn, it's thirteen hundred already? I didn't realize this movie would be so long."

"Vincent was a fascinating man. I am not surprised you got so caught up in his life story," Budreau said.

"Excuse me," Lorna interrupted, watching the exchange. "Who are you?"

Melinda retrieved the remote and paused the movie before responding. "Lorna Asher, meet Jean Proudhon Budreau of *Facilite de Mars*, otherwise known as Eridania Colony."

Budreau stepped forward and gripped Lorna's hand ceremoniously. "Ah, the traitor's wife. An absolute pleasure to make your acquaintance."

"My husband is not a traitor," Lorna barked, yanking her hand away before the Frenchman could kiss it. "He simply didn't trust you."

"A character flaw I trust you'll not share," he retorted, knowing the mental adjustments his people had placed upon her would make certain of it.

"Lorna understands what we are doing here," Melinda broke in. "There is no need to provoke her."

"My apologies," Budreau said with unusual humility.

175

"Could we speak privately?" he asked Melinda.

"This is private enough for the moment," Melinda replied.

Budreau frowned, but decided it wasn't worth an argument. "Very well. You should be pleased to note that assembly of your teleporter pad is nearing completion. We should be ready for initial trials in a few days."

"That soon?" Lorna asked excitedly.

"Yes," Budreau said in clipped tone, sparing Lorna an irritated glance before turning his attention back to Melinda. "And you should also note that we are officially ending our search for Morgan Asher. We have seen no sign of him since the sandstorm, and we must conclude that if he is not already dead out there, he will be shortly."

Lorna's head slumped and the joy left her face. It was news she'd been expecting, but it was still worthy of tears.

Melinda put an arm around her friend in a reassuring manner. "I'm so sorry, Lorna."

After a minute, Budreau continued. "Now, Ms. Faris, there are certain matters concerning the teleporter we must discuss alone, whenever you find it convenient."

"Tomorrow," Melinda said.

"Very well. Thirteen hundred again?" he asked, and Melinda nodded. "Then I bid you *adieu*. Please, enjoy the rest of your afternoon."

With a brief flash, he disappeared, leaving Lorna wiping tears, and Melinda doing what she could to support her new friend.

Chapter Twenty-Two
October 5, 2327

Armin Weitz never intended to rebel against anything. He was just an American, first and foremost, and loved the more romantic notions of the Founding Fathers. Thomas Jefferson and Benjamin Franklin were like distant ancestors who fascinated him. He had once considered pursuing a career in Constitutional Law, like his father, but his aptitudes drifted more toward his mother's line of work, in computer programming. He would have likely gone to work for a software firm had his father not been shot in a mugging on his eighteenth birthday.

Armin had grown up in the suburbs of Philadelphia, just a few miles away from where George Washington had crossed the Delaware River. Violent crime was a rare thing in this day and age, so the death of his father had come as a total shock. It had forced him to reassess his priorities. Setting aside his laptop, he joined the police academy and became a beat cop, hoping to make a difference.

He never gave up his love of knowledge, though, and he often could be found off-duty in one of any number of libraries, studying history or playing with computer files. It was there he met his future wife, Emily Holst, a grad student studying volcanology, with wild-eyed dreams of joining the Space Program. Somehow, they hit it off, despite having little in common other than a thirst for knowledge. By the time they officially tied the knot, the first group of colonists was being selected for Mars. Emily's initial application was approved, throwing both their lives down a whole new avenue.

They honeymooned in New Mexico, so Emily could attend the first orientation classes. After she passed with flying colors, Armin resigned his position with the Philadelphia

Police Department and began training for Mars. He barely scraped by, but was granted a seat on the maiden voyage of the *Plymouth*.

Armin's experience with law enforcement granted him lieutenant bars and the position of second-in-command of the Colonial Police Force. Arriving on Mars, he found his position amounted to the equivalent of a traffic cop, with a side order of anger management. There was no real crime to be heard of, only order to be maintained. Occasionally, one colonist would step on another one's toes and they'd have nasty words, but violence was absent in the cramped environment, where a majority of the citizens were highly educated and knew how to get along in order to survive.

Meanwhile, Emily was assigned to her research, examining the fascinating volcanoes of Mars. Much of her time was spent in the lab, playing with hardened lava samples, or watching remote probes burn in hot magma. She would occasionally get the chance to fly out and study one of the giant "Monses" in person, but mostly she stayed at home. Her work was tedious but rewarding, or so she told her husband.

They were about a year into their stay when the first rumors of Scife activity began to circulate. It was no secret that many thousands of colonists were sympathetic to that philosophy, and there were fanciful tales of insurrection brewing—that the Scifes would take power and create their own utopia on Mars, free from the dictates of any Earth government. There was never any substantial proof, just idle speculation, and Armin hadn't believed in any of it until the proof sat right before his eyes.

The files in Melinda Faris' database were plain as day. She'd been communicating with European agents and her logs proved it. There were even several journal entries in which she discussed her involvement with the foreign Scifes, and he had just scratched the surface. Further down, she had a list of contacts within the United States, people who were in league with her plans for an independent Martian State, many in high office.

The data he'd reviewed let him know who he could trust back on Earth, and it would be proof enough to get the attention of the President and the Joint Chiefs. All he needed to do was transmit the information, but communications were heavily restricted; only information screened by the governor or one of her proxies could be relayed.

He didn't know who to trust. It seemed everyone around him was acting strangely. His fellow officers and friends were different now. He might have just been paranoid, but he couldn't shake the feeling that they were somehow in league with the Scifes. Even though his wife remained as he had always known her, he didn't want to drag her into this mess, either. She was safe and content, exactly as he wanted her. That left him very alone in the grand scheme of things. Who could he turn to?

The answer came to him in a most curious summons— Deirdre Keene wanted to see him.

The former chief's wife had been fairly distant over the last three weeks. She'd spent a few days under house arrest for breaking her husband out of jail, but following the discovery of his body, she was granted a pardon by the governor. After giving birth to a healthy baby boy, she called upon Armin.

Armin proceeded down to the hospital, where he found her resting, but fully awake.

"Armin, come in," she invited as he poked his head through the curtain surrounding her bed. "It's good to see you."

"Likewise, Mrs. Keene," Armin said formally, feeling a little awkward. He'd always been a little nervous around her. She was such a gentle creature, seductive in so many ways, a perfect match for her spirited husband. "Are you okay?" he asked, finding it strange she was still be in bed two days after giving birth.

"Oh, yes. I just lost a little blood. They say the first time is always the roughest. I'll be fine."

"How's the baby?"

"He's perfect. The nurses are keeping an eye on him while I recover. Sit, please."

Armin sat down in the chair beside the bed and asked, "Why did you want to see me?"

"I'd like to talk about my husband. You were one of his closest friends, and I imagine he trusted you more than anyone."

"Tim was the best friend I ever had," Armin agreed. "I miss him."

"The Scifes," Deirdre grumbled. "You know they murdered him."

"That is just an unsubstantiated rumor," Armin said, afraid of being overheard. "Tim and Morgan got caught in the dust storm after breaking out of jail. That's all we know."

"It's okay," Deirdre said. "I had the nurse disable the monitor." She pointed at a tiny black ceiling panel. "Nobody's spying on us here, which is more than can be said for our personal quarters. They have them bugged."

"You're just being paranoid," Armin said, keeping up his pretense of ignorance. "There are no monitors in our homes."

"What do you think those viewscreens do when they're just sitting idle? They aren't simply providing a comforting atmosphere. They double as a network of surveillance cameras, relaying video and audio data back to the governor and her Scife allies. They're keeping tabs on everything we do, all in preparation to enforce the new anti-sedition laws. That's how they've kept everything hushed up all these months. That's how they know who to target for brainwashing."

"You're just being overly suspicious. I can understand your feelings. Losing Tim has been hard for us all, and it's difficult to accept that his death didn't have some greater meaning, but it was just a terrible accident, caused by his own poor judgment."

Armin shot the new mother a questioning stare and Mrs. Keene returned it. He could tell she was doubting his sincerity, and with just cause. Truthfully, Armin was the one being mistrustful, fearing Deirdre had been compromised. Knowing what he knew about Melinda's tactics, he didn't put it past her to be using Mrs. Keene to extract valuable information from him.

"I am telling you what I know," Deirdre growled in a hushed voice. "Tim had the viewscreen in our quarters removed several months ago, after learning they had spy capabilities. Why would he do that if they were harmless?"

"Maybe he didn't like the simulated moonlight glaring in his eyes every night," Armin lied, knowing full well she was telling the truth. The viewscreen in his own quarters had also been removed at roughly the same time, for the same reason. Of course, the governor had objected to her senior-most police officers removing her spying devices from their personal quarters, but since she wanted to keep the surveillance capability of the viewscreens top secret, hadn't voiced her discontent. It had, no doubt, made her suspicious.

"Stop patronizing me!" Deirdre shouted. "I know the truth. Why won't you believe me?"

"Come on. European Scifes here on Mars, controlling the governor? A grand conspiracy to break off from Earth entirely? These rumors have been circulating for over a year, but there's never been any proof."

"I had the proof, but Melinda stole it from me," Deirdre said.

"What proof?" Armin asked, his interest piqued.

"I had a copy of Melinda's computer files, the ones my husband and Morgan stole from her. It showed the governor had ties to the entire underground movement. The rumors are true! The governor and her allies want to establish a wholly independent Scife State here on Mars."

"You expect me to believe the governor had that kind of information logged on her computer?"

"Yes, because I know you have seen it!"

"How would I have seen it?" Armin asked, worried.

"Because I was there when Tim copied the files. He sent

two copies of the database. One to me, and the other to you."

"That's not possible. It's ludicrous."

"We both know what my husband thought the Scifes were capable of, their uncanny ability to change minds. It's true, they can brainwash us, but they haven't gotten to me," Deirdre said, sounding sincere.

"Assuming, hypothetically, that I'm willing to entertain these notions of yours and buy into this all-powerful Scife conspiracy, how can I know you haven't been compromised?"

"The pregnancy," Deirdre said. "They use their teleporter to adjust our mental pathways, but they can't teleport a pregnant woman."

"Why is that?" Tim asked. He wasn't privy to the ins and outs of the teleporter's mechanics.

"You must have seen the report labeled 'Fetal Cerebrostitial Syndrome' in Melinda's database. It's a Consensorate report explaining the kind of brain damage a fetus endures when teleported during the second or third trimesters. They couldn't brainwash me when I was pregnant without subjecting my baby to severe mental retardation, and that's one thing even *they* would never do. It's what spared me."

As Armin listened to her words, he wondered if his gut was wrong. A large part of him was reluctant to trust her, but he felt she was telling the truth. He needed help to take on the subversive elements. He had to trust someone, eventually.

"What do you want?" Armin asked.

"The files, Armin. Do you still have them? Are they safe?"

"Why do you want to know?"

"I need to know they're safe. They're our only hope."

Letting down his guard, he said, "You can rest easy. They're in good hands."

Deirdre scooted up in bed. "Who have you shared them with? Who do we have to worry about turning on us?"

"Nobody. I haven't known who to trust, so I've kept it all low key. Not even Emily knows. You should keep quiet, as well. It might buy us some time."

"Agreed, but I must have some assurance that things are proceeding as planned and the data is secure. We can't risk anyone getting a hold of it before we're ready."

"Like I said, it's safe. The files are on an isolated system in a secure location, away from prying eyes. The incriminating data is on a shadow hard drive, so anyone accessing the main system won't see that it even exists. The masked, secondary drive is keyed to my retina, so even if someone knew what to look for, they couldn't access it without me."

"I had no idea you were so computer savvy," Deirdre said.

"I picked up a few tricks growing up. My mother has been writing software for Virtucom since before I was born."

"Then there is absolutely no way anyone other than you can access the data," Deirdre concluded.

"I doubt it," Armin said, leaning in close to give her a reassuring pat on the shoulder.

Deirdra answered with a smile, and then stabbed a needle into his arm. She jammed down on the plunger, sending a full vial of clear fluid into his body. In seconds, a stabbing pain surged into Armin's chest, causing him to retch.

Deirdra pulled the needle free and stood up to hover over her victim. The smile drained from her face as she looked at Armin grabbing his chest and gasping.

"What is that?" Armin asked, as he felt his chest burn with pain.

"Polysidrine," Deirdre replied, dropping the syringe on the floor. It was a commonly used sedative. One milliliter could knock a patient out for hours. Ten would assure Armin Weitz would die in moments.

Armin should have trusted his instincts. He'd known better than to trust anyone, and his mistake cost him his life. Apparently, he had been in over his head all along. "Why are you doing this?" he asked, hoping his words could somehow reach Mrs. Keene.

"It's my penance," she said sadly. "My husband's death was my fault. If I'd left well enough alone and not been so stupid as to break him out of that cell, he'd still be alive."

"That's not true," Tim said, grimacing in agony.

"His obsession with this Scife conspiracy sent him over the edge, and now our child has to grow up without a father. This resistance has to stop, *now*, before any more people die."

"They...they brainwashed you," Armin said as his body began to shiver uncontrollably.

"Your death shall be the last," Deirdre said, tears rolling down her cheeks. "It ends here and now, forever."

Before Armin could respond further, he found his voice box paralyzed. His entire body was fading fast. The pain eased as the medicine flowed through his veins, and he pitched forward, falling on the floor in a crumpled heap.

A strange euphoria came upon Armin in his last moments of life, a sense of contentment and joy. It was truly bizarre, but somehow he felt it would be all right—this was not an end, but the beginning for him. He died with a smile on his lips.

* * *

Deirdre stood and stared at the man she had just killed. He could not have been dealt with any other way, unfortunately.

Directly after giving birth, Deirdre had been sent through the teleporter. Once her mind was properly adjusted, Melinda had told her of the plan to get information from Armin, and Deirdre had asked, "Why? Why must I kill a man? Surely you can persuade him as you just persuaded me."

Melinda had frowned and answered most sincerely, "No. We've already tried to bring him around, but nothing has worked. Every time we sent him through the teleporter, his mental pathways realigned themselves, erasing any and all evidence of the procedure. I'm afraid there is no way to change his mind."

"But you could lock him up," Deirdre argued, searching for a peaceful alternative.

"That would be ideal, if he weren't such a dangerous threat," Melinda replied. "But with the knowledge he has, we can't take the risk of him escaping, or using his computer knowledge to send a message to our enemies. He is impossible to control, so long as he's alive."

"Then we're going to kill him, just like that?"

"I know, it goes against everything we stand for, but it must be done. Sometimes, the ends must justify the means for our survival. You understand?"

Deirdre understood perfectly. Her conditioning made sure of that—and it gave her the will to do the job the Scifes had in mind for her, to be their assassin.

Thus, Armin Weitz had to die to assure the survival of Fundamentalist dreams.

It wasn't over, though. Deirdre understood that as she yanked open the curtain shrouding the bed. The knowledge Armin had given her assured this madness would go on, should the governor hear of it. Melinda would continue her quest to locate the stolen data, throwing untold thousands into jeopardy.

Deirdre had told Armin the truth regarding the surveillance camera being deactivated. It had been Melinda's idea. She didn't want any of Armin's secrets recorded, nor did she want his death televised, so she would be depending on Deirdre's testimony to learn the truth.

Deirdre knew the only way to put an end to it was for her to lie. Only she knew the truth about the shadow hard drive, and that was how it would remain. The files were as good as destroyed, anyway, so there was no harm in misleading the governor. Quite the contrary, if she lied, this mad vendetta would end and life could return to normal.

The stolen data would remain hidden, unknown to anyone, accessible only to a dead man. Nobody on Earth would see it, and the rise of the Martian Science State could continue unabated.

Chapter Twenty-Three
February 27, 2329

Eighteen months passed following the disappearance of Morgan Asher. Back on Earth, half of North America was digging out from crippling February snowstorms, while on Mars the warmth of spring was melting the frozen carbon dioxide at the South Pole. It still plunged well below zero each night, but the days were growing temperate again in the southern hemisphere.

The *USS Plymouth* was on braking thrusters, steadily slowing its approach to the Red Planet. They were still three days away, but there was no sense tearing the ship apart with a rapid slingshot into orbit. A slow and steady approach vector was all they desired.

Colonel Seth Avery was antsy, having been cooped up on board for six weeks. The time was growing near—he'd see his plans come to fruition or burn to ashes. He'd spent the better part of two years working toward this moment, and he'd twisted more arms and greased more wheels than a politician. Even so, his expeditionary force wasn't all he wanted it to be.

"Forty men. Hell, that's scarcely a platoon," Avery complained to Captain Waltham over a cup of coffee. He gave a long draw on the straw to ingest a mouthful of the strong stuff. It was an odd way to drink coffee, but in the weightless environment, you couldn't have it any other way.

"We're lucky we could put any of this together at all," Waltham said, scratching at the white stubble on his chin. "It's getting scary back there. I swear, half of Congress is under Scife control, and damn near that many of the military brass, as well."

"Enough people are noticing, at least, to keep them from taking over completely," Avery replied.

"But how do you prove there's a legitimate threat?"

Waltham asked. "I mean, how can we tell someone's being influenced through brainwashing, or whether they're an honest believer in Scife philosophy?"

"What's the difference? Both kinds are traitors to the republic," Avery reasoned. "Scientific Fundamentalism ought to be classified as subversive, and its followers barred from public service—or worse."

"Doesn't that defeat the purpose? The whole point of opposing them is for the sake of free will and liberty. By denying someone the right to believe in whatever they choose, doesn't that destroy the very republic we're trying to save?"

"Liberty has its limits, and wanting to steal someone else's liberty should be one of them," Avery affirmed.

Waltham shook his head in disagreement. "It's going to take people with a lot more brains than us to figure it out. I think that's for the best. The real victims are those poor souls who have had their minds changed for them. How do we help them?"

"General Silverman's got a team of experts working on it, seeing if we can't detect unnatural alterations and reverse them. It may take a while, but he's got a crack team of specialists, along with eleven transformed guinea pigs to work with."

"How are your men, anyway?" Waltham asked, recalling the brave marines that had first accompanied Colonel Avery to Mars.

"Most of 'em are in sad shape. Nine are still convinced they fell in love Scientific Fundamentalism of their own accord, unwilling to believe in the teleporter's brainwashing properties. The damned Scifes sure did a number on them."

"And the other two?"

"They're like me, broke the conditioning through force of will. Or so they claim. There's no telling what fail-safes the Scifes sneaked in. They could flip at any moment."

"If that's true, how can we trust *you*?" Waltham asked with an upraised brow.

"I'm the most stubborn son of a bitch ever born, that's

how."

As Avery sucked up the last of his coffee, a chime sounded, and Waltham answered his door to find a midshipman with a message. "Sirs, you'd better come up to the command deck. We're picking up something funny."

"Elaborate on 'funny,' son," Waltham ordered.

"It's some kind of communication, sir, addressed to us."

"Is it from our people or the Scifes?" Avery asked, drifting to the door.

"Neither, as far as we can tell, sir," the midshipman reported.

It was a short trip from the captain's office to the command deck of the *Plymouth*. The large, rectangular area was the brain of the most sophisticated vessel known to American science. Half a dozen computer stations monitored various ship functions, each set along the wall of a railed deck ringing a deep pit dubbed the "soup can," due to its shape. Inside the can sat the higher command functions, including the navigational controls and the communications center.

Captain Waltham and Colonel Avery followed the midshipman down into the soup can, where they met with Commander Jason Burroughs, the first officer, and ranking communications specialist, Lieutenant Bengal.

"What have you got, Benny?" Waltham asked, addressing the communications officer.

"This," the darkly-tanned officer said, handing a computer pad to his captain. The pad displayed the message they'd received, reading "Waltham-5291-0071ZHK-DaVinci."

"It came in about five minutes ago," Commander Burroughs added. "It's from Mars, but the carrier wave isn't coded, as is standard."

"It could be the Scifes," Avery mentioned, not able to make heads or tails of the message.

"What do you make of it?" Waltham asked Bengal.

"I think it's an invitation for communication, sir. The first four numbers are the time, 1925 hours. The next is

Amplitude Modulation, 1700 KiloHertz. The numbers are simply reversed."

"How did you figure that?"

"Because it's pretty obvious. Plus, Leonardo DaVinci is notorious for having signed the Mona Lisa backwards. I think that's the dead giveaway to the message."

"Sounds a little *too* obvious," Burroughs mentioned.

"Indeed," Waltham murmured thoughtfully. "Still, we'd better check it out."

Four hours passed like lightning as Waltham and his handful of trusted crewmembers awaited 1925. They sat in the command pit, tuned into 1700-AM, awaiting the mysterious contact.

Ten seconds late, a voice buzzed out. It was tinny and distorted. "*Plymouth*, this is Mars calling. Please respond."

"This is Captain Percival Waltham of the *USS Plymouth*. To whom am I speaking?"

"Someone unwilling to release his name over the airwaves, but it's good to hear from you, Captain Walther."

"If that's the case, aren't you afraid someone will triangulate your signal?"

"Not with the system I'm tapped into," the voice said, then changed the subject. "I assume you're aware of the situation here."

"There is no situation," Waltham replied, seeing Avery cringe at the thought of their secret mission being exposed. "Why have you contacted us?"

"We need to talk, but not over the air. Can you meet me?"

"If you give us the coordinates."

There was a lengthy pause. "Land at the base of Zephyria Tholus. I'll find you easily enough," came the stilted reply.

Another pause ensued, after which Captain Waltham answered, "Acknowledged. We'll be in orbit in seventy hours. Expect us shortly after that."

"See you then," the voice signed off.

As soon as the channel went dead, Captain Waltham smirked and cursed under his breath in disbelief.

"What do you make of it, sir?" Commander Burroughs asked.

"That's Asher," he said.

"Morgan Asher?" Avery said doubtfully. "Impossible. He's been dead for eighteen months."

"Missing, *presumed* dead," Waltham corrected, "but that's him, I swear it."

"How could you tell through all that distortion, sir?" Lieutenant Bengal asked.

"He called me 'Captain Walther,' and I bet that was on purpose. Do either of you remember Asher's gun collection, and that P-38 he had? Those pistols are commonly referred to as Walthers, because of the manufacturing company that made most of them after the Second World War. I think Morgan was giving me a hint."

"You're grasping," Avery said. "He could've just read your name wrong off a crew manifest."

"We'll just see who's grasping in three days," Waltham said, confident he knew the identity of the secretive caller. "Bengal, I want you to pick through that message. Go over the static, the background noise. Find anything that might be a hidden code. You know damn well he's not going to meet us where he said, not after announcing it to every Scife with a radio."

* * *

Lieutenant Bengal spent two days going over the message, filtering the layers, running the static through pattern analyzers, and trying to unlock whatever code might lurk under the surface.

He finally found what he was looking for.

In the background noise was a light tapping sound, translating into Morse Code. The pattern was hard to detect because the message was in shorthand, an antiquated form of code that hadn't been used much in centuries. In addition to latitude and longitude, there was the added request, "Bring shovel and razor."

Making the rendezvous was a secondary priority, and

Avery's plan would need to be initiated beforehand.

Swinging into orbit around Mars, the *Plymouth* announced their arrival to Villas Colony and Melinda greeted them with a jubilant gusto. After nearly two years, she was very pleased to see the good captain on her viewscreen, and Villas was ready to receive the first wave of supplies. Waltham confirmed the first shipment would be heading down within the hour, well ahead of schedule.

It was barely dawn when the first Strato-Strider landed at the colony, but it was not bringing supplies. Instead, Colonel Avery led his strike team out into the hangar bay and tasered the dozen colonists there before they could alert their superiors. No questions were asked, and nobody knew if the men were friend or foe—they'd wake up in a few hours for a proper interrogation.

Most of the colonists were in their quarters, still in bed or preparing for breakfast. They were right where Avery needed them to be, and his team went to work, uploading a computer virus into the Villas mainframe. The program went to work instantly, tricking the system into thinking there was an atmospheric leak, triggering an emergency lockdown. The colonists were trapped in their respective domiciles, and they would stay that way until Avery's men released them.

That wouldn't happen until he weeded out the traitors and shipped them back to Earth to stand trial.

Avery's men quickly secured the administration complex, locking down communications. His specialists set the colony's intercom system to broadcast a jamming wave, blocking any and all nearby radio signals.

With the communications blackout in place, Avery sent the majority of his men to search for stray colonists while he went to confront an old friend.

Colonel Avery found Melinda Faris at her desk, taken aback to find rifles leveled at her.

"Seth, I didn't expect to see you here," she said, sounding a bit surprised but not worried. "What are you doing? I thought we had an understanding."

Avery's next words were emotionless and rehearsed. "By order of General George L. Casey, US Air Force, I hereby relieve you of duty and place you under arrest, pending Court Martial."

"You have no idea what you're doing," Melinda said quietly.

"I think I've got a pretty good idea," Avery said, stepping up to her desk. "You think you could get away with brainwashing me and my men? Think again. You're gonna hang, *traitor*."

"You are the traitor, Seth. Not only to our country, but to the entire human race. You are just a pawn with no idea of the implications of his actions. Don't question my patriotism. Everything I have done has been for the benefit of our people."

Two of Avery's men burst in, forcing a pause in the hostile banter. "Sir, we've found something you'd better come see," one of them said. With a grimace, Avery followed the men, keeping his gun trained on Faris as he forced her along.

A short ride in an elevator brought them to the 'thing' three levels down.

The room Avery saw when the doors opened was something that had given him nightmares for the last two years. He looked at the teleporter pad; the giant metal disk set in the floor with control stations ringing it, and memories flooded back to him of his last encounter with such a device. Change the stone walls to steel and it was identical to the teleporter chamber in the Consensorate's compound.

Two of Avery's men wandered around in the center of the device, but they jumped to attention when their commanding officer entered the room.

"Get out of there, now!" Avery shouted.

The careless pair hurried to obey the order.

"Do you have any idea what that disk is?" Avery scolded his officers. "Stand too long in the middle of that thing and you'll find yourself teleported, turned into a damn clone."

"You're saying this is Consensorate technology?" Sergeant

Major Bisson asked, staring at it in awe.

"Things are worse here than anyone suspected," Avery said, looking at a glowing display panel, showing the unit was powered and ready to use. "The whole population's liable to have been compromised by now."

"Not compromised, Seth. *Liberated!*" Melinda said proudly.

"Liberated from free will. You've got a sick sense of patriotism, Ms. Faris."

"So said the British, regarding George Washington. Sometimes the only way to fix a broken system is through revolution. I had hoped mine would be bloodless."

* * *

As Avery took control of Villas Colony, a small jet tore through the Martian skyline. The four-seater Solox Mark-II had many superior features the larger Strato-Strider lacked. Much like a great-great grandson of the Harrier, the Solox was capable of incredible speed and vertical landings, making it an ideal craft for rough, alien terrain. Its only detractions were its four passenger capacity and lacking cargo space.

Despite the objections of his crew, Captain Waltham chose to attend the rendezvous with the mysterious voice he believed to be Morgan Asher. It was an excuse for him to get behind the wheel of the state-of-the-art plane, something he'd been fantasizing about for months. Extensive practice in simulation over the last week had honed his flight skills, where they had grown lax in recent years. Starship captains don't get much flying experience.

Dropping into the lower atmosphere, the jet flew over the Zephyrian Mountains. The impressive peak of Zephyria Mensae came and went at three thousand feet per second, and it wasn't long before Zephyria Tholus, the southern peak, was also in the rearview. Slightly south and west, a high hill appeared with a rimmed crater, the mouth of the Terra Cimmeri volcano.

Waltham magnified the terrain on his viewscreen as they neared their destination, a small valley two hundred miles farther south.

Waltham had never landed a Solox on real ground, so their descent and landing was bumpy. Lieutenant Bengal complained of whiplash.

"Buck up, Benny," Captain Waltham said as he blew the cockpit seals, exposing his suit to the native air. "Any landing you can walk away from, and all that."

"So long as I don't vomit in my suit," Bengal grumbled as he unbuckled his flight harness.

Captain Waltham flipped a switch on his control board and a side of the jet's hull hinged out beside Lieutenant Bengal, lowering down to the ground as a set of stairs. The lieutenant rushed down to solid footing, holding his stomach as if he really were nauseous, while the captain and one of Avery's trusted space marines crawled over their seats to reach the steps.

"Where now, sir?" the marine asked, his massive height and girth dwarfing his companions.

Waltham activated the viewer inside his helmet and brought up a map of the surrounding area. A pair of intersecting lines were superimposed over the image, indicating their precise coordinates. They were only a few steps away.

"Okay, we're here," Bengal said, looking around at the faint rims of impact craters poking out of the sand in the distance. "Now what?"

"He said to bring a shovel," Waltham replied. "Maybe we should play pirate and start digging."

The gargantuan marine retrieved the shovel from the Solox and dug where Waltham directed. The soldier worked furiously, and after a few minutes, hit the top of a metal hatch. The rest of the dirt was removed in short order, granting them access to the complex below.

Waltham descended the deep shaft with steady steps, followed closely by Bengal who quivered on the narrow rungs. They reached the bottom in short order, and the bulky marine shut the upper hatch, plunging them into darkness.

Waltham felt the lever in his hands, and tugged it back and forth until he found the right direction to activate the opening mechanism. The faint hiss of air sounded around him as he pushed his weight against the hatch, fighting to keep it open as the pressure equalized. Once the air had flooded the vacant shaft, he was able to fully open the portal, and found a suited individual standing before him.

"You're late, Captain," Morgan said. "Welcome to Mars."

Chapter Twenty-Four

Waltham recognized the voice coming through his suit's communicator, and his memory was confirmed as the man in front of him removed his helmet. Although the heavy beard was a new addition, the other features were clearly recognizable. "I knew it. Avery's going to owe me that drink."

"Excuse me?" Morgan asked.

"Colonel Seth Avery bet me a pint that I wouldn't find you here. I just hope he lives to pay up."

"I suppose we both have a lot of questions for each other," Morgan said. "Say, how are the dust storms topside?"

"It's early spring. The bad storms haven't started yet. Why?"

"Then there's time for me to show you around," he said, turning toward the inner hatch. "I'd hate to have the dirt bury the hatch and trap us."

Erring on the side of caution, Waltham ordered the marine back to the surface, to make sure the hatch remained clear of debris. The marine reattached his helmet and went outside, shutting the hatch behind him.

Morgan led Waltham and Bengal forward, over to one of the doors on the wall opposite the entry hatch. As they reached the door, Lieutenant Bengal spotted the mummified remains of the antechamber's original occupant lying nearby, and a jolt of emotion made him gasp.

"Never mind Al there," Morgan said, motioning toward the corpse. "He doesn't say much."

"Are you feeling all right, Morgan?" Captain Waltham asked.

"I've been down in this hole for over a year. I had to do something to lighten the mood a bit. Talking to ghosts, naming a corpse—but I'm not insane, if that's what you think."

That *was* Waltham's first impression, though he held his tongue, and followed Morgan into the hallway.

"From what I can tell, this place is something akin to Villas Colony, only a lot smaller and a little more advanced," Morgan said as he led them down the hall.

"What is it, a Scife stronghouse?" Waltham asked, glancing up at the iridescent ceiling panels.

"Hardly," Morgan said, stopping at the door to the bunk room.

"Then who built it?" Waltham asked impatiently.

"That's what I'm still trying to figure out," Morgan said. "Did you bring the razor I requested?"

Lieutenant Bengal reached into a pocket on his suit and removed a slim metal box. Morgan accepted the container and opened it to find a compact shaving kit.

Morgan ushered them into the bunk room and left them to examine the surroundings while he vanished into the bathroom to remove his facial hair. He hadn't had a razor in his survival kit.

Returning to his guests half an hour later, Morgan escorted them down to the communications center, where he'd managed to get a few of the alien consoles up and running.

"I don't know what most of this is, and it took me a year to figure out how to reactivate the hardware."

"How did you ever find this place?" Lieutenant Bengal asked as he glanced at a computer screen displaying wave patterns.

"You wouldn't believe me if I told you." Morgan paused oddly, and his facial expression shifted as if something irritated him.

"This is all quite beyond the realm of rational belief," Waltham said. "I doubt your explanation would be any less believable than this...whatever it is."

"A dead girlfriend came down from heaven and led me here. Satisfied?" Morgan said, eliciting a few chuckles from Bengal.

"Yes, very funny," Waltham said, not sure whether to take Asher seriously. "Now, what have we got here?"

Morgan sat down in a chair at one of the computer stations. "This is a communications array unlike anything I've ever seen. It interfaces with several dozen transmitters imbedded into the planet's crust, allowing for global communication without the need for satellites. As I found out, it's also capable of broadcasting a message using every transmitter at once, making it theoretically untraceable."

"How are you able to operate it?" Lieutenant Bengal asked.

"It took a lot of translation, and some trial and error. Of course, I didn't have much else to do."

"Translation?"

"Yes. See the symbols under the wave patterns and along the right edge of the screen? It turns out quite a few of them are similar to Ancient Greek, and it just so happens that my laptop has a pretty extensive translation matrix. Some overachieving scientist felt it a bright idea to include such software with the operating system of all Villas Colony computers. Don't ask me why.

"The language doesn't translate exactly. It definitely isn't Ancient Greek, though possibly a root of the extinct language, or an offshoot dialect. Either way, I was able to decipher enough of these words to operate the transmitters."

"How is that possible? The writing, I mean," Waltham asked. "Are you saying some kinda aliens visited the ancient Greeks and built this place?"

"Or maybe Alexander the Great really flew a spaceship," Bengal snickered.

"I'm not saying who built what," Morgan said defensively. "I'm only telling you what I've found, and you can see it with your own eyes."

"Yes, this is all very fascinating, but I think we'd better leave it for later," Waltham said, feeling antsy. "The *Plymouth*'s been jamming the airwaves since we got here, but there's no telling how long it'll be effective against the Scifes."

"No argument here. I can't wait to get out of this

198

compound. It's been like a lifeboat and a prison for the last year and a half," Asher said as he grabbed some things and shoved them into a bag. "I'm ready to head out.

* * *

Reaching the top of the shaft, Morgan looked up and saw the sky for the first time in ages. The sun lingered in the west, a glowing ball among the haze. He let Captain Waltham and his companions get ahead of him as he looked around at the craters and dust.

His pace slowed as his thoughts harped upon the circumstances of his current plight. It was still so surreal, the Scife plot, and his subsequent escape. He wondered if he weren't really insane, locked in a padded cell somewhere back on Earth, replaying these fantastic events inside his brain—a victim of virtual psychosis.

Rheena frowned at him as he continued to ignore her. She hadn't left his side in all this time, and without her help, he would have never been able to activate the transmitting equipment. Her hints and insights had quickened impossible work, though how she'd known how to reconnect the power relays and activate the wave guides was something she had kept to herself.

Morgan flicked off his radio, so he could have a word with Rheena in private. Nobody else could see or hear her, and he didn't want to be thought a lunatic. "You've been giving me dirty looks all day. What is it?"

"I'm not going with you," Rheena said, sounding disappointed. "I've already broken so many rules just staying around all these months, but I really don't want to go back."

"Then don't," Morgan said, suspecting she didn't have a choice.

"It was nice getting to know you for a second time," Rheena said, taking a few steps back. "Thanks for giving me an excuse to live again."

Morgan stood and watched as she walked backwards. After a few more steps, her image blurred, until it faded into nothingness.

Captain Waltham grew impatient. He grabbed Morgan's shoulder, urging him to hurry.

Morgan flipped on his radio and the captain reiterated his orders to get moving. The beefy marine helped Asher into the rear seat of the Solox, and once everyone was buckled into the craft, it took off and headed west.

It was a short flight to Villas Colony, taking barely ten minutes to pass the expanse that had taken Morgan more than a week to cross on foot. There wasn't much time for sight-seeing along the way, as the plane blasted through the sky at many times the speed of sound.

Captain Waltham set the Solox down outside the giant airlock to the main loading hangar and led his group over to a smaller, side airlock. Once the airlock pressurized, Waltham and his companions proceeded inside to check on Colonel Avery's progress.

* * *

Avery paced the floor in front of the disk, cursing at an obstinate Melinda. She was obviously stalling for time, which left Avery wondering what devious scheme she was hatching.

"So, Seth, what's your plan?" Melinda cajoled. "Are you really going to arrest all *thirty thousand* of us?"

"If I have to," Avery said bitterly, knowing full well how impossible that would be. "We've got men back on Earth working on a way to reverse this brainwashing of yours. Then we'll see how much support you really have here."

Before the hostile banter could continue, Waltham entered the room on a boisterous note. "Hey, Avery, just so you know, I like my whiskey sour."

Avery turned around, at first bewildered by the comment; but as his eyes saw the fourth man with Waltham, the answer came to him. "I'll be damned," he said, unable to suppress a smile of astonishment.

Seeing the familiar face, Melinda jumped out of her seat and rushed across the room, throwing her arms around Morgan in a most uncustomary manner. "My God, you're alive!" she exclaimed.

"No thanks to you," Morgan said with disgust, pushing her back.

Melinda remained cheerful, despite Morgan's unenthusiastic greeting. "Entirely thanks to me, I imagine. If I hadn't pulled the necessary strings, the Europeans would have done who knows what to you."

"Believe me, they tried," Morgan said.

"They only did what they felt was necessary to preserve the peace, to assure the success of our first joint venture here. And here you are, trying to throw all our futures away."

"Shut up," Avery grumbled, waving his pistol at her. "Save it for your hearing."

Melinda brushed back her hair and smiled. "Maybe you'd like to check on the rest of your men before fitting me for a prison jumpsuit."

Avery glared at her, unnerved by her demeanor. Something wasn't right, he could feel it in his bones.

One of Avery's lieutenants was ordered to do a perimeter sweep, but before he could leave the teleporter room, the officer found himself staring down the barrel of a gun. The gun-bearer wasn't a Scife—it was Lorna Asher. She stepped into the room with five other colonists, each armed with one of Morgan's antique firearms. They kept the pistols steady, their fingers on the triggers, ready to fire.

"Lorna, what are you doing?" Morgan asked, trying to draw her attention.

Her aim didn't waiver, even as her eyes darted over to the face of her long lost husband. "Morgan? You're alive?" Her voice cracked with emotion.

"Yes, it's a long story, but you've got to put the gun down," he said quietly, running his hand over his smooth face as if he was nervous being face-to-face with his estranged wife.

"Like hell I will," she hissed through clenched teeth. "I'm not going to let these soldiers bust in here and take our home."

"They're not taking anything," Morgan countered. "It's Melinda. She's controlling you."

201

"No!" Lorna shouted, tightening her grip on the butt of the pistol. "Nobody tells me what to do. Not her, and not you."

Avery had heard enough. "Listen, lady, we've got you outnumbered two to one. You might hit half of us if you're lucky, but then you're done."

"Think again," Lorna said, moving her aim to Avery. "There are thirty thousand of us, and only the ten of you."

"Your fellow colonists are locked in their quarters," Avery said, his voice unsteady, fearing the worse.

"Not anymore. You didn't really think we'd stay locked up for long, did you? Villas is home to a collection of the greatest scientific minds humanity has ever known. As soon as we knew what you were doing, it didn't take five minutes to disable the lockdown protocols."

"This doesn't make any sense," one of Avery's men said. "Once the virus was uploaded, it would have required an entire system reboot to unlock the crew quarters. The only way they could have gotten around that is if..."

"...we already had the lockdown protocols rewritten, before your arrival," Melinda finished happily, stepping away from her former captors. "I'm a colonel, as well, Seth. Don't you think I considered all possible scenarios?"

"But I saw the lockdown protocols engage!" Avery shouted, refusing to believe his carefully laid plans had failed.

"And they did engage, for about five minutes. Long enough to lure you in." Sliding behind Lorna, Melinda added, "I would suggest you surrender now to avoid unnecessary bloodshed."

There was no choice. The ten men raised their hands and linked their fingers behind their heads, then stood motionless as Melinda and two colonists removed their sidearms. Three more colonists soon entered the room and removed the confiscated weapons.

Melinda removed a small audio headset from her pocket and affixed it to her ear. "Status?" she asked into the mic, a pleased smile spreading across her youthful features when a secure status was reported.

"Right, onto the teleport pad, all of you," Melinda ordered her prisoners. Before they could obey, she added, "Except Morgan and Seth."

Captain Waltham remained beside Morgan, even after the other soldiers did as they were commanded. Melinda walked over and stood in front of him, a puzzled look on her face.

"I'm not going through that damn thing," Waltham said nonchalantly, shrugging his stiff shoulders.

"It won't hurt you, Captain. I assure you."

"You don't have a mental buffer installed. Forget it."

Melinda wagged a finger in his face, then waved her hand dismissively. "Lorna, take care of those soldiers, will you? I'll deal with these three myself."

Lorna holstered her weapon and rushed over to one of the brightly-lit control panels. Familiar with the controls, she cycled the system, sending the seven men away to parts unknown.

As the men dissolved, Morgan looked over at Melinda. "Why'd you let him stay?" he asked, tilting his head toward the captain.

"Yeah," Avery said, stepping over to Waltham. "And just how do you know that this teleporter doesn't have a mental buffer, whatever that is?"

Captain Waltham said nothing, but the look of pained satisfaction on his face exposed his duplicity.

Avery's eyes widened. His mind hearkened back to that first conversation they'd had, regarding the Scife conspiracy on Mars. Waltham had accused him of being a traitor, coaxed him into revealing his true thoughts and feelings, seemingly in the service of America. It had all been a lie. Captain Waltham had been the true traitor all along, had foiled the entire operation as a double agent.

As the betrayal sank in, Avery raised his fist and rushed toward the captain. "You son of a bitch!" he cursed, ready to pound the man. Before he could strike, one of the colonists shot him in the leg. He stumbled from the bullet's impact, falling to the floor.

"Hold your fire!" Melinda shouted as Avery grabbed his bleeding thigh.

"Take care of him," Melinda instructed a couple of the armed colonists. They complied, grabbing Avery by the shoulders and walking him out of the room.

As the door shut to the teleporter room, Avery squirmed, seeking to get free from the grip of his captors. "Let me walk, damn it. I'm not an invalid."

"Your leg's bleeding pretty heavily," one of the men said.

"So what? I've had worse," Avery said. "It's not like I have anywhere to run, if that's what you're worried about."

The colonists granted Avery's request, and let him stand on his own. He stepped carefully, finding the light, Martian gravity making the task easier. He still had to limp, but at least he could carry his own weight.

Walking down the hallway toward the elevator, Avery felt he was headed to a gallows. At least he'd do it under his own power.

***

Morgan shifted uncomfortably as Melinda turned her attention to him, her last opponent in the room. Standing in front of him with a wide grin spread across her face, she said, "I would never have imagined you'd still be alive."

"What are you going to do to me?" Morgan asked.

"Nothing, if you behave," Melinda replied. "I'm quite glad to have you back."

"Even after I betrayed you?"

"You didn't understand what I was doing and you acted on your fears. I won't condemn you for that, and your opinion of me will change in time, as you come to see the results of our work here. Someday, I'm sure you'll willingly choose to be a part of our new society."

"Never," Morgan said quietly, resiliently.

Melinda shook her head in doubt. "Lorna, would you escort him back to your quarters?"

Lorna stood up from her seat. "I'd rather not," she said.

"He's your husband," Melinda said, taken aback.

204

Lorna walked over and stared into Morgan's eyes, searching his face. Her expression was cold and lifeless, as if she were looking at a faceless cadaver. "No, he's not," she finally said, and then turned and marched out of the room.

Morgan's blood ran cold as he watched Lorna leave the room without him. He knew she was right, somehow. She wasn't the same woman he'd married six years ago. The body looked the same, but her attitude was different.

"Give her some time, Morgan," Melinda said. "I'm sure she just needs time to adjust."

Morgan said nothing, paralyzed with remorse. He couldn't help but blame himself for her rejection. He'd abandoned her all those months ago, but that wasn't the worst of it. They were here because of him, because he hadn't had the will to tell her no in the first place. He may not have thrown Lorna into the teleporter, himself, but he was still culpable.

If Morgan had been a little more selfish, and rejected Lorna's desire to come to Mars, none of this would be happening. Instead, his desire to please her had condemned them both.

Chapter Twenty-Five
March 3, 2329

For eighteen long and lonely months, cut off from civilization in the underground alien stronghold, Morgan had awoken every day with the hope that he would return someday to his wife and put an end to the treasonous conspiracy that had thrust them apart. The dream was over, he realized, as he opened his eyes on his first day back in Villas Colony. Although he had spent so much time alone, never had he felt quite as isolated as he did now, sitting up in the familiar bed he had once shared with Lorna. His perfect marriage seemed like another lifetime ago.

Lorna was nowhere to be seen. Sleeping somewhere else, she didn't want to see her long lost husband. The depressing memory of her rejection forced him back under the covers, until another lady's voice ordered him out of bed.

He poked his head out from under the covers and saw Melinda's face on the viewscreen beside the bed. She was sitting at her desk, looking very pleased with herself.

"It's nine o'clock, local time," she said. "I know you've been away from civilization for quite a while, so I figured you could use a wakeup call."

"How thoughtful of you," Morgan groaned, resistant to rise. "Say, how's Colonel What's-His-Name doing?"

"Colonel Avery is still in the infirmary. That bullet nicked the femoral artery and he almost bled to death."

"He wasn't bleeding that badly when your goons carried him out."

"It must have ruptured in transit. He was half-walking on his own. Regardless, he's stable, but definitely out of it for the time being."

"I guess that makes your job easier. He can't fight back if he's in the hospital." Morgan dragged himself to the edge of his bed, letting his muscles adjust to being vertical again.

"I never wanted anyone to get hurt," Melinda said defensively, "but I'll do whatever is necessary to protect my people."

Before Morgan could give a response, the door opened and the morose figure of Lorna Asher walked into the bedroom. Her once vibrant hair was cut short, which reminded Morgan of how she'd looked when they'd first met; though instead of smiling, she looked stone cold. Her baggy clothes drooped down to match her lips. She shut the door behind her and glared at her husband.

Morgan didn't know what to say. Looking at her, he still saw the woman he loved, despite her unnatural change. His heart pounded nervously as excitement and fear overwhelmed him.

The silence was deafening.

"Well, I'll give you both some privacy," Melinda said. "I'm sure you have a lot to talk about." The monitor went blank.

"Lorna..." Morgan started.

"I'm here because I owe you an explanation," Lorna interrupted. "This is difficult, but please try to hear me out."

Morgan stood up and walked toward her slowly. "I know I've been gone a while, and you wrote me off for dead long ago, but I still love you. We should try to work things out."

"It's not that simple," Lorna said, her cold demeanor fading into discomfort.

"You met someone else," Morgan surmised, stopping in the middle of the room.

"No," Lorna said. "I *am* someone else. Maybe we should both sit down." She took a seat at the small eating table, the one where they had once shared hundreds of meals.

Morgan followed suit, and took his chair. "I understand you're not the same person you were. Neither am I, entirely."

"That's not what I mean," Lorna said.

"What *do* you mean?"

"I mean I really am not the Lorna Asher you knew. Not in any physical or mental sense. I am a new being altogether, a

207

copy with her thoughts, memories, and genome sequence, but I'm not the same person. She died long ago, to give birth to the woman you first met the day before you left here. She, in turn, died to give birth to another copy, and to another and another, until I was born almost a year ago."

"What?" Morgan asked, his mind reeling with confusion.

"I know it's hard for you to understand, and it may be harder for you to accept, but every time Lorna Asher went through the teleporter, she died and a new copy was invented. I remember dying several hundred times."

Morgan could hardly believe what he was hearing. "Wait, you're telling me that you're just a copy of my wife, an exact copy in every physical way, with all her thoughts and memories. If that's true, what else is there? I mean, you're you, aren't you?"

"Yes and no," Lorna said, putting a hand over her eyes to hide the forming tears. "I am her, but I'm not. You just have to believe me."

Morgan began to realize what she meant. A person is made up of more than just thoughts and feelings. There is an indefinable uniqueness in everyone, something many would call a soul. Beyond biological existence, there are certain elements that cannot be duplicated or fabricated, the spiritual tether that gives people awareness and a true sense of self.

"When did you first realize this?" Morgan asked gently, regaining control of his emotions. The more he talked to her, the stronger he felt, and the more hopeful he grew that he could somehow reclaim her love.

"About three lives back, Lorna started to sense there was something wrong; something different every time she came out of the teleporter. The technicians assured her it was all in her mind, but the last few deaths took their toll. When I was born on that telepad last year, I swore I was not going to go out like the rest of them. This version of Lorna Asher was going to stay alive.

"Since the introduction of the teleporter, all work crews

have been required to use it for daily transport, so there was no way I could keep working on the dome. Melinda laughed when I told her I wanted to quit, but she humored me, assuming I'd get over my 'irrational fear' before long. After it became apparent that wasn't going to happen, she let me join the police force."

"You're a cop now?" Morgan asked in disbelief.

"I was an Amazon when you met me, remember? I can scrap with the best of them, not that there's much action around here."

"*You* were an Amazon when we first met?" Morgan asked shrewdly. "But you just spent the last five minutes telling me you aren't that Lorna Asher."

"Yes, I meant when she met you. It gets so confusing sometimes," she growled.

The outburst was familiar, and Morgan was glad to see a little bit of the old Lorna still in her clone. She wasn't nearly as far gone as he had feared. "So, where do we go from here?" he asked.

"I don't really know," Lorna replied.

"We could always start over," Morgan suggested, wanting nothing more than to hold her. "The original Lorna and I were really great together."

"You were, weren't you?" she mused, a smile playing at her lips as she entertained the notion for a fleeting moment. "But I can't. Not yet. I mean, I'm feeling so much right now, but I don't know how much of it is really me, or what I'm supposed to do about it. I have all these memories that keep rattling around inside my head, but they're not mine. I didn't do any of it, see any of it. It's like I was born with a lifetime of memories, but I know deep down how young I am. I'm not ready to be a wife to you."

Morgan didn't push, choosing to give her the space and time she needed. He was relieved to know she hadn't moved on, and she didn't hate him. Somehow, he was going to make her his again, but it would have to wait.

There were, after all, greater things at stake than their love life.

"Lorna, how do you feel about Melinda's plans now, after all she's done to you?" Morgan pried gently.

"Melinda said you'd try to get to me like this, by suggesting she had betrayed me," Lorna said, sounding strangely pleased. She stood up, leaned across the table, and whispered in his ear. "You don't have to."

Morgan wasn't sure what to make of her statement, but he suspected it was good news.

Lorna straightened and let her expression grow sedate once more. In a cold and formal voice she said, "We'll talk again later, after you've allowed reality to sink in." With a slight nod, she turned and departed.

Morgan stared at the door. Things might be looking up, after all.

* * *

The mineshaft was cold and gloomy, and the air was thin. It was certainly a shock to the system whenever one would enter this side passage from the oxygen-rich botanical labs. It didn't officially exist, which allowed certain individuals a modicum of privacy.

Lorna came here infrequently, as did those she was about to meet. If they made a habit of conducting secret meetings, somebody might notice and put an end to their teleporter boycott. Only when urgent matters arose did they come to their hidden sanctuary, away from prying eyes.

The shaft shrank, and for thirty feet Lorna hunched down, after which the passage flared out once more and she came to a heavy iron hatch blocking her path. She turned the knob and stepped into the crowded room beyond.

"Hurry up!" a squeaky female voice greeted her. "You'll let all the air out."

"The condenser's running hot," a short, stocky man said in response, "but don't worry, Becky, my dear. You're not going to suffocate."

Becky Sousa slapped her husband on the chest in a show of irritation. She then brought her slender hand back and let it rest on her very pregnant belly. "Where's Travis?"

"He's been assigned to guard Colonel Avery," Lorna answered. "We'll have to proceed without him."

There were two dozen people sitting around the room, on old packing crates or hunks of rock. It wasn't the most sophisticated of conference rooms—just a niche in the wall, a natural formation with some poly-sealant patchwork that made it airtight. A small shaft led out to a canyon wall several hundred yards away, blocked by a large condenser and carbon scrubber, a device that transformed the native Martian atmosphere into breathable air.

So much effort had been expended to elude the governor's scrutiny.

"Let's get started, then," their unofficial ringleader, Graeme Carlow, said. He stood out from the others in more ways than one. His black hair grew longer than that of most men on Mars, and he sported a pair of lamb-chop sideburns to compliment his long mane. His distinct Irish accent was a gift from his parents, who had immigrated to America directly before his birth.

"First, the European front. Snyder, what's the word?"

The stocky man stood and cleared his throat. "I picked through the latest recorded meeting between Faris and Budreau, mostly just a bunch of gloating. They played that marine colonel like a fiddle, made sure he only talked with people sympathetic to the cause, which includes some frighteningly powerful generals. They already got forty new soldiers to add to the colony, and they're even thinking of doing this again, sending the colonel back to gather another team after they adjust his memory."

A few people in the room grumbled.

Carlow clapped them into silence and continued. "Do we have any new names to add to the list of accomplices?"

"None. Faris wasn't specific, but we must assume she has associates throughout the military chain of command. How else could Avery have been tricked so thoroughly?"

Carlow stood up from the rock he was sitting on and paced

around the room, deep in thought. "We have three senators, half a dozen representatives, and a couple dozen NASA administrators—but that isn't good enough. We need a full list of conspirators, or the ones we miss will simply cover their tracks and start over again, and likely make our lives short and miserable in the process."

"But we've learned how to detect them now," Lorna reminded their leader. "We can prove brainwashing."

"True," Carlow said. "A thorough encephalographic scan does the trick in revealing any lasting alterations to brain chemistry, but there's no telling how many of our enemies on Earth are truly victims of the teleporter and how many genuinely believe in what they're doing. Let's face it, we need more names."

"We've got as many as we're liable to get," Becky complained. "We can't wait any longer. It's now or never."

"We mustn't jump the gun," Carlow argued.

"I'm not going to wait another two years for you to act. My baby's due next month and I have no intention of being subjected to the teleporter after its birth."

"The rest of us find excuses to avoid it," Lorna said.

"Yeah, for how much longer?" Becky rebutted. "How long will our illustrious governor and her Scife slavemasters tolerate those of us with a 'phobia' against their technology?"

"Speaking of which," Carlow interjected, "how is work progressing on the mental buffer, Chan?"

A tall Asian man stood up to respond. "Honestly, we're still in the theoretical stage at the moment. I don't see it being feasible any time in the near future."

"What's the problem?" Lorna asked. "Millions of mental downloads are performed on Earth every day."

"Yes, in conjunction with virtual environment technology, but there are several high hurdles to overcome in adapting the mental transference equipment to function with a teleporter," Chan explained, " The key to virtual downloads is the state of a person's physical brain at the time it occurs. In order for a successful download, a body must be brought to a state of near death. Mental data can't be transferred until the subject is approaching a state of suspended animation. At that time, various electro-chemical impulses permit the transfer.

"Someday, it may be possible to transfer someone's mind while they're fully up and kicking, but for the moment, I don't see how. Our current technological development isn't sufficiently advanced."

"That settles it. We can't wait any longer," Becky said, her palm pressed against her distended abdomen. "I'm telling you, it's now or never. Let's get on with it!"

Most of the crowd agreed, leaving Carlow with a headache. "All right, all right! Calm down before you set off a seismic sensor. If we're really going through with this, we've got some serious work ahead of us. What's our timetable with the *Plymouth*?"

Reginald Matheson answered. He was a muscular, dark-skinned laborer currently assigned to the hangar bay, assisting in offloading supplies from the *Plymouth*. "We're getting a lot of heavy industrial equipment. It'll likely take a full week to get it all down here."

"Good, then we have time," Carlow replied, sounding pleased. "It's still going to be tough, and we'll need all the help we can get. Speaking of which, Mrs. Asher, what news do you have regarding your husband?"

Choosing her words carefully, Lorna replied, "He seems to be every bit the man my memory recalls."

"Then he can help us?" Graeme asked.

"At the very least, we will be helping him," Lorna answered.

Chapter Twenty-Six

The quality of Morgan's meals sharply declined. Where he was used to the meat and produce of the alien complex, the reconstituted soup of his current lunch left his taste buds reeling. It was bitter, salty, and lacked substance. Like it or not, he'd have to get used to it again, and he gingerly sipped the stuff. It's not like he had much else to do, locked in his quarters, alone, without even a book to read.

Two hours had passed since his rousing conversation with Lorna, and he kept going over it all in his head. When he wasn't feeling confused, he was disgusted. He was powerless to fight back, and could only sit and watch as Mars went to hell before his eyes.

Drinking the last spoonful of broth from his bowl, Morgan stood and went to the sink. After rinsing the dish, he returned to the small table and tried not to go stir-crazy. It wasn't long before the door opened, and Lorna came in without so much as a knock.

"We have to talk," she said, sounding agitated.

"Sure," Morgan said, hoping it was a positive sign to have her return so soon after her last visit.

"First things first," she said. Stepping up to the table, Lorna kissed Morgan passionately. She left her lips on him as she half-dragged him out of the chair, but pulled away once he was on his feet. Surprised, Morgan hesitated for a moment before returning her kiss.

"Wait," she said, digging into a pocket. She removed a small metal block and waved it in Morgan's face. "No sense in anyone spying on us." Rushing over to the blank viewscreen, she flipped open a small panel beside it and slid the block into the circuitry.

Turning back around, the love was gone from Lorna's eyes. "Now we can talk in private."

Morgan was disappointed her display of romantic interest

was for someone else's benefit. He had enjoyed the kiss. "What are you after now?"

"First, a little more background," Lorna said, sitting down at the table. She folded her hands and rubbed her thumbs together, thinking of the right words. "I am not alone in my hatred for the teleporter, and those of us who avoid it also blame Melinda Faris for killing us more times than we can recall. She is a murderer. We've formed something of a resistance group, digging up whatever information we can against Faris and her Scife allies, and we're planning to escape this nightmare, go back to Earth."

"Return to Earth? How?" Morgan asked.

"We're going to hijack the *Plymouth*," Lorna said with a bold smile.

"Okay," Morgan said dubiously, drawing out the two syllables, "and exactly how are you going to accomplish that?"

"It's simple. We switch places with the offloading crew in the hangar bay and take control of the Strato-Strider during one of its supply runs. Once we're aboard the *Plymouth*, it should be easy enough to pacify the crew, though I hope it doesn't come to bloodshed."

"You're liable to get yourselves killed doing this," Morgan ground out, unable to control his pessimism.

"Not when we're the only ones with any real firepower. So long as we don't tip off the police forces down here beforehand, taking over the ship should be a cakewalk. They don't have any real guns, just those taser sticks, remember?"

"Captain Waltham was always bitching that he didn't have any real weapons aboard. Just hope he hasn't upgraded recently."

"He hasn't. We checked," Lorna assured him. "Tasers will be no match for the guns you brought to Mars, and with any luck, we'll be blasting back to Earth this time tomorrow."

"By '*we*' I assume you're taking me with you," Morgan said, realizing her plan had a reasonable chance of succeeding.

"That's why I'm here. I don't want to leave you stuck here

and the resistance is shorthanded. We could use your help pulling this off."

"How many of you are there?"

"Twenty six," Lorna said.

"*Twenty six*?" Morgan repeated in disbelief. From her talk, he'd expected there to be hundreds of rebels. "You think that'll be enough for a successful hijacking?"

"That's one of us for every crewman aboard the *Plymouth*, plus one, if you come along."

"Even so, this won't go down quite as smoothly as you imagine. I mean, what are you going to do after you take over the ship? Can anyone fly it, or do you expect the 'pacified' crew to do your bidding?"

"Flying the ship won't be a problem. It's not like a fighter jet where you need to get the feel for the controls. It's all computerized. So long as you've got a basic grasp of calculus and astronomy, it's a cinch. As for the crew, any of them loyal to the Scifes will be put off the ship."

"You mean vented into space," Morgan assumed.

"Put into a Solox jet and sent back to Mars," Lorna corrected. "We're not interested in killing people. We just want to stop being killed."

"Yes, speaking of which, what do you think will happen if you get back to Earth? You explain everything that's happening here to the authorities, and then what? Sure, the testimony of a few dozen colonists will get their attention, but you don't have any real proof, do you? The bureaucrats will launch some drawn-out investigation, and before it's all over, most of the people behind this Scife conspiracy will cover their tracks and likely kill all of you in the process."

Lorna didn't bat an eye at his reasoned response. "That's our biggest problem. We don't know who to trust *or* distrust. However, we suspect the information may exist in the database you stole from Melinda last year."

"Do you actually have the files?"

"Not exactly, but when you and Tim Keene downloaded the files, he sent copies to a couple of different people, one of whom we suspect was Armin Weitz. Of course, Armin's been dead for quite some time."

"If he's dead, it means Melinda had him killed—which means she also found his copy of the database," Morgan said.

"Not necessarily. From what we've been able to determine, nobody ever found his copy. If that's the case, then there is one person who might know where to look."

"And if you find what you're looking for?"

"It'll be our ticket to freedom," Lorna said wistfully.

Morgan knew joining the resistance was his only real chance at survival. He didn't expect Melinda's lingering hero-worship of him would last forever, and her co-conspirators didn't share her affinity for him in the least. How long would it be before he woke up on a teleporter pad, or simply had an "accident?" Sticking around was not an option— not if he wanted to live.

"Okay," he said, "I'm with you. Tell me what to do."

"Just keep quiet," Lorna answered. "Things are already set in motion. I'll be back later tonight."

Standing, Lorna walked over to the kitchen sink and ran a little water into her cupped hands. She splashed the small amount of liquid into her short hair and rubbed it around to simulate sweat. A few drops trickled down her forehead and she rubbed it around evenly before rushing back to the monitor and removing the small surveillance disruption device. She smirked at the blank screen, expecting any spy would see her looking hot and sweaty, as would be expected after a private encounter with her husband. She tugged on her collar to straighten it, and kissed Morgan on the cheek on her way out, completing the illusion.

As she left, Morgan's thoughts flipped between dreams of freedom and memories of love.

* * *

Deirdre Keene's quarters were full of rocks. She enjoyed studying the geological samples. Her eighteen month old son had the habit of getting into her sample bins and using them as toys, so the rug was always dusty and cluttered, but at least he wasn't at the throwing stage yet.

Before his death, Deirdre's husband had asked to name their son Theodore after some ancient historical figure. Deirdre had wanted none of that nonsense and had insisted on naming him Roland, after her father. Of course, his untimely death had worked to persuade her otherwise, and so Theodore Timothy Keene was so named.

Deirdre spent nearly every waking moment with Theodore. Her work took a back seat to motherhood, so instead of studying the dried river beds and mountain caverns, she settled for cataloging samples while her colleagues had all the fun out in the field. She didn't second guess her decision to dedicate her life to raising her son. A family she'd wanted, and she was devoted to that most rewarding vocation.

Raising a child alone could be trying at times, but she had many friends to help her. There was always someone there when she needed time alone, to take a shower or attend a meeting. Even Governor Faris stopped by to help on occasion, though her maternal instinct was nonexistent.

Overall, Deirdre was well-liked, though few people knew of her bout of momentary insanity, which had claimed the life of Armin Weitz. In truth, even she didn't have a clear recollection of the traumatic events, and she felt it was for the best. It drove her mad to think she could act so violently, with utter disregard for human life. Even if it was a necessary evil, she could never believe what she'd done was right.

When a couple of friends stopped by and asked her out to dinner, Deirdre thought nothing of it, and gladly accepted, leaving her son in the care of a trusted neighbor. When she stepped into the elevator, it quickly became apparent they weren't taking her to eat—they threw a cloth sack over her head and she felt an electric twinge that forced her body to go limp.

Time passed quickly as she was dragged around. Before long, she found herself sitting in a cold, clammy room. Life was returning to her muscles as the sack was lifted from her head. The gloomy cave frightened her, as did the masked individuals hovering in front of her.

"What do you want?" she asked, frightful.

"Answers," one of the masked individuals said. She didn't recognize the voice as it was distorted through an audio synthesizer.

"I don't know about anything. Please, let me go. I have a young son" she begged.

"We know you murdered Armin Weitz."

"It was an accident," Deirdre explained, shaking her head. "I didn't mean to..."

"Melinda covered it up, but we know the truth," the leader of the group persisted. "Tell us what you know and you won't be harmed."

"I told you, I don't know anything!" Deirdre cried.

"You know where Armin hid Melinda's files," the leader declared, leaning over her quivering body. "Tell us."

"No, he never told me."

"*Tell us!*" the leader shouted, grabbing her hair and pulling her head back to stare into his covered face.

Deirdre bawled and shook all over. Her captors waited for her to stop hyperventilating before continuing their interrogation.

"You talked to Armin before you killed him," the leader said. "We want to know what he told you."

Deirdre wiped tears off her cheeks and answered in a frightened ramble. "It's all so hazy, but I remember I wanted him to tell me. I needed to know what he'd done, what he was going to do. I asked him to tell me about the files, but he wouldn't do it. He just said they were on a shadow hard drive that could only be accessed by him. And then I stabbed him. Why did I stab him?" She broke out into tears again.

Her captors couldn't get anything else out of her in her frazzled state, and they promptly stunned her again and dragged her to an unobtrusive corner of the colony. After they had her limp body where they wanted it, they stabbed a needle into the back of her neck, knocking her out with sedative.

Deirdre Keene awoke hours later with no memory of the last few days, and she wondered how she'd come to be locked in a storehouse full of fertilizer.

* * *

It wasn't much to go on, and the trail was over a year old, but at least they knew what they sought actually existed. Now it was all a matter of deduction and hoping they could unlock the shadow hard drive when they found it, assuming they found it in time.

There really weren't many places to hide a data storage device in Villas Colony. All computers were owned by the government, and a log was kept of who was using what. Records were meticulous, and each piece of precious hardware was accounted for over the last four years, meaning Armin hadn't stashed his computer in a wall or otherwise disposed of it. Somewhere out there, someone was using the system that contained the incriminating files.

Police headquarters was the first stop. Lorna, along with a pair of computer savvy specialists, picked through every laptop and data pad used by the force, but nothing turned up. Rechecking the use allocation records, they determined no computers used by the force had been transferred in two years, leaving only one other probable location for the hidden files.

Armin's personal quarters were still occupied by his widow, Emily, who had grown secretive and reclusive since her husband's death. She didn't much care for Lorna showing up on her doorstep and forcing her way inside.

"What do you want?" Emily demanded.

"We have reason to believe your husband stored stolen property on one of his computers. We are here to locate that data and dispose of it, if found."

"My husband was no thief," Emily protested, pulling a knot out of her tangled, black hair. It didn't appear the tangled mess had been combed recently. "What about my Fifth Amendment rights?"

"Villas Colony and all of its contents are government property. Therefore, the Fifth Amendment doesn't apply. We don't need a search warrant."

Unable to defy the authorities, Emily went over to a cabinet and retrieved the laptop and a data pad still assigned to her husband. They hadn't been touched since his death, or so she told Lorna.

The two computer specialists took the devices to the eating table and began dismantling them, searching for any hidden accessories.

"My husband was right about you people," Emily said as the technicians worked. "I didn't want to believe him, told him he was just falling for his boss' paranoia, but it's true."

"What's true?" Lorna asked rigidly, playing up her role as an impassioned police officer with little regard for anyone's feelings.

"That you Scifes are just a bunch of fascist pigs, looking to push us around," Emily replied spitefully.

"I take it you no longer enjoy living on Mars," Lorna surmised, her voice dripping with sarcasm and her eyebrows raised.

"No, I love Mars. Working here was my dream, but you people are screwing it up. Do you know I was downgraded to a Class-D researcher, all because I refused to use that infernal teleporter? If you want to go anywhere nowadays, you're ordered to use that thing. But if you understood half of the physics involved, you'd think twice about having yourself killed every day."

"Why didn't you file an official complaint?" Lorna asked.

"And be forced into the teleporter in order to cure my 'phobia?' I don't think so. That's what they do to most people if they decide the teleporter's a death trap, which it is. That's policy, but of course you're not allowed to say anything disparaging against policy, now are you? The anti-sedition rule imposed by the glorious ICB means you can't even think about disagreeing with the establishment."

"If things are so bad here, you're free to leave."

Emily laughed. "Nobody leaves Mars. You can't without prior approval from both the governor and the ICB. Last I checked, nobody's been so approved."

"That's probably because no one has ever applied," Lorna said.

"They make sure nobody applies, and you know it," Emily corrected. "Do you really think Melinda Faris and her Scife collaborators would let any of us go back to Earth, knowing what we know about their plans? Face it, we are all State property."

The computer specialists interrupted, saying they could find no hidden drives on either of the computerized devices.

"See? I told you," Emily chided. "Now, why don't you go goose-step your way back to the governor like a good little puppet?"

"What about that?" Lorna asked, pointing to a laptop sitting open on a corner desk.

"No, that's my personal work computer," Emily objected. "I use that every day. There is nothing hidden on it."

"Then you won't mind if we take a look at it," Lorna said arrogantly. She pointed at the specialists. "Bobby, check it out. Yuan, call up Mrs. Weitz's records. I want to know if her story checks out."

"What story?" Emily asked. "Wait, let me guess. You want to make sure I really am a malcontent before arresting me for my antisocial rhetoric. Guess what, I don't give a damn anymore."

"That much is obvious," Lorna said. *Perhaps a little too obvious*, she thought. *Could this spitting viper be a trap of some kind?* It was just the sort of deceptive trick she was afraid would foil their plans.

Yuan accessed the Villas mainframe with his personal data pad, and after a brief search, determined that at least one thing was true about Emily Weitz—she'd never been teleported, and had been downgraded because of it. He handed the pad to Lorna, who subsequently read a summary of the incident.

"On the fifth of December last year, Emily E. Weitz was slated to lead a team of Vulcanologists to study the Tyrrhena Mons volcano. Weitz was subsequently ordered to teleport out to the Cimmerium airstrip where a Solox was waiting to fly her to the research location. Upon refusal to teleport, the research mission had to be rescheduled and restaffed, causing unacceptable waste of time and human resources. Weitz was therefore downgraded to Class-D researcher status until she proved herself willing to utilize all available technology in the performance of her job."

"Satisfied?" Emily asked.

Lorna wanted to believe Emily Weitz was as disgruntled as she claimed to be, yet there was no way to tell for certain without exposing her to certain truths—truths that could spell doom for the resistance.

It was a risk, but Lorna trusted her instincts. "Mrs. Weitz, if you really want to leave, I think I could arrange a seat aboard the *Plymouth* for you."

"How gracious of you," Emily said cynically, "but, no, it's impossible. Even if you really wanted to, I can't be permitted to leave."

"Why not?" Lorna asked, growing frustrated.

"I've already taken the anti-aging therapy. Armin and I did it as soon as we got here, and there are special conditions regarding the use of that treatment. The colonial contract specifically bars anyone from ever returning to Earth after receiving it, and it's perfectly understandable. If word of this got out to the general public, our planet would be doomed. So, instead, *I* am doomed."

"That's very noble of you, but you don't have to condemn yourself to Mars. It would be years before anyone noticed your condition, and you could easily move around to avoid suspicion."

"But, like I said earlier, nobody leaves Mars. The powers that be would never allow it."

"You don't understand what I'm offering," Lorna started. "We—"

"Got it!" Bobby shouted, hastily screwing the outer casing of the laptop back together.

Emily's eyes flared and she looked ready to do something impulsive. Lorna grabbed her shoulders before she could run over and attack the computer or the technician.

"Emily, listen to me. If you want to get out of here, you've got to let us take your computer. The files Armin hid on it could mean the difference between life and death, literally."

Emily kicked Lorna in the shins, but heavy boots prevented any harm. "Whatever's on that computer, my husband was murdered for it. I'm not going to let you get away with this!"

"Nobody's getting away with anything!" Lorna shouted. "If we can unlock those files, it'll mean justice for your husband and everyone else Melinda Faris has betrayed here."

"What do you mean?" Emily grumbled, yanking one arm free from Lorna's grasp, glaring at her with suspicion.

It was dangerous, but Lorna felt she owed Emily the truth. "We're not working for Melinda Faris. We want to expose her and her fellow conspirators back on Earth, but we need the data your husband stashed in your computer to do it."

Emily shook her head. "I don't believe you. You're just trying to shut me up long enough to get away!"

"You want proof? Come with us. We're all leaving aboard the *Plymouth* tomorrow."

"How do I know you're not trying to trick me?" Emily asked, feeling as apprehensive of Lorna as Lorna was of her.

"You can't. It's either trust me or stay here and rot until the Scifes change your mind—literally."

Chapter Twenty-Seven

The pot of water was just starting to boil on the stove when Morgan's door chime sounded. He thought it considerate for someone to actually announce themselves before storming in on him. Though, when that person entered a few minutes later, he found his mood soured.

"I hope I'm not too late," Captain Waltham said, looking over at the pot on the stove. "The governor requests your presence at dinner."

Morgan flipped the dial on his stove and let the range grow cold. He turned his eyes onto the captain and noticed he looked much younger with a clean shave and his sharp dress uniform. No doubt, he would also be supping with the Gov.

"Can it wait for another day?" Morgan asked.

"I don't think so," Waltham replied, holding onto a pleasant tone. "She expects you to make an appearance."

"Then it's not really a request, is it?" Morgan asked rhetorically, then muttered, "Accursed trappings of fame."

Waltham escorted Morgan to the governor's library, and once there, they each took a seat at the table. It was a larger arrangement than Morgan remembered, and lifting up the purple tablecloth, he found there were now two rectangular tables buttressed together, allowing for extra room, though there were still only four place-settings.

There was no one else in the room when they arrived, though that quickly changed, as Melinda Faris entered with a curious looking man in tow. Morgan may not have recognized the man's face, but he had a pretty good idea where he came from. The cut of the suit was one popular among the upper echelon of western European society.

"Ah, Morgan, I'm glad you came," Melinda greeted him as she approached the table.

"How could I possibly refuse?" he replied, trying to sound amiable.

"Allow me to introduce Jean Proudhon Budreau of Eridania. Jean, Morgan Asher."

The Frenchman extended a hand for Morgan to shake. "A pleasure to meet such a notorious figure."

Morgan shook the hand ceremoniously.

Taking her seat at the table, Melinda said, "I hope this proves to be the beginning of a most beneficial friendship."

Morgan was about to reply in a negative fashion, but he caught himself. This was not the time to be recalcitrant and incur the wrath of his captors. It would only serve to complicate matters and could negate any chance of escape. He had to slip under the radar, play along, but only so much.

"I take it you're settling in again," Melinda mentioned after a long silence.

"As well as can be expected," Morgan replied.

"I hear you and Lorna have patched things up."

"Who told you?"

"Oh, word gets around," Melinda said with a smirk. No doubt her spies had given her a full report on Lorna's performance.

"You didn't invite me to dinner to chat about my love life, I hope," Morgan answered.

"Not really," Melinda said as the waiter rolled in a cart loaded with food. The savory aromas filled the air, stimulating the senses in many ways. It certainly seemed to be far better fare than standard colonial rations.

"I'm sure you'll recognize this," Melinda said as the waiter began setting out platters of sautéed meat. "It's from your alien compound."

"So, you've already begun plundering it," Morgan said.

"It is hardly plunder!" Budreau said, sounding offended.

Morgan smiled obnoxiously at the reaction. Melinda saw him, realized what he had done, and was unable to restrain her chortles. "Jean, he's just trying to rile you."

The Frenchman grumbled. "I see you two are much alike."

It was Morgan's turn to feel riled, but he didn't show it. Instead, he grabbed a serving fork and brought a cluster of brown meat strips to his plate.

"Jean and I had a look around that place earlier today. It truly is a wonder to behold. Beyond imagining, really," Melinda said, "and it could very well change our understanding of existence."

"More importantly," Budreau added, "it could help facilitate our independence. Should we unlock the secrets that lie within, they could make us more formidable opponents, protect us from future assaults. Assure the survival of the new Scientific Republic."

"Good luck," Morgan said. "Do you really think both the United States and the European Consensorate are just going to stand by and let you take Mars?"

"What choice will they have?" Melinda asked. "Our people control the only ships capable of making the journey here, and we have enough influence in both governments back home to forestall any efforts to derail our plans. By the time we declare our independence, we will have adequate infrastructure to be self-sufficient, and we won't need Earth at all."

"And when they launch a few missiles at your domes, then what?"

"I doubt they'll waste their time trying to fight us," Melinda said, unperturbed. "It would be a waste of time, and neither government would sanction our wholesale slaughter. We aren't a threat to anyone. We just want to be left alone."

"But anyone here who disagrees with your vision of the future has had their mind forcibly changed," Morgan countered. "How's that being left alone?"

"Sacrifices have to be made. Sometimes the ends *do* justify the means," Melinda replied. "I'm not proud of what we've had to do, but we can't afford dissent at this time. In the future, if our children want to live differently, they'll be free to think that way and leave, but I doubt many of them will. After we've expanded our colonies into—as my colleague so aptly put it—a flourishing Scientific Republic, everyone will want to join us."

227

"We'll have to be damned selective by then," Waltham added. "Especially when none of us will be dying of old age to make room for the newbies."

"As long as you know what you're doing," Morgan said, seeing no point in arguing.

"Quite so," Budreau said, pouring himself a glass of red wine. "I only hope the vines will flourish before long."

"I didn't think real Scifes were allowed alcohol," Morgan mentioned.

"Nonsense," Budreau replied. "Wine is beneficial to the heart, when used in moderation."

Melinda took the bottle and filled her wine glass, then passed the bottle over to Morgan who ceremoniously poured a small quantity of the red substance into his own.

"Now, about your alien compound," Melinda said as the bottle was handed down to Captain Waltham. "It would be a great help if you could share whatever insights you may have regarding its workings."

"I really didn't learn that much," Morgan said, stabbing at his food. "I'd be glad to give you an extended tour, go over what I know and point your researchers in the right direction."

"That won't be necessary," Melinda said, "but there is one big favor you could do for me."

"What?"

"Give me the password to your laptop."

All of Morgan's personal possessions had been confiscated upon his capture, including the laptop he'd had with him throughout his ordeal. Eighteen months worth of journal entries, personal ruminations, and off the wall theories about everything he had seen, sat inside it. A lot of the data was quite private, most of it quite trivial. Some of the entries made him appear absolutely mad, particularly those that prominently featured discussions with Rheena Liszt.

The fact that Melinda was asking for his password was odd. "Don't you have hackers for that?" Morgan asked.

"Yes, if I only want the files," Melinda said. "But I don't

want to treat you like some dangerous felon. I want us to trust one another, to be on the same side again. I know it will take time, but I'd like to start here, with a little consideration."

"So, if I don't give you my password..."

"The laptop stays locked, you have my word."

Budreau almost spit out his wine.

"You really mean that?" Morgan asked.

"Morgan, I may have hidden things from you in the past, but have I ever lied to you?"

He realized she hadn't, which left him wondering if he could cut a deal. "Okay, Melinda, here's how it goes. I will give you full access to all of my files, but only if you give me back the laptop."

Budreau laughed, "That is absurd!" he slurred. Morgan wondered if the wine was loosening his emotional restraint.

"All right," Melinda said thoughtfully. "That sounds fair enough."

Budreau threw back the contents of his second glass and refilled it again.

Melinda continued. "You do understand that you won't be able to share your data with anyone, not even Lorna, without my prior authorization?"

"Once you have a look at my files, you'll realize they're mostly personal notes that I have no intention of publicizing."

"Then it's a deal," Melinda said happily, raising her glass. "A toast, to peaceful resolutions."

Morgan put his glass up and Melinda's tapped it. They both took a small sip.

"It seems only fitting. This whole thing started with you stealing my files, and now it ends with you giving me yours. May it lead us to a greater truth."

* * *

"I think we should blow it up," Morgan said.

It was shortly after dinner and he was back in his quarters with Lorna, who had brought along Graeme Carlow to go over their plans for the morning.

"You believe it's that big of a threat?" Lorna asked.

"You bet it is," he replied. "The technology in that alien domain is years ahead of anything we've developed, and I just barely scratched the surface. You know the geniuses around here will be able to figure out a lot more of that stuff than I could."

"So your answer is to just blow it up and the hell with the consequences?" Carlow asked, disgusted. "How could you be so barbaric? You must have some faint glimmer of the ramifications of your discovery. It could change the way we view the world, the universe—our very existence!"

"I know, but we can't risk leaving it in the hands of Melinda Faris. She believes it might hold the key to her establishing an independent Scife nation on Mars. Someday that knowledge could very well come back to threaten all of mankind."

Carlow wasn't convinced, but changed tactics. "Say, for a moment, that I accept your reasoning. What can we really do about it?"

"I figure we'd fly out there in a Solox tomorrow morning, plant a few explosive charges, and let her rip."

"And you're certain that would destroy the complex?" Carlow asked. "Is your survey of the place detailed enough, and your understanding of demolition extensive enough, to calculate the explosive yield required? You've done a metallurgical analysis of the structure to rate the concussive force needed to bring the whole thing down?"

"No," Morgan said, ready to argue further.

"Then it's not much of a plan, is it?" Carlow surmised. "On top of everything, it would be suicide. Granted, it might be possible, but even if you could procure enough explosive compound from storage without being caught, *and* you managed to fly out there and plant the charges successfully, you would never avoid apprehension afterwards."

"I thought *we* could do it in conjunction with your capture of the *Plymouth*."

"No, it would threaten our entire mission. If we waste our time trying to blow that place up and the Scifes catch us, it won't matter to us if it's there or not. We'll all be dead, in one manner or another."

Lorna gripped Morgan's hand in a familiar way. "We all want to live," she said. "We can deal with Melinda Faris when we get back to Earth."

"Look, we've got one good shot at this," Carlow said firmly. "If we stick to the plan and don't do anything stupid, we're home free. You can help us and escape, or stay behind. Make a choice."

There was no choice. "I'm with you," Morgan said.

"Good," Carlow said. With a slight nod, he turned and headed for the door. "Get some sleep, both of you. You'll need it for the morning."

Morgan was pleasantly surprised when Lorna decided to stay the night, though when they got ready for bed, his hopes were dashed when she left on her clothes.

"I'm a virgin and I intend to stay that way—for the moment," she said, lying down.

Morgan let it go and lay down beside her, bare-chested. They slept well together.

Chapter Twenty-Eight
March 4, 2329

The hangar was getting cramped. Half the floor space was filled with crates of supplies and industrial machinery that had come down the previous evening. None of it had yet been cataloged and assigned warehouse space. The morning crew was trickling in to work, and the sixty laborers began reading off numbers and running them through the Villas mainframe. Nothing would get moved for another few hours, as the quartermaster's office needed to sign off on the transfers.

The clutter worked to the advantage of the rebels. Six of them were on the hangar staff and Reginald Matheson was the foreman for the shift, which gave them a definite advantage.

About half an hour into the sorting, after rebels in the communications center had disabled hangar surveillance, Reginald called everyone to order and had them assemble in one particular corner of the room, a spot mostly cordoned off by highly-stacked crates. Once all of the Scife loyalist workers were lined up, the foreman raised a pair of condensed energy pistol from under his overalls. They were the only two modern weapons the rebels had been able to procure from the police armory without detection, but two was all it took to drop fifty four people in the cramped space.

Most of the victims would live, though with varying degrees of neurological trauma. Either way, they wouldn't be posing a problem for the next phase of the plan.

A few crates were moved to hide the bodies and, one by one, rebels trickled in to replace the stunned laborers. Even with the addition of Morgan Asher and Emily Weitz, they could barely make up for half of the regular workforce, but it would have to do.

The Strato-Strider came down right on time and the rebels waited patiently for it to land. Several watched through a view window as the giant metal plane glided to a stop on the airstrip outside and taxied to the giant airlock that would grant it access to the interior of the hangar bay. It took a few minutes for the airlock to fill with air, and by the time the inner seal was broken, the craft was running on auxiliary electric motors that rolled it slowly inside to be unloaded.

A rear panel of the Strato-Strider hinged downward, leaving a short ramp leading into the cargo hold. The rebels started working, lugging out cases of food and dragging out the larger crates of industrial equipment using motorized lifters. It wasn't going to take them long to offload the supplies, even with half the intended number of workers. They would have to act quickly if they wanted to succeed in procuring the craft.

"Hey," Reginald shouted over his radio to the three figures lounging around inside the cockpit. "We're a little short-handed this morning. Do you mind lending us a hand here?"

After a few minutes, the two copilots exited the craft and began moving crates. The senior pilot remained at his post, which complicated matters slightly.

Carlow and Lorna called Reginald over to the back of the plane to discuss the matter privately.

"We've got to get him out of there," Carlow whispered. The copilots were nearby, but didn't appear to notice their discreet grouping.

"We can't just slip in and blast him?" Reginald asked.

"No," Carlow said, glancing up the ramp to the cargo hold. "We can't risk firing a weapon in there. A condensed energy blast could fry the circuitry, and a bullet could puncture the hull."

"We'd better think of something fast," Reginald said. "That hold's almost empty."

"I'll deal with it," Lorna said, sounding disinclined to do so.

Running up into the cargo hold, Lorna crossed the large, vacant chamber that had been packed full half an hour ago.

The last time she had been inside this plane, two years earlier, much of this space had been filled with passenger seating. Those had been stripped out now, for there were no passengers on this trip, and it made more room for cargo.

It was a long walk across the metal floor to the cockpit door, and when Lorna finally reached it, she found it locked tight. She rapped her knuckles against the door, hoping the pilot would answer. "What is it?" he promptly asked through the intercom.

Pushing a button beside the speaker, Lorna said, "Your friends said I might get a look at the controls."

"Sorry, no civilians. Captain's orders," the pilot said.

Lorna breathed a disparaging sigh, feeling quite uncomfortable with her own plot, but she had to go through with it. Pushing the button again, she used the most alluring voice she could muster and said, "Oh, but I've always been interested in flying, and what would it hurt for me to have just one little look? I won't touch anything you don't want me to, and I promise not to tell your captain."

There was a long pause and Lorna feared she'd put on the performance for nothing. Before she could turn away, she heard the locks disengaging. The ruse had worked.

As the door slid open, Lorna removed a small knife from a hidden scabbard strapped to her hip. As soon as she spotted the face of the pilot, she flicked her wrist, releasing the sharpened blade with deadly accuracy. The shiny metal stuck into the man's left eye and he dropped to the floor, twitching.

She had learned to be lethal with both swords and knives in the virtual realm of Fantasan, but this was her first real kill. Remorse and adrenaline made her want to throw up, but she didn't have time to be sick. This was about survival, and she was determined to do whatever it took to live.

With the cockpit secure, the other rebels easily subdued the copilots and proceeded into the Strato-Strider. They carried several crates aboard, and Carlow cracked one open as the ramp was lifting and the plane prepared for departure. Inside lay the guns of Mars, a dozen pieces from Morgan's collection that would assure they stood a fighting chance of commandeering the *Plymouth* and escaping back to Earth. Three more crates contained the rest of Morgan's collection, as well as the few pieces once owned by Tim Keene. In all, they had two guns for every rebel.

The weapons were distributed while the Strato-Strider waited in the airlock, and as it rolled out onto the runway, everyone positioned themselves against the back wall and grabbed onto whatever they could for support. It would be a rough ride without seats or strapping, but they'd survive.

"I wish we could take Colonel Avery with us," Morgan said. "It doesn't feel right, leaving a fellow patriot behind."

"If he hadn't gotten himself shot, he'd be here," Carlow assured him.

The plane took off with a hard blast, pinning everyone against the sides of the craft. A few stragglers ended up getting slammed harshly, Emily among them. She bruised her shoulder when she hit the wall, but didn't break anything.

After a few minutes, the plane leveled off and the passengers were able to breathe for a minute, but then the pilots kicked them into a rapid secondary ascent, and everyone felt the crushing force of eight gees as they climbed steadily toward the upper atmosphere. Soon the scream of the jets vanished as they entered outer space.

The sky outside the windows turned from hazy gray to starry black, and soon the plane approached the *Plymouth*. The hangar bay was sealed, so they docked up against the cargo bay. The top of the plane gently glided up against the side of the huge ship and locked into place. A few clicking sounds ensued, and the roof of the Strider began to retract.

The rebels were starting at a disadvantage, for they didn't have any magnetic boots to help them move. Also, the *Plymouth's* crew were on alert, since the rebel pilots hadn't followed standard docking protocol, nor responded to repeated radio signals.

When the roof fully retracted, half a dozen white pellets came flying at the rebels, hitting several with shocking results.

The electrified tips fired by the taser sticks did more than just tickle, and those hit were not going to be putting up a fight right away.

A volley of lead was the rebel response, causing mixed results for everyone. Five of the bullets hit their targets, but the ensuing recoil from the weapons left their users flailing wildly in zero gees. One man had two front teeth busted when a rifle barrel flew back at him, and several others got elbowed and kicked by out of control allies. It was fortunate only seven shots had been fired, or it could have been much worse.

"Let's move," Carlow shouted to everyone who was still able to fight. Nineteen in all came floating out of the plane and into the brightly-lit cargo hold. Drops of blood floated in the air like a foggy mist from the men they'd shot.

Two of the crewmen still put up a fight, and using the solid end of their taser sticks, managed to zap three rebels before being subdued. Morgan and Reginald strangled their opponents into submission, but only left them unconscious.

"Why are you doing this?" one of the wounded crewmen asked the pack of rebels. He was nursing a bleeding shoulder, stuck to the floor by his mag-boots.

"We need your ship," Carlow replied. "Anyone who surrenders will not be harmed."

"A little late for that," the crewman shouted.

"You fired first," Carlow said, moving on. He led the rebels across the cargo bay, toward the lone doorway at the back of the room. After they traversed the large chamber half-filled with storage crates, they encountered more resistance.

Two junior officers barred the way, but they promptly stepped aside when they saw a dozen rifles leveled at them. The rebels ordered the men to hand over their tasers. When the crewmen did as they were told, they received a jolt from their own weapons, and were put out of action.

The rebels drifted down the hallways until they reached the spacious commons. They pulled themselves along the wall of the giant room, toward the forward hatch that led to the command center.

Reginald was the first to reach the hatch and he found it shut tight. It was only a minor obstacle, as someone handed him an electronic scrambler to release the magnetic locks and grant them access. He slapped the black strip against the number pad beside the door and the device did the job.

The hatch slid open and a shot rang out. Reginald slumped forward, drifted limply in space, as streaks of blood floated out of his mouth and chest.

Commander Burroughs stood in the open hatchway, holding Waltham's personal sidearm. "Drop your weapons," he ordered, staring down the pack of armed men and women.

The rebels didn't oblige. Instead, several of them opened fire, putting an end to the commander's defiance. Before he dropped, he let off another round from his pistol, hitting Graeme Carlow in the leg.

"I thought there weren't any real guns on board," Emily screeched, her voice tinny with fear.

"There aren't supposed to be," Carlow said as he inspected the bleeding bullet hole above his right knee. "Keep moving. The command bridge should be straight ahead."

Thirty feet down the corridor was another hatch. It was opened with the scrambler and the rebels entered the cramped command center of the *Plymouth*. The three officers present promptly threw up their arms in surrender.

Drifting into the command pit, Snyder, their resident computer and communications expert, found all command functions encrypted. "I'll need ten minutes to get us underway, at least."

"You won't succeed," one of the subdued officers countered. "Captain Waltham has been informed of your piracy. Once he's back aboard, you're finished!"

"Get him out of here!" Carlow shouted, and the *Plymouth* crewmen were dragged out of the cockpit.

After a few minutes, Snyder managed to unlock the ship's surveillance and sensor grid, confirming the young officer's boast. Waltham's Solox was already airborne and en-route.

"You can bet he's not alone," Carlow said. "Four armed soldiers might put an end to us."

"We can take them," Morgan said with bravado. "A couple of us could set an ambush and drop them before they leave the hangar."

"Easier said than done," Snyder said, staring at a monitor. "You can't ambush him before he gets on board, and by then, it'll be too late. Waltham's command codes will still work while this encryption is in place, but he'll need a secure connection. He'll be able to access ship's system remotely once he breaks the upper thermosphere. If he gets a hold of this computer, we're finished. He'll vent our atmosphere, or electrocute us with one of his damn security protocols."

"How long do we have?" Carlow asked.

"Five, maybe ten minutes," Snyder replied.

"Then I'd better get going," Carlow said, pushing himself toward the hatch.

"Where are you going?" Morgan asked.

"To the hangar bay. There are two more Solox Mark II's waiting there."

"You're going after Waltham?" Lorna said, sounding surprised.

"The bridge is yours, Mrs. Asher. Get our people home," Carlow said, disappearing down the hallway in haste.

"I thought those Solox jets were unarmed," Morgan said.

"They are," Snyder replied, as he returned to clacking on a keyboard.

"He must be planning to ram Waltham," Lorna added sadly. "It's the only way."

Emily Weitz asked, shocked, "He's going to kill himself, just like that?"

"He's sacrificing himself for the sake of the mission," Snyder growled. "It's either that, or we're all dead. What would you choose?"

"He's your leader, right?" Emily asserted.

"Which means it's his decision," Morgan replied,

understanding the situation.

"Let's just hope it's worth it," Lorna concluded.

* * *

Graeme Carlow reached the hangar door, confident in his course of action. His leg stabbed with pain, and even with a tourniquet, blood still seeped through the makeshift bandage. He only hoped he wouldn't black out or become otherwise incapacitated before completing his mission.

The door opened to his scrambler, and he drifted to one of the sleek jets nearby. The silver craft was a familiar sight. In his youth, he'd been an aerospace engineer, and had worked to design the first Solox craft for use on alien terrain. The curve of the fins was his personal addition, and a sour reminder that the dreams he'd spent his whole life working for had turned to ashes. He'd believed in the space program, in the benefits of Scientific Fundamentalism, until those benefits turned into lethal mandates.

He'd known the physics involved in teleportation, but until his first trip through, he'd never really understood it. He hadn't believed in anything beyond his fleshly body, had thought that becoming a digital clone was only a technicality, a superstitious concept used to discourage the advancement of science. Materializing after his first teleport, he realized how wrong his progenitor had been, as he, the clone, was born.

While most people could undergo teleportation hundreds or thousands of times before catching on, something in Graeme Carlow's mind had permitted him to understand the difference right away. He quickly expressed his concerns to Melinda Faris, and after much debate, convinced her to explore the concept of developing a mental buffer for the newly acquired teleporter. In the meantime, Graeme and anyone else who shared in his "phobia" were exempt from using the technology, with certain consequences.

Of course, it didn't stop Melinda or most of the other colonists from using the teleporter, and they gladly killed themselves on a regular basis without knowing the dangers.

239

If the buffer concept had been viable, this all might have been avoided. But as it stood, his fellow dissidents could not remain under Melinda's control. She put the dictates of science and the concept of technological advancement ahead of human rights, and that was too great a threat to those who sought the right to live.

Sealed into the cockpit of the Solox, Carlow accessed the hangar controls, depressurized the bay, and opened the doors. Flicking a switch, he activated the primary thrusters and glided out into space, ready to make the ultimate sacrifice. He hadn't wanted it this way, had always intended to escape with his friends, but nothing ever turns out the way one would dream. Mars had taught him that lesson the hard way.

If he hadn't been shot in the leg, he might have hesitated, asked for someone else to volunteer for this suicide mission, but the wound had decided for him. He was the weakest link, the most expendable member of the group. The bullet had shattered the bone, and such a wound would be difficult to treat in space, especially when none of his rebels were in the medical profession. It only made sense that he lay down his life to assure their escape.

The sensor grid displayed on a section of the rounded windshield, and in a few moments, a red dot appeared, exiting the upper atmosphere below him. He set his navigation system to home in on the signal, and the Solox dove toward the planet below. Waltham's craft was approaching at a steep vector, and he couldn't alter his trajectory until he broke free of the atmosphere, making him an easier target.

It was a race to the finish. Could Carlow get there before Waltham triggered a remote link with the *Plymouth* and executed anti-intruder measures?

He would never know of his success. Thirty seconds later, he collided with Waltham's Solox. The cockpits of both jets blew apart, and the shredded passengers were exposed to the vacuum of space. Death came quickly with excruciating pain.

* * *

"I've unlocked the navigational controls," Snyder said excitedly.

"Becky, get to work," Lorna prodded.

The pregnant blonde floated into the command pit and began programming their return trajectory. A minute later, she replied, "Ready on your command, *Captain*."

Lorna turned to Morgan and asked, "Ready to go home?"

"Let's get our asses back to Earth," Morgan said, eager to put this disastrous chapter of his life behind him.

The command was given, and the *Plymouth's* drive engaged, pushing the ship into a slingshot around the planet. They were underway and home free.

Chapter Twenty-Nine

Six hours after breaking Mars' orbit, the *Plymouth* received a call from Melinda Faris, demanding answers. Lorna told her everything about the resistance, her feelings, and the desire of the rebels to escape the growing tyranny.

Melinda didn't take the news well. "You have no idea what you've done here!" she cursed over the video screen. "How could you betray me like this?"

"You gave us no choice. If we stayed on Mars, you would have killed us for opposing you."

"That's not true! And you killed over four dozen of your fellow colonists, not to mention Captain Waltham and his crew, over irrational fears."

"We never wanted anyone to get hurt, but you kill thousands every day when you feed them through your teleporter. America needs to know what you're doing *and* what you're planning."

"They never will," Melinda said. "I've already been in contact with Earth. Congress and NASA both agree with me. You had no right to mutiny!"

"When they learn the full story, things will be different," Lorna replied, lifting a slender laptop in front of the viewer. "This belonged to Armin Weitz. It's the reason you had Deirdre Keene murder him. There's some pretty incriminating stuff on this thing."

"No, that's not possible. Deirdre assured me he didn't have the files."

"She must have lied to you because I have the proof in my hands," Lorna said. "By the time we get back to Earth, everyone will know the truth about you and your coconspirators. I expect your little science project will be ending badly."

Morgan was nearby, trying on a pair of pilfered mag-boots. Overhearing the conversation, he joined the conversation and gave Melinda his two cents. Lorna stepped aside and let her husband vent.

"Morgan," Melinda said. "I thought we'd gotten over our differences."

"I wasn't going to sit back and watch your dreams of utopia morph into a dictatorship."

"You still fail to understand what I'm trying to do for our people," Melinda chided.

"No, I understand perfectly, but you are so blinded by your dreams that you can't see you've abandoned everything that makes them admirable. When you start believing the ends justifies the means, the ends inevitably *become* the means."

"You're wrong," Melinda said. "I wish you had stayed around long enough to realize that."

"You won't get the chance to prove anyone wrong. Pretty soon, it will be all over."

"Oh, no," Melinda said bitterly. "It's only just beginning." With that, she signed off.

* * *

During the first few days of the trip, everyone got settled in. The eighteen surviving Space Force crewmen were confined to quarters and guarded day and night by the wary rebels. They were provided with everything they needed to live, even permitted board games for amusement, but never did they get to step outside of their chambers.

On the fourth day of the blast back to Earth, Becky Sousa gave birth to a healthy baby boy. It wasn't the first child born in space, though it was certainly an adventure for those involved. They were lucky to have someone with limited midwife training among their ranks. The child was named Graeme Reginald, in honor of their fallen compatriots.

Lorna sequestered herself in the captain's cabin for most of the journey, spending only limited time in the command center, getting updates on the ship's status. She didn't eat with the others, and her exercise was done during the night, when everyone was asleep. She was clearly avoiding one person in particular.

243

Morgan missed Lorna, and every day that went by—as she hid herself away—pained him more. It would have been easier to lose her entirely, but things were strange between them. She was, and yet wasn't, his wife. She loved him, but didn't understand her feelings. Their relationship was a mess, their future was unknown.

Cracking Armin Weitz's database was difficult. Without his retina to unlock the encryption, the hard drive didn't want to give up its secrets. As computer savvy as Armin had been, however, he was no match for half a dozen top notch hackers. After three weeks of around the clock work, the ingenious rebels managed to access the information.

When the final bits of Melinda's files were extracted, and all the pertinent data was sorted and made ready for transmission back to Earth, the group voted Morgan the official leader of the rebels. He didn't want the honor, but it was a very pragmatic move. If someone else were the figurehead of the rebellion, they would be more easily marginalized by Melinda's colleagues. But if the one and only Morgan Asher spoke, people would listen—even if only out of curiosity—and the truth would be heard.

So, with a week left to go on their journey back to Earth, Morgan composed a short message explaining the situation. It was sent to every major government official in Washington, along with the data files exposing hundreds of those officials to be traitors. It wasn't long before the *Plymouth* was deluged with replies from politicians and reporters, who all wanted to talk to the man responsible. After the first dozen interviews, several of which included nasty threats from powerful senators, Morgan declined further comment and let his original message speak for itself. When that didn't stop the calls, other rebels took to the airwaves to give their version of events, making their case ever stronger.

When the *Plymouth* reached Earth's orbit, a welcoming committee was waiting. Half a dozen XLC Hellcats, high altitude American war planes that weren't ordinarily allowed outside the atmosphere due to international treaty, flanked the shuttle on its final decent to Earth. With all the controversy brewing and the death threats being bandied about, the Secretary of State had negotiated for a one-time exception to assure the safe return of the rebels and crewmen of the *Plymouth*. A freshly outfitted Strato-Strider arrived to transport the crew, and they were taken to Patterson Air Force Base, where they were given safe accommodations.

Twenty four hours seemed like twenty four years to Morgan as he lounged around in the VIP room ninety feet underground. He felt restless, but his muscles ached too much for him to pace. His body would need several weeks to adjust to Earth's gravity, even with the rigorous workouts he'd performed aboard the *Plymouth*. At least he had plenty to do without moving. The television got every channel imaginable, and it was placed directly across from his padded recliner.

Still, Morgan couldn't enjoy the accommodations. He didn't know what was going on outside of his quarters, or what his ultimate fate would be. It grated on him in the early morning hours, as his second day back home began. He couldn't help but expect the worst.

At nine o'clock, he received a most unexpected visitor. A pair of airmen stepped inside first. Seeing that Morgan was dressed and alert, they signaled the all-clear for the guest.

Morgan's eyes widened when he saw the man standing before him. He would never have expected the President of the United States to call on him, but there he was, the six-foot-three retired quarterback-turned actor-turned politician, Harold Steyn.

"Morgan Asher, it's a pleasure to meet you," President Steyn said, holding out a hand for Morgan to shake.

"Likewise," Morgan said, his hand crushed by the man's impressive strength. "I'm sorry I didn't get the chance to vote for you last fall."

"Yes, you were out of the country, as it were," the president remarked, sitting down on a nearby coffee table. "Though, I didn't come here to discuss elections. Rather, I wanted to see how you were and discuss what we're going to do with you."

"It sounds like a fairly mundane job," Morgan said, surprised he wasn't talking to some staffer instead of the important leader.

"Not at all. And to be honest, I've wanted to meet you for quite some time."

"Yes, I know. I'm everybody's favorite historical relic."

"I wouldn't go that far, but you must admit you are a unique individual."

"I guess I'm just not one for fandom," Morgan said.

The president laughed boisterously, drawing a peculiar stare from one of the watchful airmen by the door. "We have quite different personalities, Mr. Asher, I assure you."

"How so?"

"I've spent all my life trying to get as much attention as possible. I won three Superbowls, two Oscars, tried for a Pulitzer, but it turns out writing's not my thing. And then I got into politics, became Governor of Washington State for two terms before finally landing the Presidency. Do you know why? Because I want to make my mark on history, to be remembered for being someone who stood out, who made the most of their life, and left something behind that people could respect and understand. Like it or not, you are that kind of person, too. You've already made your mark."

"And you said you didn't come here for hero-worship," Morgan said, a little embarrassed by the praise. He was finding President Steyn to be far more personable than he'd imagined.

"No, I came because of the tremendous gift you've given me," the president said furtively.

"Gift?" Morgan asked, confused.

"The names of all the Scife traitors in Congress, the State Department, NASA, the works. You can't imagine how much this is going to help me in my second term. You've painted a giant bulls eye on every one of my major opponents in the House and Senate, and given me a mandate to bring this country back into line with its founding principles. You have lived up to your reputation, and I might even give you a medal in a few years, assuming everything works out."

"I'm glad I could be of service," Morgan said, less than thrilled by the president's overzealous reaction.

"Yes, now let me be of service, to you," President Steyn offered.

"You could start by letting me out of this box," Morgan suggested, wishing to breathe the fresh air of his home world again, and taste the freedom he'd missed these past years.

"That might be difficult," Steyn replied. "I don't expect you'd last long outside. You and your rebel friends have stirred up a hornet's nest, and there are some powerful players gunning for you right now. I can't guarantee your safety outside these walls, which leaves us with something of a dilemma."

"You need me to lie low while the dust settles. I understand," Morgan grumbled, irritated. He could take care of himself.

"I'm afraid anything above ground level isn't low enough," President Steyn warned. "We are talking about a hundred and sixty congressmen, and God knows how many Consensorate officials, all hot for revenge."

"Then what's the plan?" Morgan asked.

"We need you to disappear for a year or two, just until the hearings are over and those behind this despicable scheme are out of power. We have a number of options I hope you'll find agreeable."

"These 'options' of yours wouldn't happen to involve Simworld, would they?"

President Steyn chuckled. "You're perceptive, Mr. Asher. Yes, that is our intention. As you know, we have plenty of sway with the virtual reality companies, and you'd be quite safe with your body on ice and your mind downloaded into a program until everything gets sorted out here. Then you'll be free to do whatever you wish, without fear of assassination."

"Do I have a choice in the matter?"

"Of virtual reality programs, yes. But you must go under."

247

"Mr. President, I somehow doubt it will ever be safe for me again," Morgan said. "I mean, you can't get rid of every Scife in the country, and even if you remove them from power, what's to keep the Consensorate from exacting revenge?"

"You're right. We can't get every one of them, but you shouldn't worry about the Consensorate. They have officially condemned the actions of the Eridanian colonists, denied any connection with the Scifes in our government, and swear they have never brainwashed a single American."

"Do you believe them?" Morgan asked, incredulous.

"Not really, but to back up their lies they're offering us technical data that should help us to develop safeguards against the teleporter technology, to prevent brainwashing in the future."

"Why would they do that?" Morgan asked, perplexed.

"For many reasons, but primarily because things aren't as orderly and controlled in their society as they'd like us to believe. They're having difficulty keeping their people in line—I imagine the splinter group on Mars is proof of that— and increasing hostilities with us would only make their troubles worse. Keeping the peace is to their advantage, for the moment."

"Lucky us," Morgan mused, still not entirely convinced, but willing to let it go. "What are you going to do with the other rebels?"

"They'll be offered a virtual trip, same as you, though we'll need to keep a few of them around for the hearings."

"Then why don't you keep me around to speak in court? Let me lead the charge."

Steyn shook his head. "I'm getting tired of arguing, Mr. Asher. It's not an option. It may be a bit self-serving, but I can't afford to be remembered as the president who let the great Morgan Asher get murdered by his political rivals. If one of the others gets whacked, it won't be so bad—we can thaw out another to take his place."

Morgan realized he wasn't going to have it his way, so he gave in. "All right, but do me a favor. Don't give my wife the option of staying out. I'd rather she not be one of your expendable witnesses."

"You got it," President Steyn promised with a million dollar smile.

"Can I get that in writing?" Morgan asked, only half in jest.

"I'll tack it onto your Simworld contract, how's that?" Steyn answered, standing. He stretched and offered his hand again.

"I guess it's back to Fantasan, then," Morgan said, feeling his knuckles being crunched again.

"They've already got a slot reserved for you," Steyn said. "We're prepping a jet to take you to Seattle."

"Can I speak to Lorna before I go?"

"I'll instruct the airmen to bring her in before escorting you to the surface. Good luck." With that, he departed.

Morgan sat alone for a few minutes, considering what was about to happen to him, again. It seemed he couldn't get away from that accursed program, but couldn't think of an alternate, safer scenario. At least he had a friend or two in Fantasan, people who could keep him comfortable until he had the chance to get back to reality, and maybe, finally, have a normal life.

A light tapping sounded at his door, followed by the entrance of Lorna. She rolled in reluctantly in a motorized wheelchair, looking unusually nervous. "I hear you're getting shipped out, but they won't tell me where."

"I'm heading back to Fantasan. I'd like you to come with me," Morgan said, hoping she might be tempted. It was where they'd first met, the site of their honeymoon. Perhaps she could find herself there again and they could rekindle their relationship.

"I'm not sure I'm ready for that."

"Please, Lorna, don't let it end. Not like this." He reached out to grasp her hand, but she pulled away from his touch.

"I'm not...It's just... I need some time to think."

"You've had almost two months!" Morgan snapped, scared he was about to lose her forever.

Tears welled in Lorna's eyes, and she turned her chair around, preparing to head back out of the room. "I'll see you around, okay?" she said softly.

As she left, Morgan felt his heart go with her. His life would never be normal again.

Epilogue

Martian independence came fast and furious, following the revelations of Morgan Asher and the Villas Colony rebels. Faris and Budreau had had little alternative but to follow through with the next phase of their plan, and so the *United Scientific States of Mars* was born. It may have happened far earlier than intended, but they were certain they could make it work.

Jean Proudhon Budreau sat in his small office at Eridania, reading the latest parley from his former superior at the Consensorate Space Agency. The time lag between Earth and Mars prevented them from having a direct conversation, so a series of scathing letters back and forth was the preferred substitute.

Budreau smiled as he read the first paragraph. "Jean, you fool! Do you not realize the position you have put us in? How much you have threatened the security of our people? The Americans have blamed us—*us*—for your ignominious actions, and we have been forced to cooperate with them, to purge our allies from their ranks, in order to preserve a precarious peace. Did you truly seek to start a new Great War on Earth? Surely you understand we cannot let that happen, yet appeasing the barbaric Americans is almost as undesirable. Almost."

Budreau hadn't planned it, but had hoped for it. It appeared the two great powers were keeping each other busy, which meant neither would be likely to turn their attention back at Mars immediately. It could give their fledgling nation the time it needed to become secure and autonomous.

The second paragraph brought him more critical news. "Not only have you threatened our foreign affairs, but our domestic tranquility as well. Your petty defiance has emboldened dissent among several of our own Nation States. Macedonia is threatening to withdraw from the Scientific

Accords, and others may follow. We are looking at Ireland all over again, but this time it could lead to the dissolution of the entire Consensorate Federation."

One could only hope, Budreau thought vindictively. *It's the least they deserve for abusing Scientific Fundamentalism, and everyone under their care.*

The letter continued, "You claim to remain faithful to the dictates of science, yet you behave much like an Irrationalist savage. To think, my wife once bore your child! I certainly hope your rebellious nature is not genetic."

There was a twinge of resentment in Budreau as he finished that hunk of text. He thought of all the children he had artificially fathered, that the Consensorate had made from his genetic material with women they deemed compatible with his genome. So few of them were really his, for he hadn't been there to raise them. What was the point in perpetuating a bloodline with a dozen different ladies, most of whom you never met? He had been little more than livestock, as were all people under the Consensorate, and that understanding kept his resolve firm.

A true father passed on far more than his genes. He was supposed to be there to share his love and his knowledge, so his heirs would understand where they came from and who they could become. They deserved a real family, just as their parents did in rearing them.

Following a few more insults, the letter moved into threats. "Your new nation will fall. It is futile and foolish to deny it. You cannot survive without us, and so long as you persist in this illogical defiance of Consensorate rule, you shall be banned from ever calling upon us for aid. Do not think the Americans will help you, either, for they are of a like mind in this regard. You have betrayed us both."

Budreau wasn't worried. As much as the Martian colonies had now isolated themselves from their originating nations, there were still plenty of other countries on Earth who would welcome a new trading partner. None of them had the ability to reach Mars yet, but the USSM had control of the

Consensorate's only space-liner, the *CFS Archimedes*.

The *Archimedes* was already on its way to Mars, carrying a fresh load of supplies and three thousand new colonists. The crew and passengers were loyal to Budreau's dream, and several of them were stowaways from the Space Agency who had fled mere hours before Martian independence had been declared. They'd all be safe and sound in a little over a month, and the ship would be their lifeline back to Earth.

As it currently stood, neither Villas nor Eridania could produce enough food for subsistence living, and it would remain that way for many more years. They would need to find new allies to trade with, but their prospects were good. A mining crew at Villas had recently struck a fresh vein of gold, and a few thousand kilos could buy enough food to keep them alive until their farming projects bore fruit. Perhaps they'd start trading with the free Macedonians. Barring that, the Persians were always eager for a good trade, and their neutrality gave them access to all the produce of Asia.

The letter concluded, "You wanted your independence, then you shall have it. The Consensorate council has decided to grant your request and leave you to your ultimate demise. Perhaps time will show you the error of your ways. And when you are alone and starving, you will once again return to the true path of Scientific Fundamentalism."

As he closed the laptop and reflected on the words, Budreau could not help but feel increasingly bold. It was all happening so perfectly. No potential hardship could perturb him.

His thoughts drifted back once more to fond memories, those precious few years he'd spent with his dear Janet. For two decades, he had longed for her touch and dreamt of seeing her loving smile every morning. At long last, he was to get his wish, for she was returning to him.

Over the years, they had remained in contact, even though their government barred them from talking openly. Short emails were sneaked through the system and it was enough to keep their love alive. Budreau had never discussed his plans with her, but had promised they'd be reunited someday.

Budreau's last message to Janet fulfilled that promise in the form of two Space Agency technicians, who offered her a seat aboard the *Archimedes*. After a brief explanation, she accepted their gracious offer, and was now on her way to Mars to spend the rest of her life with the man of her heart's desire, who had been unjustly ripped from her arms all those years ago.

Jean Proudhon Budreau had caused countless deaths, betrayed his homeland, and founded an entirely new nation on an entirely different world—all in the name of love. So much he had sacrificed, so much he had gained, all for the sake of that all-consuming emotion. There was no stronger force in all the universe, and it would truly be irrational to deny its power.

Appendix:
Scientific Fundamentalism in Europe
(2105-2330)

After the Last Great War, Europe was in shambles. Governments had been toppled throughout the chaos, and by the beginning of the twenty-second century, there was no controlling legal authority over much of the continent. Tin-pot dictators and loosely-organized citizen councils struggled to fill the power-vacuum, but they were unable to cope with widespread food shortages, epidemics, and utter economic devastation. Infrastructure was gone and ethnic tensions perpetuated violence.

There was to be no outside help. America and her remaining allies were struggling to maintain order elsewhere in the world, and had to cope with their own economic hardships. The nations of central and western Europe were left to fend for themselves.

Out of the depths of doom and depression came a new philosophy, which amalgamated several failed socialist systems of the past and united them with modern scientific principles. This new philosophy was Scientific Fundamentalism, a system designed to bring both order and security to the world through strict adherence to rational logic and the laws of science. Before long, it swept across the continent, and those Nation States that adopted the credo were united by a governing council calling itself the European Consensorate.

The Consensorate instituted controversial reforms to cure the rampant chaos and devastation all over Europe. Their new brand of collectivism was tempered with scientifically-based ideology. Instead of the State being omnipotent, it was a servant to science, and the consensus that humanity must progress socially and genetically toward a purely rational being. Human existence became a series of equations, and individuals were conformed to serve the whole of humanity in whatever way the Consensorate's scientists deemed appropriate, based on rigorous genetic screenings.

"Human Rights" was a relative term in Consensorate Europe. Each person was provided with all the necessities of life, and in exchange, they worked at their assigned tasks to the best of their abilities. With the conformity of the majority, the State facilitated a safe and secure society, free from the inconvenient and inefficient side-effects of individual liberty. Crime was unknown and everyone had a purpose. It was the dawn of utopia, or so the ruling scientists believed.

At first, the war-weary citizens of Europe heralded the Consensorate's reforms as salvation, for they ended decades of death and destruction nothing else had been able to stop. In many places on the continent, freedom had been unknown for generations already, so it wasn't missed. The people were accustomed to strict order and pervasive government policies, and after the recent chaos any form of stability was a welcome change.

Of course, there are always objectors to any new system of government, and the rise of the Consensorate was not without its detractors. However, the Consensorate did not rule with terror, and they sought to deal with dissent peacefully, within the confines of their pervasive and controlling charter. If someone refused to obey the dictates of the State, they were shipped off to a comfortable rehabilitation community, where they were shown the error of their ways through various psychiatric means. It was rare when someone could not be convinced peaceably, and no jail-breaks were ever reported.

That raises two great questions, the first being why the Consensorate would be so kind. It was all part of their scientific doctrine, which sought to be beneficial to all humanity. It was their philosophy that everyone had a purpose, and it was harmful to society when even one person was deprived of the opportunity to live up to their full potential. This concept required the State to impose a purpose upon those who did not seek it; that, in turn, leads us to the second question, which is why anyone would seek to reject utopia.

To fully answer that question, one must look at the totality of the oppression at hand. For example, under the scientific governance codes, marriages were all regulated by the State. Couples were paired off according to their genetic prerequisites to assure the advancement of the race, and in many cases monogamy was thrown out the window when a particular genome showed favorable pairing possibilities with multiple suitors. Those with desired genes could not be wasted on just one lover when polygamous relations served to genetically advance the human race.

The Consensorate's Reproduction Board went far beyond the primitive eugenics which other regimes had played with in the past. With a mapping of the genome and the establishment of sophisticated laboratories and a computer database of all genetic makeups, Consensorate doctors could determine who should breed with whom with rational authority. There was no courting, no love or emotion attached to State-mandated couplings. People were matched according to a complex set of calculations, and the concept of a "family" was fluid.

The Consensorate switched its policies in regards to breeding on many occasions. Early on, sexual intercourse was the standard method, but as infrastructure advanced and medical service became more readily available, natural conception was discouraged in many cases. Embryos of matched couples were created in labs en-masse, and only the most viable and superior were permitted the gift of life.

In some cases, couples with unremarkable genomes were assigned surplus embryos from more genetically advanced couples, to perpetuate superiority. The Consensorate held no desire to continue the bloodlines of those it deemed inferior. If the geneticists proved your prospective offspring would be inherently flawed, or less superior, you were obligated to accept surrogate embryos and raise them as your own. In fact, you were supposed to be grateful for the opportunity to place your surname on such an advanced child beyond your own ability to conceive. To be spared the shame of an imperfect heir was meant as a blessing, both to you and society.

There was no consideration for emotion in the Consensorate. They were primitive, animalistic impulses which restrained human advancement. Feelings were irrelevant, sentimentality a sin. Although you couldn't help but tolerate irrational behavior in young children, adults were expected to be cold and calculating. Public displays of emotion were greatly discouraged, and unwarranted outbursts could result in serious penalties.

Despite the restrictive nature of the Consensorate, their order helped Europe to flourish, and, after a century of their constructive rule, they had wiped out much of human suffering. Nobody went hungry, genetic and communicable diseases were virtually unknown, and the ancient concepts of racism and nationalism were all but forgotten in most places. To cure these problems, all it took was pervasive government controlled by scientific mandates, and a people willing to surrender their individuality entirely.

Still, there were some cultures under Consensorate control that had a hard time eliminating their cultural heritage and traditions. The Irish, in particular, objected to the eradication of their historical identity and religious beliefs. After half a century, the troubles of the past that had coerced them into Consensorate membership were long forgotten, and modern day oppression was all too obvious. By the end of the twenty-second century, the Celtic people had had enough, and they began to rebel.

The initial uprisings were easily snuffed out, but the violent action taken against the people only encouraged more rebellion, and generated sympathy far and wide for the cause of Irish liberation. Rebel manpower grew, and American sympathizers persuaded Congress to send provisions. With a revitalized sense of nationalism among the populace, and the right military equipment to put up a real fight, Ireland finally won their independence in 2256. The fact that the Americans had had a hand in the affair only vexed the Consensorate even more.

The American aid had not been provided out of purely humanitarian concerns. Many political groups in the United States had been growing wary of the Consensorate for a long time, as the totalitarian state grew in all respects and their strict adherence to Scientific Fundamentalist Doctrine naturally conflicted with the individual liberties granted by the Constitution. A new cold war had been brewing, and liberating Ireland was seen as an important step toward undermining the European powerhouse and establishing a staging point for possible future operations.

Despite the animosity, neither superpower was eager to start a new Great War, so peace was maintained. The diplomats shook hands and flashed each other smiles on a regular basis, exchanging sycophantic platitudes while hating each other vehemently. Both powers pretended to like each other, and their armies pretended not to be supporting rebels in dystopic pockets around the globe.

Although militant warfare was off the table, a new form of conflict arose, one of scientific advancement. Truly, the future belonged to the nation that could grow and expand the farthest, and with most of the world already claimed, both nations looked to the stars.

A new space race was hard to sell to the American public, as they had grown more accustomed to trivial pursuits and virtual simulations, but two key events helped to stimulate support for renewed scientific advancement. First was the critical exposure given to a virulent computer virus within virtual systems that had caused psychological damage to untold millions. That, coupled with the animosity toward the Consensorate after the Irish Revolution, stirred a growing majority to agree that space colonization was necessary for the future of the American way of life.

To help foster positive sentiment, the government employed a series of media campaigns, utilizing the ideals and testimony of numerous American thinkers and philosophers, including the limited works of Morgan Asher.

After a century of a new space race, America was seemingly on top. They had the only lunar colonies, and were in the middle of establishing the first Martian settlement, but the Consensorate was no less a participant in space exploration, as was made apparent by the Asher Rebellion on Mars in 2329. That uprising exposed the truth behind the Consensorate's covert space program, as well as their morally questionable teleporter technology.

Following the Asher Rebellion and Martian Independence, the European Consensorate has shown signs of disunity. Several member nations have taken steps to secede from the Scientific Union, though the Consensorate Authority has thus far prevented any secession through show of force. Though news is widely suppressed in Europe, word of riots and civil disobedience has been leaked from several member nations, including Macedonia, Greece, Portugal, and even France. It is unclear how long the unrest will last, but it is clear the Consensorate government will have its hands full in maintaining order for the foreseeable future.

Appendix II
Deleted Section

Author's Note: In the original draft of "The Guns of Mars," the beginning of what became chapter twenty-three started with a bit of wordy philosophy, which was originally designed as a scene break, as 18 months passed between chapters 22 and 23. During preparations for publication, editorial opinion was that this particular hunk of text was too incongruous with the overall theme of the book, and therefore it was cut.

Now, for the first time, I present the following "deleted section" in print. Enjoy it, despise it; it's all up to you:

The universe thinks, in a philosophical sense. As time goes by, every electron flowing in the universe drifts in a preordained pattern, determined by a complex set of laws that not even the brightest human scientist has ever been able to determine with relative accuracy. The subatomic flow dictates the actions of yesterday and tomorrow, shaping what the future will bring based on the movement of today. The future is set in some ways, determined by that which has come before, yet the question of fate is one that has plagued thinkers since the dawn of time.

The Heisenberg Uncertainty Principle dictates that the universe at large is unpredictable, that you cannot tell where any particular particle is going at any given time due to the overall randomness of existence. Though modern experimentation with teleportation helped determine that you could cheat that rule a bit, it was still impossible for modern science to predict the future.

Therefore, there is born the ultimate of philosophical debates. Is there such a thing as free will, or is it simply an illusion, that we are merely doing what we have been "programmed" to do by the nature of the universe? If all things in existence are ruled by a certainty principle, and all motion of all particles is preordained since the dawn of time, are we actually locked into a set of events, and unable to change because the future of the universe has already been written?

Which is it? Fate or free will? Perhaps it is both. Things are set, but there remains enough uncertainty to alter the future, but only so much. There may exist certain focal points, where the flow of history can be turned onto a different track, but once certain factors are in place, decisions made perhaps centuries beforehand, then future events become destiny. Therefore there is both the reality, and the myth, of choice.

The universe itself does not give up its secrets easily, and mankind has yet to advance anywhere beyond infancy in the grand scheme of things, so everyone is free to be right and wrong at the same time, relatively speaking.

Also by Martin T. Ingham:

THE "WEST OF THE WARLOCK" SERIES: THREE BOOKS—ONE CAPTIVATING SAGA

A dwarven gunslinger, a warlock sheriff, an independent elvish widow, and a scandalous elvish barkeeper, along with a whole host of Wild West characters set the stage for thrilling Fantasy Western adventures.

http://www.martinus.us/books.html#westwarlock

West of the Warlock: ISBN#978-0-9887685-1-2

The Curse of Selwood: ISBN#978-0-9887685-

0-5

The Man Who Shot Thomas Edison:
ISBN#978-0-9887685-2-9